Sign up for our newsletter to hear
about new and upcoming releases.

www.ylva-publishing.com

OTHER BOOKS BY GEORGETTE KAPLAN

Ex-Wives of Dracula

SCISSOR LINK

 GEORGETTE KAPLAN

PREFACE

Many thanks to Carl Hoffman for permission to use extracts from his book, *Hunting Warbirds: The Obsessive Quest for the Lost Aircraft of World War II.*

CHAPTER 1

"OVER THERE, WHAT ABOUT HER?" Regan asked with the proxy desperation of the married friend.

Wendy glanced over, feeling like she needed binoculars to see through the strobing lights and the mist that was rolling around like the Hound of the Baskervilles was about. Yeah, she was cute. Black, with a modest afro, about Wendy's age, maybe a little older, pushing thirty. Dressed not too shabby, but not trying too hard either.

"Okay," Wendy said. "I'm going to try to psychically implant in her mind a desire to come over here and make the first move, while she tries to do the same to me. Brace yourself. Psychic combat on this level can be a hard thing to watch."

"Or you could just go over and talk to her."

"No, no, this is the lesbian way. Loser has to speak first. It's a time-honored tradition."

Regan sighed and sipped her drink empty. "Well, you have me as a wingman. How does one lesbian wingman? Do I just go over there and loudly mention how hot and single you are?"

"You're my sister, so no, that would be creepy."

Not that either of them needed a reminder. Five years older, and infinitely more mature, Regan looked like the finished model of what some sculptor was trying to do with Wendy. She was several inches taller, with long, limber legs and yoga-tightened arms, and the fashion sense of a swan turned into a human. Her face was narrow and elegant, (whereas Wendy's was round and 'cute'), with a pert nose, high cheekbones, long dark hair that obeyed her will out of loyalty to the crown. A face made for rouge and eyeliner and smiling. Her eyes were a piercing shade of blue not found in nature, while Wendy's were an unremarkable brown. Wendy didn't consider herself unattractive unless she was on her period; Regan just looked like some ethereal elf queen or something. It made Wendy want to start an Instagram account: *My sister wearing white and quotes from Tolkien.*

Wendy looked at herself in one of the many mirrored surfaces that composed the bar. She liked the way she looked, she did: sweet and natural, and she fashioned herself a little mischievous, even with eyebrows that she couldn't quite bring herself to love (after all, they might've been proof her mom fooled around with Peter Gallagher behind Dad's back). But one day of looking like Regan, and she would have no problem finding someone. And she could wear a corset, just because.

Regan jostled her again. "You're feeling sorry for yourself again, I don't know why. You have a great job, you're young, you're pretty—who cares if you have a girlfriend?"

"That's good, let me down easy."

"Oh, you're a pill."

"A pill with a great job." Wendy toasted it. "Great job."

Wendy Cedar worked for Savin Aerospace, a small but lucrative company that built helicopters for military and civilian use. Her job was in Safety & Risk Management. She worked as an intern directly under her manager, Donnie Parsons, whose job (and thus Wendy's job) was to collate the various findings of safety experts within the department and submit a recommendation on the technical risk margin (TRM) up the ladder.

"It pays well," Wendy reasoned.

"Not when you're an intern."

"So I used the wrong tense. It *will* pay well. It's important work."

Wendy grumbled the way she did when the person she was arguing with was right. Successfully distinguishing between a design flaw and random chance within the testing apparatus could mean millions of dollars, not to mention lives. So she tabulated and calculated, took one memo and ground it down to its essential points and wrote it out again in the proper formula and passed it on to another department. Six years for a Master of Science in Engineering and she double-checked figures. It was frustrating.

"Fine. I won't be frustrated with my boring, monotonous, grindstone job—"

"That everyone does as an intern," Regan finished with her, singsong in the way all sisters were when they got a chance to torture their siblings.

"What did you think, that they were going to let you build a Heli-Carrier fresh out of college? Or—" Regan gestured around in the impressed-with-herself way all mothers had when they stumbled on a teachable moment "—that the perfect woman is just going to fall into your lap while you sit at home wondering which crappy horror movie Netflix should shoot into your eyes next?"

"I know that was meant to be discouraging, but all I can picture is some kind of *Die Hard* situation where terrorists have taken over my building and some lady cop is crawling around the air vents in a tank top."

"Terrorists haven't already taken over your building? How do you explain the rent?"

"You're the one who took me out. I could be getting my money's worth right now, working on my bike or something."

"I don't think 'money's worth' and 'your bike' belong in the same sentence." Regan took another sip, then slapped her empty glass down on the bar. "If you didn't want to go to a gay bar, then why'd you let me take you out? We could've gone to a cheese-making class."

"Do they let you eat the cheese?"

"Yes!"

"You're right, we should've gone for that." Wendy tried to signal the bartender, who was gazing soulfully into a soft butch's eyes, getting ready to give her a free drink. Christ, if Wendy worked here, she'd be doing better. "You wanted me to meet someone. Your idea. I blame you. My plan was working perfectly."

"What was your plan?"

"I grow old, I die, in heaven I get married to Tallulah Bankhead."

"Or you could use Tinder."

"I'm not using Tinder," Wendy said definitively. "If I get murdered by a psycho, I want it done the old-fashioned way."

"Would you listen to yourself? I would never have gotten married if I had your attitude."

"Maybe it's your fault. Maybe you're giving everyone unrealistic expectations. They look at you, they think 'hey, it could happen', then they look at me."

"No one thinks I'm prettier than you. We're two tens."

"I look like Megan Fox about to sneeze."

"You do not!"

Wendy grinned. "I look like the face Megan Fox used to have before the face Megan Fox used to have."

"I think you're pushing the Megan Fox thing too far."

"I look like…shit." After a moment's hesitation, Wendy had one. "I look like the Megan Fox who would actually end up with Shia LeBeouf."

"Now you just sound depressed. Do I have to take away your razor blades?"

"I need those to shave my legs. 'Cause hair actually grows on my legs, unlike yours."

"It's a genetic disorder, I didn't ask to be born with it, and it actually slightly raises my risk of leukemia. But come on, it's not like people can tell the difference."

Wendy could barely hear her. The music was too loud. Wendy was far too young for the music to be too loud for her. But she didn't know if the current music would be safe at any volume; even with the volume turned all the way down, it might irritate dogs. It was loud, repetitive, and not much more than a beat when you came right down to it. Sounded like one of those comedy sound effect CDs being played inside a washing machine. Dubstep. What the hell was a gay club doing playing dubstep? The gays had David Bowie! You'd think people could take some pride in it.

And the lights were flashing, and there was some kind of mist being sprayed around and all in all, she'd have preferred it if someone changed the flickering lightbulb (oh, those were strobe lights), put on some damn pop, even Taylor Swift, and maybe just served coffee. Heck, she didn't care how cliché she was. Tea. She'd take tea.

She knew that wouldn't exactly make for much of a nightclub, but how was it only nightclubs had ended up being gay? Couldn't there be a gay martial arts dojo? Gay bookstore? She could meet people like in a Meg Ryan movie.

Gay arcade! She didn't care if no one went to arcades anymore, she would stay there all day playing *Time Crisis*, and when the only other lesbian who liked light gun games and *Street Fighter* came in, she would marry her.

Lesbian movie theater for showing lesbian movies. Shit, though—once they'd shown *D.E.B.S.* and *Imagine Me & You*, who would come? Maybe if it was winter, some hobos would sneak in for the central heating. Not if they were showing *Bar Girls*, but otherwise…

The bartender picked then to set a tequila sunrise in front of Regan. "From the lady in the back."

They both looked over. It was from the woman with the afro. She waved and flashed a smile. Wendy groaned. It was a cute smile. Yeah. Wendy wouldn't mind playing *Time Crisis* with her.

"Get up," Regan stood, gripping the drink.

"What is this?"

Regan pulled her to her feet. "I'm being a wingman."

"Oh God no—"

Regan gripped Wendy with a bouncer's hold on her upper arm and ushered her toward the cute girl. She worked out surprisingly often. Had a weight set where other housewives would have a sewing room.

"Sit down beside her," Regan ordered. "Don't think. Just sit."

"Abort. Abort. Abort—"

Regan stranded Wendy on one side of the cute girl, setting her drink down on the bar between them. "Hi!" she said brightly. She could talk to strangers as easily as a normal person might talk to a stray kitten they found on the road. "Thank you *so much* for the drink. I'm Regan."

"Alice," the cute girl said. Shit, she had a British accent. "I didn't know you needed a stunt double."

"This is my sister, Wendy."

"Oh," Alice said, her face doing some maneuvers it didn't seem to be cleared for. "I'm not really into that. Don't get me wrong, if I could be into that, you two would certainly have me into it."

Regan let out a deep breath, and Wendy was somewhat gratified by her frustration. Even her sister wasn't good at the lesbian dating scene. "I'm married, actually, but my sister here is single! Very single!"

Wendy elbowed her in the ribs. "Thanks, sis."

"So, married—" Alice said. She sounded deep in thought.

Wendy supposed she would have to be, to get the conversation back on some kind of track.

"Do you and your wife…like to party, say?"

"Married and straight. Excuse me, I have to go to the bathroom." Regan straightened and looked around theatrically. "Oh good, no takers. Last time I did that, the whole club came with me."

"She thinks she's funny," Wendy told Alice. She gave Regan a look. "I'm gonna tell Keith you turned that one down," she stage-whispered.

"Don't you dare." Regan headed off.

Alice picked up the drink she'd bought Regan and sipped.

Wendy wondered if that was a good sign. *You know, a good sign, like sitting in silence with someone who wanted to fuck your sister.* "So," Wendy said, "you looking forward to the next *Star Wars* movie?"

"Excuse me?" Alice replied.

"*Star Wars Episode 8*. Rian Johnson's directing it? He did *Looper*, *Brick*, *The Brothers Bloom*... Some people say Rey is going to go Dark Side, which I think would be really cool, because then maybe Finn—"

"I don't watch *Star Wars*."

By the time Regan came back, Alice was long gone.

"You know we have pretty much the same genetic code?" Regan asked. "I'm not sure how you can mess up with someone who's already into you on a genetic level."

Wendy held up a finger. "I opened with *Star Wars*," she said defensively. "Not *Star Trek*. Not *Farscape*. Not *Stargate*. *Star Wars*. If she's not into that, what's she into? What's that leave? *The Fast & the Furious*?"

 АVА

Well, Wendy had wanted to pay her dues. She just didn't think dues had included making coffee runs because her boss insisted on Starbucks, even though she'd worked there in high school and honestly, the stuff in the Savin Aerospace break room was exactly the same. She could even do the little leaf in the foam if he wanted. No, that would be too much brownnosing.

She walked through the lobby on autopilot, appropriately enough, flashed her identification to the security guard and then swiped her pass for good measure, then headed to the elevator bank where she would swipe her pass again because if someone wanted to steal industrial secrets, by God, they would use the stairs to do it.

And it was there, waiting for her elevator, that Wendy saw the most beautiful woman in the world.

The most beautiful woman in the world was standing there, at the elevator beside Wendy's, waiting for her car to arrive. And just by standing there, she appeared to Wendy more *vibrant* than her immediate surroundings; a whole different species from everyone else embroiled in the drab rat race. Her clothes seemed more fitted on her, a second skin: gray on white, a midi skirt bridged to black high heels by a length of stockinged calf that seemed shockingly naked—unarmored, really, especially in comparison to the black leather gloves that shrouded her hands.

But it was her face that nearly overwhelmed Wendy. The rest of her was all tight control, humming power in deliberate muscle, all sorts of things projecting and drawing in. And then her face was stone. Square, symmetrical, with a neat point of a chin, light pink lips, a pert nose and smooth cheekbones cutting into that white-gold tan of hers. And reigning over it, a pair of Wayfarer eyeglasses, black and sturdy and somehow timeless. More than anything, Wendy wanted to see what that cool, composed face would look like with the iota of remove that the glasses provided gone.

Wendy stared. How could she not, it being so important to her to find out how a person could *look like that*? People weren't supposed to look like that, right? Maybe Helen of Troy, Cleopatra, Angelina Jolie in *Gia*, but not just a *person* at Wendy's *job*, where she worked, like, how was that fair?

The woman noticed she was being stared at. She looked at Wendy and Wendy looked away. Because staring at people was creepy and rude and wrong, even if you thought they might possibly be a Greek goddess seeking out the Chosen One. She felt the woman's eyes on her; a quick, appraising scan. She really wanted to look back. She really wanted to make crazy-mad eye contact, even if it might cause spontaneous human combustion. She took deep breaths and wondered if the woman was still looking and hoped she wasn't looking and hoped she was. Could she still feel herself being stared at? Was it just wishful thinking? Maybe she should flash the most beautiful woman in the world and see if she reacted. *No Brain, bad idea, get it together or I'm punishing you with shots.*

Her elevator arrived. Wendy stepped inside the glass capsule, pressed the button for her floor, and reminded herself that no one has a heart attack in their twenties. It was passé. The elevator car rose, climbing steadily up the building's atrium, and Wendy casually looked around as if that hanging scale-model F-14 that she passed every day could take her mind off possibly seeing a Terminator (indeed, a Terminatrix) built to be able to both seduce and destroy any human resistance.

And Wendy saw the most beautiful woman in the world *again*, in the elevator beside her, and if seeing the most beautiful woman in the world once was shocking, twice in one day was getting into *Die Hard* sequel territory. How many times could one man run afoul of independent gangs of terrorists? How many times could Wendy abruptly want to volunteer for sex slave duty?

Wendy was not an unintelligent woman. She wasn't MacGyver or Machiavelli, either. While a quick-thinker, she was more likely to come up with the proper tip in a few seconds than any sort of master plan. So Wendy was a little proud of herself for coming up with this scheme: she would get out her phone and call someone as she looked at the most beautiful woman in the world.

She called Tina Thuy, whose number was labeled BFF in her phone.

"I am so gay," she said, right off the bat. "Holy shit, am I gay. I am just… I'm even gayer than previously expected. I didn't know my gay could go that high, but it can, and it has."

"Good for you." Tina punctuated her reply with a yawn. Working from home meant she didn't have to know if time had letters other than P.M. "Are you coming out again? Do people do that? Like a second wedding?"

"No, I'm just *really fucking gay.*"

"Because if you can come out again, don't throw anything at the clown this time, he meant well—"

"I'm not coming out again! But I feel like I should, because if I was at a hundred percent gay before, now I'm at two hundred percent!"

"What, did Donald Trump make a pass at you?"

Safely on her phone, Wendy looked over into the other elevator. It was still rising with hers, and the most beautiful woman in the world was still the most beautiful woman in the world. The way she stood, *God*, all power and control and just a little slinky, not at all like a man but maybe kind of macho? It was the way Xena would stand. Or the way a female director of the FBI would stand as she gave orders to Agent Scully—that was a happy thought.

"I'm looking at a woman who is, like, *unfairly* sexy. She's overloading my gay circuitry. My homosexuality is not rated for this level of hotness in a woman."

The most beautiful woman in the world made a minute adjustment to her wavy platinum hair. A chic short cut, side parted, with the fringe windswept. It reminded Wendy of the ropes on a cat o' nine tails. Not because it was stringy or anything, just in that there was something coiled there, something with an edge of threat.

"I think I just came," Wendy said.

"Wendy, doll, how much does this call cost after the first minute?"

"You're making light of a deeply spiritual experience I'm having with my gayness. I'm at the mecca of my homo right now."

"All right, take a picture, I need to see her."

"No! That would be creepy—"

"You're the one staring at her and wondering how her hair smells."

Wendy raised her hand to her mouth. "Oh God, I bet it smells amazing."

She had just been thinking that it was even more unfair that their elevators had come up together for so long, submitting her to more and more of the sight of the most beautiful woman in the world. It was like being forced to stare at the sun. But then Wendy's car arrived at its destination, and the Khaleesi's kept going: up and up and up, far out of sight behind the opaque ceiling of Wendy's elevator.

Then the doors of Wendy's elevator started to close again, having apparently opened, and she got out. "So," she said into the phone, "I'm just gonna…weep somewhere. Curl up on the floor. Pray for death. My heart's broken. Business as usual."

"Wendy's got a girlfriend, Wendy's got a girlfriend—" Tina chanted, singsong.

"Please don't joke about that. It's…too soon."

ÅⱯÅ

The food court in Savin Aerospace was about the size of a high school gymnasium. It boasted several restaurants in kiosk form: McDonald's, Chick-fil-A, Popeyes, Starbucks, even a Dunkin' Donuts and a recent strain of artisanal offerings. Wendy told the girl at Smooth Runnings, the smoothie place, to blend her something surprising and promised to drain the whole thing in fair trade for neglecting her StairMaster. Anything that tasted this bad had to be *great* for her.

The food court was pocketed between the building's atrium and exterior, wrapping around half of an entire floor. There were three big TVs in the room's corners: one along the white walled expanse where the restaurant business hadn't yet expanded (Wendy guessed they were trying to figure out how to park a food truck there), and the last corner of the room taken up by a Dairy Queen that only offered desserts.

Each TV was tuned to something different, and the quadrants of the room formed factions as carefully chosen as a favorite Star Trek captain. At the northeast corner, opposite the empty one, the TV played MTV11—the MTV that still played music. At the northwest corner, the TV played the Game Show Network, which occasionally tempted Wendy when something from the seventies was on. And at the southwest corner, there was a TV showing films from the Silent Movie Channel.

Trust a bunch of engineers to game the system. With their petition successful, they basked in the comparative quiet of orchestral music and either read their tablets or did incomprehensible things with their phones. One of this crowd was Elizabeth Smile. If someone had told Wendy that Elizabeth had worked out a way to go for a PhD on her smartphone, she would've believed them.

With her chic ensemble and glamorous makeup, the executive assistant looked more like a model doing a 1950s-themed photoshoot in their office. And was so out of Wendy's weight class that she felt abashed to look at her, as if she'd been caught doing something wrong like participating in the office sport of 'Look At Elizabeth.'

Nonetheless, Wendy pushed past it, sitting down across from Elizabeth. "I'm looking for a woman."

Elizabeth scantly looked away from her smartphone. "I like where this is headed. I can work with this."

"An older woman. Seems kinda dominating, tightly wound, position of power, but you just *know* she's worn a strap-on? Like, you want her to sneer at you while she wears Gucci and shoves a file folder into your arms and says 'Fix it!' in a really tense voice?"

"So, like a MILF?"

Wendy scoffed. "I actually don't like that acronym, that's a straight man acronym, and lesbians were into older women before it was cool. And they totally diluted the brand anyway, because it used to be just cougar, if a lesbian were in charge, it would've stayed at that, but there are leopards and pumas and jaguars and black panthers. I would've had sex with Helen Mirren before I saw her in a bikini!"

"So you're looking for Helen Mirren?"

"No, she's a lot younger, forties, aging like a Spielberg movie. And, uh…" Wendy held circled fingers in front of her face. "Glasses."

"Oh, is that what glasses look like?" Elizabeth set down her phone. "Sounds like Janet Lace. You've heard of her?"

Everyone had heard of her. Janet Lace was the rising star of the company's production division, no pun intended. She'd flown jets, not just approved overhauls for them. She knew the product line inside and out, could take apart a turbine and put it back together. If Janet's flight got delayed at the airport, she could probably get it working again with a thump of her fist.

"That's *her*?" Wendy boggled. "I thought she would be, you know…less like the teacher in a Van Halen video."

Elizabeth's phone dinged and she picked it back up, instantly engrossed in something it displayed. "What do you want with her, anyway?"

"I'm in love with her. I want her to quit playing these games and make me an honest woman."

"Is that even possible?" Elizabeth replied.

"Tell me everything about her. How high are her heels? Where was she born? How many adopted kids does she want? Is she okay with friendly back massages—"

"Would you like me to tape her sleeping, too?"

"I'm not stalking her. I'm just making sure she's not a serial killer or anything."

"Well, I don't think she'd be too happy about me writing a Wikipedia article on her, given that she's my—"

"Hold up," Wendy said.

Donnie Parsons had just come through the door.

Every time she saw him, he reminded Wendy of one of those yapping little dogs that were bred to fit into the purse, much the way rich people had to be bred not to find them annoying. He was a pretty normal boss—

Wendy thought she could've met much the same if her job were delivering pizzas or serving up fries—but he wore his goatee in the Frank Zappa style. It was doing a lot to ruin a hairstyle that Wendy had previously found pretty inoffensive.

"Duty calls," Wendy said. "My lunch break's almost over."

"Oh, come on, sit and gossip, this place could use an office romance to spice things up."

Wendy stood. "I'm in love with keeping my job."

"It's an unhealthy relationship. Your job doesn't pay you."

"It's called an internship."

"It's called slavery."

"Get out, it's not like they whip me."

"They make you wear heels."

Wendy shrugged and hurried over to the line at Subway's, where Donnie was looking at his watch. "Mr. Parsons, hi, one second of your time?"

"Cedar," he replied, managing to fit 'you again' between the letters. "It's lunch. Eat something."

"I had a power bar," she replied. "Listen, you remember telling me to submit the TCB report?"

"I remember it still not being done."

"Yeah, that's the thing, I still haven't gotten the proper numbers back from R&D." Wendy tried to diffuse her aggression with a slightly confused laugh. "I can't submit a report about their findings without their findings, you know?"

"You have their findings," Donnie interrupted, shuffling forward in line. "I uploaded them all onto the cloud myself, and I know you have access—"

Wendy had to dodge a stanchion to keep up with him. "I do, yes, but the findings aren't…" Wendy struggled for the right word "…exhaustive. I really need more information for the TCB report."

"Just put the report through, they'll clear it up somewhere above your pay grade, same as always."

"Yeah, but here at my pay grade, it's my job to clear it up now—"

"Cedar. It's Friday," Donnie interrupted. "Do you really want to hold everyone up and make a bunch of people, including us, work on the weekend just so we can dot a few I's?"

Wendy stopped moving to avoid colliding with the line to McDonald's, formed on her side of the stanchion rope. "It's not the weekend for three hours yet. I'm sure with your help, we can get what we need from R&D, finish the report—"

"I'm a busy man, Cedar. I have better things to do than hold your hand while you do your job. Send the damn report before you cost us all our weekend. You don't want that, do you?"

"No, sir."

Donnie was at the front of his line. "Good. Now get out of here, I don't know what to order."

"Sweet onion chicken teriyaki," she told him, then hurried off to figure out why she'd said that.

CHAPTER 2

WENDY DID NOT WORK ON Sundays, but she'd been called in, and as an intern, she wasn't expected to have a life. So, since her usual commute was only on weekdays, she hired an Uber, did her best to learn Greek to hold up her end of the conversation, and went into the deserted weekend workspace. Blank, flat monitors; some noisy grinding sort of janitorial work being done; and no one presenting themselves, no matter how many doors Wendy knocked on.

This meant she had the kitchen all to herself, and Wendy thought to put on a pot of coffee for when the others arrived. She also thought to have a sip of fresh coffee, made the way she liked it, instead of the indignities to which her co-workers subjected the coffee beans. Selecting her favorite roast from the cupboard in the break room, she set about cajoling the coffee machine into doing her will. The machine, for its part, kept hectoring her to connect to it with an app on her presumed smartphone. This would tell her when her coffee was done if she forgot how to tell time.

Wendy did not forget how to tell time. It was exactly seventeen minutes after she'd shown up when she heard the dogged footsteps of Donnie Parsons, along with a clearer, more intently pitched noise. Heels on linoleum, striking with a determined repetition. Like Wendy imagined a thief would use as he worked on a safe with a chisel. *Click, click, click, click.* Rapid succession, but not rushed. Purposeful.

Donnie came in followed by Janet Lace, and if Wendy didn't fall in love at first sight, or even at second sight, she was definitely ready to fall in love.

"Wanda! Did you send a *memo*—" Donnie began, and his pinched voice was as shocking to Wendy as having a water cooler explode in her face.

Janet silenced him with a wave of her hand. Her nails were quite short, black, neat little claws on slender fingers.

Wendy stared at them and was very hopeful.

"We apologize for our lateness." Janet's voice was clear, restrained, powerful. It seemed perfectly suited to that set of lips. "Traffic," Janet concluded; not apologetic, but with a slight growl like a mine threatening to cave in. An expression of anger toward the obstacle that had robbed her of her punctuality. "You know who I am," she stated by way of introduction.

Wendy nodded, trying to keep phrases like "Mrs. Wendy Cedar-Lace" and its variations indoors rather than out.

"It's fine. The traffic. Not that the traffic is fine, I'm sure it's very bad if it delayed you, but you being delayed by traffic is…" Wendy got through all that in one breath. Upon the next breath, she reconsidered. "Coffee?"

"Wanda!" Donnie insisted, his voice pinching in harder than ever, one of those submersibles that went too deep and was imploded by the pressure.

Janet strolled past him—she walked like a woman who did everything at a stroll—and wordlessly communicated to Wendy a question of where the mugs would be. Wendy gestured to a cupboard and Janet opened it up, fetching out a black mug with one sly finger.

"Her name is Wendy," Janet said. When her voice cooled, it was rich as chocolate. "It's on the memo. Which you did send, yes?"

"Yes." Wendy nodded. Then she moved hurriedly out of the way as Janet went to the coffee machine behind her. "I assume—I mean, I pretty much know—yeah, you're here about the TCB memo? To upper management?"

"My memo!" Donnie said. He nearly squeaked. "To my upper management!"

The sound of coffee cascading into a cup cut through him like a knife into butter. He seemed to sputter at every little mitosis in Janet's cells, which was Wendy's first real indication that Janet was as important as she assumed. Of course, she just *was* important to Wendy. Anything else would be like looking at the Pope and saying 'what's with the dumb hat?'

"Donald, please." Janet seemed infinitely concerned with the aroma of the coffee she was pouring, and not at all interested in the meeting she was attending. "If it's anyone's upper management, surely it's mine. I am assistant vice president, after all."

"Yes, miss, ma'am, of course, you are, of course, I just mean—" Donnie stopped and cleared his throat. "It's my office's responsibility to send out all communiqués, *with my express permission*—" He eyed Wendy like she was something he'd stepped in, and he was wearing really nice shoes. "Not hers."

"Yet she does work in your office, yes?"

"It was my project, yeah," Wendy answered.

Donnie took being cut out of the conversation as if it were his father's will. "It was not your project, it was mine. I *assigned* it to you, you were supposed to bring it back to me."

"For a rubber stamp," Wendy retorted.

"For my *approval*. As your boss—"

"This is very good coffee." Janet had taken a sip. "You made it?"

"Yes," Wendy said, flustered by the recognition. It suddenly felt like a long time since anyone had really noticed her. "I'm glad you—"

"Company beans?" Janet asked.

Wendy tried her best not to preen. "I bring some from home."

"Tastes expensive." She pursed her lips to underline the hint of approval.

Wendy restricted herself to only quasi-preening motions. Her main imperative was not playing with her hair. "Well, everyone here works really hard, and no one likes the coffee you can make with the, uh, provided beans."

"So you buy coffee for everyone?" Janet asked.

"Just the people who want to use it." Which was everyone, Wendy thought, but also thinking that would sound too full of herself to say.

Janet favored Donnie with a look. "How much does she make?"

"She's an intern." Donnie managed to make it sound like something for which you could be deported to Australia.

"That doesn't answer my question," Janet said, with another sip.

Donnie took a breath. "We don't pay our interns. Especially not when they take it on themselves to deny approval to multimillion-dollar contracts integral to this company's—"

"I thought we suspended the unpaid internship program." Janet set down her cup of coffee. "The Old Man himself wanted it done away with. Said that even if we just want someone to make paper airplanes, we should pay for the paper airplanes."

Donnie waved his hand as if some insidious smell was making an attempt on his nostrils. "That's in the Chicago division, this is New York."

"Do people in New York not like money?" Janet asked. She pointed at Wendy. "Is this some kind of Amish woman, doing her work out of Christian charity?"

"I really don't need the money." Wendy tried to smooth over the defensiveness she saw on Donnie's face, the rampant disapproval she saw in Janet's eyes. "I'm doing this for the experience, to learn the trade—"

"Well, I do need the money," Donnie interrupted. "And I'd rather not be out of the job because this company has no new helicopters to produce!"

"He does have a point about needing money. Ms. Cedar, please do tell us why you want to cost your company hundreds of millions of dollars?"

"To save us billions in lawsuits!" Wendy gritted her teeth. She knew people would be mad, but after they saw the problem, how could anyone not take her side? She grabbed a stack of napkins and, taking a pen from her pocket, began to sketch out a diagram. "Look, this is the swash plate, right? Two plates connected to each other. The upper part moves with the rotors, spinning them, while the lower part is stationary and moves under the pilot's control to direct the helicopter."

Wendy stopped drawing and blotted up the napkin. The diagram wasn't really helping. She regretted not taking more art classes in college, if not the additional hundreds of thousands of dollars that would put on her tuition.

Janet crossed her arms. "Please assume that the executives at a company that manufactures helicopters know how a helicopter works."

"Yeah, right, sorry—but this is very important. The scissor link connects the two, right?"

"Ten seconds," Janet said.

"Scissor link connects the two, allows them to move somewhat so that the pilot can control it, but restrains excessive movement so that the helicopter doesn't—well, worst-case scenario, crash."

Janet raised an eyebrow on the word 'crash.' "Ten more seconds."

"So the scissor link has to be about the *most* durable part of the helicopter, otherwise it won't stay in the air. We have to know it's rated to withstand the stresses the rest of the helicopter takes, if not more."

"And Mr. Parsons here assures me it will."

"The *tests* assure you it will," Donnie said, seeming very pleased to correct her.

Wendy threw her hands up. "Maybe! Here's the—" She paused on the 'fucking' she so dearly wanted to say "—the thing, though." Grabbing another napkin, Wendy wrote '20,500 feet' in big letters. "That's the service ceiling of our last chopper. Here's the service ceiling for our new chopper." She wrote '25,000 feet', nearly taking up the entire napkin. "The air pressure at 20,000 feet is 13.74 inches of mercury. The air pressure at 25,000 feet is 11.10. Less air pressure means less resistance."

"The rotors move through the air faster," Janet surmised. "And are the scissor links rated for that speed?"

"I don't know!" Wendy cried. "I e-mailed R&D, asking them for their stress test findings at 11.10 inches of mercury. They would only give me the rankings down to thirteen inches of mercury. So maybe the scissor link will be just fine, or maybe it'll fly apart."

"Those findings are classified," Donnie said.

"From who? We're the same company."

"You can't expect to have the clearance of a DARPA-certified asset—"

"I expect to be given the resources I need to do my job."

"It's my job!" Donnie insisted. "R&D says it'll be fine, it's our job to approve the specs, that's what we do!"

"We stop helicopters from crashing. That's what I do."

"Do you have a contract?" Janet asked.

"What?"

"What?" Donnie echoed.

Janet picked up her coffee again. "With your internship. Do you have a contract guaranteeing you a position at the company once you've finished the program? That if there's an opening, they won't just hire someone else off the street instead of giving it to you?"

"Well, no," Wendy admitted. "But I'm pretty sure—"

"Ms. Cedar," Janet interrupted, then held a moment's silence while she sipped her coffee again. "We are under a deadline to submit a proposal for the Navy contract. If we don't have a project drawn up and green-lit by that time, ipso facto, we won't get the contract."

"If the prototype crashes, we won't get it either."

Janet nodded. Then she folded her hands together, ringing her fingers around the warm coffee mug, and Wendy had the unmistakable impression of a snake coiling up. And the equally unmistakable desire to feel that snake around herself, squeezing tighter and tighter… "All right, I think I've heard enough. Mr. Parsons, please deal with the situation as you see fit."

"Thank you," Donnie said. "Now, if we're through wasting time, Ms. Cedar, your services will no longer be required. Please clear out your desk and turn in your security badge. It'll be expected within the hour."

"But you can't fire me," Wendy protested, giggling a little at the nervous absurdity of it. "I'm—"

"Don't waste your breath trying to save your job," Janet said. "Or volunteer work, as the case might be. Regardless, I would like to hire you for a position in my division."

"What?" Wendy asked, followed by Donnie again repeating the question at a higher pitch.

Janet looked from one of them to the other. "I have an opening. I have Wendy here, who's done conscientious and professional work despite the pressures put on her. If she were working at another company, I wouldn't think twice about snatching her up. And I'd usually offer her twice her pay, but since she isn't making anything, that's not really possible. Oh well. We'll hammer something out."

"You're just going to promote her?" Donnie demanded. "Someone who'll question your authority? Someone who won't follow orders?"

"How do you think I got promoted?" Janet asked. "Now, please see to it that R&D sends over the stress test rankings for 11.1 inches of mercury to *my* department. We wouldn't want to miss the deadline, after all."

It was then that Wendy Cedar fell hopelessly in love.

ΑΫΑ

That afternoon, Wendy skipped down to her sister's house in the suburbs to do her laundry. Regan's place was a neat little stucco thing, short and plump, and so lovely it looked more like a gingerbread house than anything else.

Regan graciously took the laundry basket and while the machine worked, Wendy went out into the front yard to wait on the swing.

Keith was mowing the lawn, wearing jean cutoffs and a muscle shirt that showed actual muscle, and he gave Wendy an impeccably neighborly nod and smile as she loitered.

When Mac brought her his basketball for a game with the hoop up above the driveway, Wendy agreed to shatter the domestic tranquility. "Okay, Ewok," she said, "we're gonna practice some free throws. You know free throws?"

Mac nodded. He had Keith's eyes and Regan's hair.

Wendy shot and felt like a badass as it swished in.

Mac ran, impressed, to retrieve it.

"All right, now you do it," she said.

He shot, and managed to brush the hem of the net before the basketball hit the garage door and rebounded.

Wendy caught it before it went into the street.

"You're taller than me," Mac complained. "It's not fair."

"Oh yeah?" Wendy got down on her knees and shot again. The ball wobbled on the rim for a moment, but went in. Wendy smiled smugly in the way only someone who was a badass to a seven-year-old could.

"Your arms are bigger than mine!" was Mac's follow-up.

"Joke's on you, I'm a lesbian, my people are very into big arms."

Mac rolled his eyes.

Wendy wondered when Regan was going to teach the Ewok respect for his elders already. "Fine. Bring it in. I'm gonna make this shot lying on my belly."

Mac returned the ball to her. She did not make the shot lying on her belly. "Let's see you do it, smart guy."

After retrieving the basketball once again, Mac got down beside her and tried to shoot. The most he managed was to get the ball to roll all the way up the driveway to the garage door.

When it rolled back, Wendy caught it and had another try, just as Regan wandered out the front door with a tray of lemonade in hand.

"Finding a way to play sports lying down," Regan said. "I'm impressed."

"I thinking of calling it Wii Sports. Is that taken?"

Regan brought the tray over to Keith, who paused the mower to take a grateful swig and give her a kiss on the cheek. Wendy shared Mac's sense of 'oh, come on'. Then she rolled over and sat up as Regan brought the lemonade to her.

"Hey," Regan said, "I know it's short notice, but Keith and I won this radio contest for a vacation in Hawaii. It's just three days over the weekend, so do you think you could watch Mac while we're gone?"

"Yeah, no probs." Wendy tried to Harlem Globetrotter the basketball on her finger, without much success. "My man Mac and I will play co-op, a little *Gears of War*—or I don't know, something rated Teen, whatever. Is he old enough to watch R-rated movies yet? I mean, old R-rated movies, like *Friday the 13th*, where they're so tame they're basically a seventies PG?"

Regan sighed and Indian-sat, balancing the tray on her lap. "We're not going to Hawaii."

"You're not?" Wendy replied.

Keith stopped the lawnmower. "We're not?"

Regan looked over her shoulder. "No, honey, I was proving a point."

"So we didn't win the contest," Keith reiterated.

"No, we didn't."

Keith moved to pull the ripcord again, but stopped with it in his hand. "Wait, did we lose or have they just not announced the winners yet?"

"We didn't enter the contest."

Keith pulled the ripcord, getting the lawnmower to fizzle but not turn over. He let go of it instead of giving it another pull. "Well, why didn't we? I would love to go to Hawaii!"

"There is no contest!"

"What is going on with this family?"

"Just…finish mowing the lawn," Regan said. "It's a sister thing."

"That's what you said about why we couldn't get a clown for Mac's birthday."

"It's for the best," Wendy assured him.

Regan took the basketball from her. "Hey, Mac, could you go play somewhere else for a little bit? Your Aunt Wendy and I need to talk."

Mac took the basketball and tried to spin it on his finger as he walked away, with even less success.

Wendy swiped a glass of lemonade from Regan. "You know, if you want to go to Hawaii, you can probably go to Hawaii. It's really not that expensive as long as you clear your cookies before you go to the airline website, because they will jack up the prices on you—"

"This isn't about Hawaii. It's that my sister is in the prime of her life, I just asked her to spend the weekend looking after a seven-year-old, and you agreed to it without thinking."

"I know, I'm a wonderful sister." Wendy ran her fingers through her hair with care, as if taking pains not to dislodge her halo.

"Wendy! You have no social life."

Wendy sighed. "I have Tina. And very many Tumblr followers. Some of them even reblog my posts. And if this is about the girlfriend thing, look—"

"It's simple," Regan insisted. Then, God help the single, she started counting on her fingers. "Step one, you put yourself out there. Step two, you see something you want—a career, a relationship, whatever—*you go after it.*"

Wendy waved her hand in the air. "Okay, maybe it's that simple in Straightland, which is admittedly most places besides San Francisco, but I don't have it so easy. Pussy in Straightland, it's a seller's market."

"Trust me, it is *not.*" Regan set down the tray, then checked automatically to see if Mac was in earshot of a conversation about the market value of pussy. He wasn't. "I see plenty of twenty-something straight women in therapy and relationships aren't easy for them, either. All the good men are either married or gay."

"You're married," Wendy pointed out. "Look at him, he has...*arms*! He's mowing the lawn! What else can you ask for? You have the perfect relationship."

"It's nice," Regan admitted. "But I got in on the ground floor; I've been dating him since elementary school."

"Exactly my point. How many gay women do you think went to our elementary school?"

"Suzie Mendler."

"What, really?" Wendy's face went blank as she helplessly reviewed every interaction she'd ever had with her. Not so much as a high sign.

"Yeah, she came out last year, it was all over her MySpace page."

"Well, MySpace, of course I didn't hear about it."

Regan reached out to take Wendy's hand. "Wendy, you are my sister and I love you and I promise, it doesn't matter to me whether you're straight or gay or bisexual or a furry."

"I can't believe that's what comes fourth for you."

"Sure. The point is: I just want you to be happy with whoever it is that…makes you happy! Whoever that very lucky person is! Or whatever kind of animal they pretend to be."

"No, it's fine," Wendy told her. "And it's not like there's no one—"

Regan reared up, crossing her arms. "Oh, so there's someone?"

"I didn't say that."

"That's literally what you just said."

Wendy mouthed 'fuck' and drained her glass of lemonade dry. When she finished, Regan was tapping her fingers on her bicep, patiently awaiting an explanation.

"You know," Wendy said, "you really should get a shorter basketball hoop, he is a small child, he cannot throw a ball that high. In fact, you might want to give up on basketball altogether, see about raising a jockey."

"Don't change the subject." Regan laughed. "I'm doing your laundry, c'mon, you owe me."

Wendy groaned and lay back, pillowing her hands behind her head. "She's this…co-worker in my new department and she is very…cool."

"Oh, so she's laid-back, kinda Zen, like a surfer, that's good." Regan crossed her fingers. "Like goes with like."

"No, I mean she's a little frosty, on the outside? Tightly wound? You'd like her."

"Okay then, a bit of a Type-A personality, something of a realist to keep your dreamer ass grounded. Excellent." Regan held her two index fingers apart and then brought them together. "Opposites attract."

"Also, she's an alien from the Omega Theta galaxy and she feeds on human brains."

"Does she want children?" Regan asked without missing a beat.

Wendy unspooled her leg to kick at her sister.

"Watch it, watch it—" Regan scooped up the tray. "You're gonna spill my lemonade. It's all organic, you know."

"It's made from lemons, water, and sugar, what else would it be?"

"C'mon, c'mon, your office crush, she's Type-A, what else?"

Wendy bit her lip. It almost ached to think of Janet. A good ache, but if she let herself forget that, it was almost certainly not going to happen.

Well, let Regan think it was possible, at least. She deserved to live in hope for a few more years, at least.

"She's passionate…very passionate. Powerful. It's all interior." Wendy tapped between her breasts. "In here, you know? But you can tell it's there. Just looking at her, you can see that she's all…" Wendy shook her head. "She's just amazing."

"You know what you should do?" Keith said. He'd finished mowing. "You should get one of those side-cuts. Those look great!"

"They *do*," Regan agreed.

Groaning again, and only partially because of exercise, Wendy got to her feet. "Do you two mind planning the grand seduction without me? I think my clothes are done, so I should probably get going."

Regan picked up her glass and handed it to her. "Take one for the road." Then she lowered her voice. "And by the way, I was with Keith when he went through puberty. I've put in my time."

CHAPTER 3

WENDY LIKED HER NEW WORKPLACE in the Efficiency Optimization Department (a title so relentlessly buzzworded she was surprised that there were actual plaques with it written down in the right order). The carpet was thick and decadent, the lighting bright and full and mainly suborned by the giant windows that had most of the floor sunlit. There were no cubicles either. Her office space was the space in an office. It wasn't in the corner or anything, but there was something psychologically soothing about being able to close a door behind you. Went back to the primitive hindbrain; being able to hide from dinosaurs or something. If dinosaurs hadn't been able to open doors. She would have to ask a paleontologist or something.

She was just getting her desk moved into when something went *thunk* in her headspace and made her think, *Fuck, T-rex!*

It was a vase. Not even a particularly reptilian vase, just a normal vase with a few pansies in it that Janet Lace had set on the upper portion of her desk.

"Housewarming gift," Janet explained, making minute adjustments to the flowers until they looked fit for van Gogh to paint. "How are you finding your new 'digs,' so to speak?"

"It's very…windows," Wendy replied, nodding to hers. "And everyone's very well-dressed."

"We have a group discount at my tailors," Janet explained. "It's all right if you don't want to go," she added insincerely.

"Those are really nice flowers," Wendy said.

"They're from my garden. Funny how I killed them just so you could feel welcome here."

"What?"

Janet sidled down onto Wendy's desk in a way that made Wendy resolve never to put pictures of her family—okay, cat—in that space. "I would just like to say something to clear the air. Efficiency Optimization is my department, you are my subordinate, and I absolutely believe in an open-door policy. You did exactly the right thing back at Safety & Risk Management, keeping the company from making a costly mistake. That being said, this is still my department; I am in charge, and I like control. So if you're going to go over my head, you should be damn sure you're right, or I'll pull you like a weed. Like a fluffy little dandelion."

"I…don't want to go over your head," Wendy said. Her voice sounded as if it was sweating.

"That's good." Janet sounded as if she was commiserating with Wendy. "I don't want to pull you like a weed. So do your job, follow my instructions, and I promise I'll take care of you. But always remember who's in charge. All right?"

"Yeah."

"I think you're going to fit in well around here. I think you're the kind of employee I like to have." Janet reached over and picked up a snow globe from the cardboard box Wendy had been unpacking. "I like this. What is it—Hoboken?"

"Yeah, my dad got it for me on a business trip. You might know him, actually, he's—"

Janet set the snow globe down by her vase. "I think it would look good here, don't you? Well, I'll leave you to it. And remember, don't hesitate to come see me if you need anything. I like to keep my employees happy."

"Yes. Thanks. I'm very happy." Wendy smiled for Janet.

"You have a nice smile," Janet told her, and left.

Wendy waited until her new boss was gone, then moved the snow globe a half foot away from the vase. She nodded in satisfaction—it looked much better there.

⚸

At night, the office shone white. The big windows turned black, the absence of sunlight throwing a pall over the floor, even with the lights still blazing away. The furnishings, the load-bearing pillars: all shades of white. Even most of the computers were gray, save for the monitor screens themselves. Coupled with the oppressive darkness, they seemed to brighten to a spectral glow, overwhelming any variety in color, any knickknacks that might've introduced a different hue. Coupled with the desertion of the 9-to-5 crew—which technically should've included her—Wendy felt like she was on a literal ghost ship, sailing dark waters, maybe taking flight among clouds in a starless sky. Outside the window, her floor was too far off the ground to see anything but the distant, rolling hills outside the city. Not a light among them.

The mood it put Wendy in pleasantly reminded her of her teenage goth years, and she abandoned her cramped yet cozy office to sit out on the main office floor with her laptop, finishing her work under a nice massage from the AC unit that never quite reached her workspace. On the far side of the elephantine room, the lights were on in Janet's office. They burned like a private moon.

Wendy typed away, sending e-mail after e-mail to wait for morning in sleeping in-boxes. She felt a sense of communion with Janet, working this late. Despite the difference in ages, in position, they had the same drive, or so Wendy fancied. They wouldn't quit until the work was done, exceptionally so. Being the best was their reward.

And so was explicit validation and approval. No one said the best couldn't be self-aware.

She looked up from her laptop, some reptilian brain impulse driving her head up. She saw that the lights to Janet's office were off. The communion vanished, replaced with a stark fear of being caught…doing what? Working late?

"Interesting attire for a janitor." Janet Lace was standing right next to her.

Wendy turned her head, saw a tower of nylon-encased leg, goddamn *leg*, and looked back at her laptop. Felt like she was back in high school, trying not to get noticed staring at the head cheerleader.

"And I didn't know defragmenting hard drives was part of your duties."

Wendy forced herself to look up. They were co-workers. All she was doing was talking to a co-worker. "I was just finishing up."

"Everyone else went home four hours ago. That's not finishing, that's working. And if you like it so much, there's always tomorrow." Janet offered her hand.

Wendy took it, maybe a little too quickly, or maybe a little too slowly— weird to think of Janet Lace as someone you could touch, no matter how casually. Janet helped her to her feet, Wendy shutting the laptop and tucking it under her arm. Now she was face to face with Janet, and Janet was taller than her. By a few inches. High heels. Wendy wore sneakers.

"You're here too," Wendy pointed out.

"I'd never ask an employee to do something I wouldn't do myself. Speaking of, since you're up…" Janet brought a dossier out from her briefcase, and Wendy could do without the image of Janet's fingers sliding over glossy black leather. At least, she could do without it until she was alone. Very, very alone. "Your new in-pile." She handed a dossier to Wendy, thick and heavy. "I'll expect it to be done with your usual alacrity."

Usual alacrity? So she was usually…alacritical? That sounded like praise. But what the hell was alacrity?

"Of course," Wendy said. "I'll get right on it. With lots of alacrity!"

Janet rolled her eyes, a little fondly, Wendy thought. "*Tomorrow.* When you're fresh and well-rested. A good sleep cycle is something you don't appreciate until it's gone."

"I went to engineering school. I don't remember what one of those is."

Janet smiled in commiseration and Wendy felt like she'd won the lottery. *We have something in common!*

"Well, we'll just have to see about getting you to mind your bedtime, won't we?"

Why had God put sweat glands on Wendy's thighs? It felt like a monsoon season in the backs of her knees. Was that normal? Maybe she had a gland condition.

Wendy clutched the dossier tight to her chest, bundled with her laptop—hugging them, really. Was this what getting the team captain's letterman jacket felt like? "It's not my bedtime just yet," Wendy said, because a demon had suddenly possessed her and someone with a voodoo doll of her stuck a needle into the 'say stupid shit' part of her brain. "Why don't we get a drink?"

Janet blinked, a bit like a particularly lazy lizard might.

Wendy found that hot. Slightly frightening.

Then Janet's head tilted forward, her glasses catching a beam of light and becoming two brilliant oval jewels, gleaming too bright to be looked at directly. "I think you've misunderstood our relationship," Janet said, her voice affectless.

Wendy said, "Oh," and would've liked to be anywhere else. In a split-second, she thought of all the 'anywhere elses' in the world, from North Korea to the South Pole, and decided that all of them were better than here.

Janet raised her hand and pressed two fingers, fore and middle, into Wendy's chest. "I think you're going to make a fine employee. I appreciate the contributions I foresee you making to this company. And I recruited you in that expectation. But we're not friends. I'm not your mentor. I'm not some sister helping you out of feminist solidarity. I'm your boss, you are my subordinate, and our relationship—our *working* relationship—is strictly that."

She went on from there, trying to let Wendy down easy—as easy as she could, anyway. But Wendy wasn't listening anymore. She'd seen what was on Janet's left hand.

There was a very good reason why Janet had not fallen hopelessly in love with her as well. She had already fallen hopelessly in love.

And, naturally, Janet had married him.

CHAPTER 4

Dear Roberta,

I remember you suggested a marriage counselor some time ago. Despite how things have deteriorated, I still believe that's unnecessary. I've read numerous texts and internalized them quite thoroughly. We're two reasonable people—we can resolve our issues without an outside party. If that's what we both want.

Frankly, I believe you want a counselor because you think they'll take your side. Let me disabuse you of the notion. From any outside, unbiased perspective, I am in the right. My decisions and my career have consistently benefitted us. What do you have to complain about? The home my work has provided you? The luxuries? The respect? You treat my good fortune like an oppression of you, my career aspirations as your embarrassment. It's aggravating me and shameful to yourself…

Janet stopped writing. Too aggressive. Too angry. She usually never let herself get this angry. At a certain point, too much fire stopped fueling an engine and started damaging it. But that was the problem, wasn't it? Bobbi had grown tired of putting up with a wife who was more successful than she was.

Or she'd just grown tired of Janet.

Janet set her fountain pen aside with her notebook—both in the cold space where Roberta had once slept—and rolled over to see her bedside clock. It was 7 a.m. Saturday, no work. Still, she wouldn't sleep in. She would keep her habit. Otherwise, it was useless.

Exercise regimen: an hour every day, seven days a week. She wasn't a kid anymore. She couldn't afford to be lazy. Cardio. Jump rope. Light weights. Treadmill to cool her down to a finish. Her earbuds beat out a rhythm, she followed it. No peak, no summit, just control. She wasn't trying to burn fat, lose ten pounds, or build muscle. She was trying to maintain. Keep the statue polished to a sheen. Keep chipping away at it, because there was always something underneath. She pushed her limit to the almost comfortable frenzy, hard sweat, harsh breaths, burning in her arms and legs. The rhythm pushed into her and she didn't have to worry, didn't have to think.

She guzzled from her water bottle after. The bottle was by Alexander Wang. The water was by Angelina Jolie.

Shower routine: warm water. She preferred to be scorched, but lukewarm was better for her skin. Shampoo rubbed into her scalp, especially at the nape of her neck. Sixty seconds. Conditioner. Brush. Soap. Scrub. Blast of cold water to seal the cuticle for shiny skin. Then, as the steam hung in the air, she moisturized. She didn't admire the tautness of her own body, but she did appreciate it. All her exercise, her dieting, her care, they'd given her this raw material that she could now play with. Make something out of.

Beauty routine: she washed her face with cleansing crème. Moisturized with Luzern lotion, adding a mist of rose water and a light helping of sunscreen. She considered a perfecting mask, but no. Once a week was enough.

Makeup was minimal. Highlighter, mascara, rose balm. A touch of lip sheen. Then a dab of fragrance on her wrists, the nape of her neck, by her ears. She used her hands for as much of the application as she could. She liked to be sure with her makeup, to know what she was crafting. Brushes and other tools were always so imprecise.

She put on a cream-colored shearling and cashmere vest underneath a beige long-sleeve sweater tunic. Then a suede pencil skirt. Brunello Cucinelli. Pink underwear beneath. Kitten heels in sable-black. A low-key look. Light, but ascetic. She stared into the reflection of herself and saw nothing to chisel away, to grind down or excise.

Not yet.

9 a.m. She'd finished breakfast, but the notebook sat in the kitchen nook, the pen an unsteady bookmark to an unfinished page. She gave it a wide berth, as she took her dishes to the sink, rinsed them, then placed them into the machine. The job seemed unfinished, though—she'd tried to think what hadn't been done.

Of course. She hadn't washed Roberta's dishes.

Dear Roberta,

I know you think that if you'd stuck with your legal career, you would have become a senior partner by now. You were a fair legal mind, but in all honesty, the point is moot. You became a paralegal. You supported me as I pursued a career at Savin. We moved here. We built a life here. I attained a position of respect and responsibility. And now you want to throw it all away to start a law firm with some college buddy and pretend you're fresh out of law school?

Clearly there's something lacking in our life. Fine. Tell me what it is, because I can't see it. You have a wife who loves you. A wife who is intelligent and successful. A wife who looks practically the same as the day we met, and I am well aware of how long ago that was. What else must I contribute to your happiness?

The maid arrived slightly behind schedule. Janet left little for her to do, but whatever there was, she did it.

Janet sat in her living room, listening to the spritz of spray bottles, the squeak of washcloths, the burr of brooms. She didn't know why—after seven years, surely she could trust the woman with her homestead.

Perhaps it was just her place, as it was the maid's to clean.

She tried to concentrate on her book. *Unfriendly Skies: The Air Battles of World War II*. It was hard to be engrossed in it. The author made the most basic errors, confusing the SBD and SB2C dive bombers, mistaking the caliber of the IJNS Yamato's guns. She tossed it aside and lifted another from the tower of To Be Reads. *Hunting Warbirds: The Obsessive Quest for the Lost Aircraft of World War II* by Carl Hoffman.

On February 21, 1947, the *Kee Bird* crashed on a frozen lake in the Arctic. A Boeing B-29 Superfortress bomber, the *Kee Bird* had been one of the last of its kind—at the time, the pinnacle of American engineering. Its development had cost a billion dollars more than the Manhattan Project, and two of the *Kee Bird's* brethren, the *Enola Gay* and *Bock's Car*, had ended the war they'd been designed for.

As part of Project Nanook, the *Kee Bird* was sent on a top secret mission to search for possible Soviet military activity in northern Greenland. Encountering bad weather and the North Pole's compass-killing magnetic anomalies, the *Kee Bird's* crew became disoriented and flew off course, burning fuel for over nine hours, until they had no choice but to crash land and await rescue. Three days later, they were rescued by First Lieutenant Bobbie Joe Cavnar aboard the C-54 *Red Raider*.

And the *Kee Bird* stayed in the ice. Ninety feet long, its wingspan 141 feet wide, its only damage was the props bent from a wheels-up landing and a leak in the number-three engine. The plane that had won the Second World War, still fully functional, still a beauty of a machine, was now only so much scrap metal.

Janet closed the book before she started, blaming her sudden emotion on the overall melancholic day she'd had. She wanted literary comfort food, an old familiar friend in paperback, but she didn't want to taint a good book with her present mood. She wanted to slip out of herself, just for a moment, and fill her lungs with something other than this numbness.

The maid started vacuuming. Janet could hear the steady thrum of air being sucked in, the slight rattle of chunks disappearing into the intake. Morsels of food. Particles tracked in from inside. Outcroppings on her perfect life that just had to be chiseled away, sanded down, made pure.

She didn't know the maid's name. She'd forgotten it.

Roberta would know.

The maid was done by 11 a.m. Janet had an appointment at her nail salon for noon.

She got there early. Someone else had canceled. She got to have her manicure at 11:40. Janet liked saving time, even when she didn't know what she was saving it for.

The manicure took twenty-five minutes, the pedicure thirty-five. Five minutes of drying. She tipped thirty percent.

She spent fifteen minutes on the letter after, to make it an even hour and a half. She wanted to be back on track.

Dear Roberta,

Is it control? Is that what you miss so dearly? Is that what you've starved for, more and more hungrily, during all our wedded bliss?

Can you not enjoy our good fortune because it's under my name instead of yours? Do you think you'd be happy, an over-the-hill paralegal playing greenhorn lawyer in this day and age, simply because all your disasters are your own?

Every choice we made, we made. You agreed to all of it. I supported you as much as you supported me. It's been a good life.

What decision have I made that you can't live with?

Was it the baby?

Her hair salon appointment was at 1:30 p.m. It was within walking distance of the nail salon. Because she had finished early, she took the brisk walk rather than an Uber. She tried to think about the letter some more, about Roberta, about control, but her thoughts circled each other, chased their own tail and refused to yield dividends. It didn't make sense and she couldn't make it make sense and she wished someone could explain it to her and she felt guilty that she needed it explained.

And more and more, she wondered if there was an explanation, or if it mattered that she knew it.

Inside the hair salon, there were no cell phones, no eating, and no loud conversations. A stereo played a song Janet didn't recognize. It was low and soothing, a curtain thrown up between her ears and the sound of snipping. Denise, her preferred stylist, was there and, as always, she asked if Janet would like to try something new. She always had an idea for a new look and sometimes Janet indulged her, but she was in no mood today. She asked for the same look, asked if Denise needed to see the picture on her phone again. Denise didn't. She'd done the cut enough times.

Just little tendrils of hair, pushing out of her short, neat side part. Slowly pulling the lines of her silhouette out of alignment, adding one more frizzy deviation to her overall look, then another, then another. They were all stripped away. Scoured. Until all that was left was her undiminished, unencumbered perfection.

Two hundred dollars for an hour's work. She tipped thirty percent. It was 2:30 p.m. She had nothing else to do with her day.

She went back to her apartment. It was quiet. Not too quiet—she didn't believe such a thing existed. The four-bedroom was spacious, she knew, but its real virtue was quiet. That was the premium, the rarity, the value. Only the most wandering sounds made their way up from the streets below—tires, horns, but no people; nothing as messy as that. Divorced from context and shorn of environment, the sounds became little semaphore flags against her windows. The world politely trying to contact her, and Janet refusing its attentions.

The living room was like a reverse painting. The appropriately bold whitewashed walls, the hardwood floors, the prints on the wall of a ballet company in repose (Roberta's) and the models of the furnishings of airplanes in flight (hers)—they were all framing for the TV, the sound system, stereo equipment, and plasma screen just abreast of the dappling of light from the shuttered windows. She filled the frame. Powered on the TV, the surround sound, the Blu-ray player in ritualistic sequence. Selected Netflix. Checked her watchlist.

She settled on a documentary. At an hour long, it wasn't in-depth enough to be informing, but also didn't dramatize the subject well enough to be engaging. Eventually, she just let the noise of it play; it compelled being watched only so that she could say it did not get any better. It didn't. At 3 p.m. she left it playing to make herself a late lunch. She'd forgotten to eat again.

After a salad, she turned Netflix back on. Checked the new releases.

Nothing of interest. Everything was too old to be intriguing, but not old enough to be classic.

Horror movies. Serial killers she wasn't afraid of—too easy to deal with so long as you had a brain in your head, which none of the characters did. Ghosts she didn't believe in. Zombies she was just bored of.

Action movies. Nothing with a budget high enough for so much as a decent explosion. Starring the washed-up and those who would never be famous enough to ever wash up. They would just disappear one day when they walked around a corner out of sight, like something unloved.

Dear Roberta,

Twenty-five years in this business have convinced me that I have my managerial style down, and down so well that I can apply it in any aspect of my life with similar success. When faced with a dilemma, I weigh my options, I solicit advice, I decide the right course of action, then I apply myself to it with all my strength.

Maybe I've treated you as just another team member, giving me advice, when you're not. You're my wife. That's not fair to you.

But I can't regret my life. I can't take back my career. This is my home. This job is what I do.

Janet stopped. She crossed out the last sentence. She wrote:

This job is who I am.

She wondered why she'd written that. She wondered if it was the truth. It seemed like it, and she had no one to tell her otherwise. Funny as hell: all this time, she'd never had to choose between work and a relationship until now. And it hadn't been hard at all.

"It should've been, right?"

The words surprised her. She hadn't spoken since she'd left the hair salon. The silence had been perfect, completing, inviolate.

She didn't like how the words reverberated, even when they were her own.

Her laptop was still on. She stared at it as the background became a long-forgotten inside joke—a modern-day flying toasters screensaver. Flying…had to be engineer humor. She watched them go by without seeing them.

The screensaver blinked back to her desktop. She'd jiggled the touchpad. Janet blinked, pumped her eyes shut then open, trying to come to and remember what she'd been intending. Yes. She went to the address bar, typed in Wendy Cedar, and pressed *Enter*. Her Gmail account disappeared into a Google search. There were few results, at least for a person, but one was a Facebook account. Janet clicked on it. It hadn't been updated since 2013, at least not publicly, but there were a number of pictures.

Wendy looked very different than she did at the office.

It wasn't boudoir photography or anything like that. The pictures didn't frame her or pose her; they were just casual snapshots, probably taken by a friend. She wasn't even dressed immodestly. She wore a white half shirt, exposing only a smidgen of taut, firm belly. Printed on the front were two lines: 'Fem in the Streets, Butch in the Sheets.' The fabric was white, the text black, and the cups of her bra were just evident behind the obscuring letters. An undercurrent of black underlying the words that drew in the eye. Demanded it.

She wore an olive-drab army jacket over it, one elbow worn thin, a lining of plaid just visible on the sides between shirt and jacket. Her pants were hip-hugging jeans, holes in the knees yawning open so wide they could've been cut with a straight razor. A red belt holding them up.

But it was her hair that really caught Janet's eyes. The way it was tousled, disheveled, falling in shaggy, perfect locks to her shoulders, down the front of her face in erratic patterns, barely missing her eyes. In half the pictures, she seemed to be lazily corralling it out of the way. In one set, she pushed it back out of her eyes, only to drag her hands back through it, down over her forehead. Her hair bustled out in a crazy mane after that, one strand slinking down to catch at the corner of her wet lips, a sweet scar just waiting to be healed...

She had hair like she'd just been fucked. Not bedhead, but bedroom hair. Unconsciously, Janet reached behind her glasses and combed her fingers through the fringe of her own hair. Would Wendy's hair feel like that? Soft and smooth? It looked that way. Layer after layer of midnight black, soft as a summer night, and under it that face. Her eyes. The challenging smile of those lips.

But the eyes. Everything else was a bit challenging, a bit butch, *don't fuck with me*, but the eyes were soft and alluring, a gentle warmth in them. There was one of her looking at another woman—a friend? A girlfriend? There was an insouciant smirk on her lips, a raised chin like a boxer inviting a jab, but the eyes sent a more complicated message. The eyes asked...the eyes almost pleaded...

The look Janet had always imagined a woman giving her before she slipped the blindfold over her eyes.

Janet shut the laptop. Jesus. Wendy was her *employee* now. Maybe not in 2013, but that woman—soft butch Wendy Cedar, she might not even exist as far as Janet was concerned. She had Worker Bee Wendy Cedar. Good Employee Wendy Cedar.

'You've misunderstood our relationship' Wendy Cedar.

Janet went to the wine rack. It had to be late enough in the day to drink by now.

A glass of port helped her come up with the problem in writing to Roberta. Janet was trying to tell her how she felt, but she couldn't summon it up. The prospect of Roberta leaving her was foolish, and she responded to the foolishness, tried to tell her how foolish it was, but aside from that— when it came to Janet—how she felt was like the ocean at night. Too deep and black to be penetrated.

She turned the TV back on. The Blu-ray player had a few videos in its memory. They'd put their wedding video on there. Janet couldn't remember ever watching it.

She watched it now like a hawk, an avid viewer of her own past melodrama. She tried to see signs of artifice in herself—it would be so easy to hide under all the pageantry, the white dress, the traditions. But she couldn't find any. Whatever had happened, it had crept in between then and now. It had been patient.

Because she'd been happy then. She didn't know what she was now.

Dear Roberta,

I don't want to be alone.

She called Bobbi. She'd never intended to send a letter, not really. She'd just wanted to get her thoughts together. All it had done, though, was show her that her thoughts were as 'together' as they'd ever get.

Roberta picked up on the first ring. She supposed that was the courtesy a few decades of marriage got you. "Janet," she said. Her voice didn't sound like it had on the tape.

No point in putting pleasantries before something unpleasant. "Are you coming back?"

Roberta didn't answer. She *waited.* Janet waited. She could feel Roberta trying to be diplomatic, trying to explain.

Oh Bobbi, I've been trying to do that all day, and you're only starting now?

Finally, there was her voice again, small and stagnant in all the quiet she'd brought. "I've met someone."

Janet tried to say something, just something automatic and thoughtless. "Oh" or "I see" or "I understand." One of those lies that came in so brutally useful. But none presented themselves. She couldn't even pretend anymore.

Roberta continued. It took her less time than it had to speak in the first place. "She makes me feel the way I used to feel."

Janet resisted the urge to ask how that was. She hung up. Like it'd all been some obscene harassment. Roberta didn't call her back.

Janet tried to think if there was anything else to say and there wasn't. Even the prenup was ironclad. All that'd been left after the separation was deciding if they wanted to keep trying or not.

She guessed Roberta had finally gotten to make the choice for both of them.

She didn't remember sitting back down at the couch, opening up the laptop again. She must've. There were the pictures of Wendy. Taunting her. Young and alive and unhurt.

She was beautiful, yes, but she'd been beautiful at the office. No, what drew Janet's eye was her confidence. She was so collected, so composed, so brazen in her dykishness. The center of her was firmly rooted. She leaned over girls, eyed them, flirted with them, fucked them, not with the kind of poise Janet favored, but with her own slouching, cocky swagger.

Except for her eyes. Sometimes she looked a little lost. Maybe it was just late and dark and she was tired, drunk, wanted to go home. Maybe she just needed someone with a little bit more experience to take her hand and tell her it was all right and to take her away. Maybe, if Janet had been there in 2013, Wendy would've given herself over with the same unvoiced desperation she'd tried to show in the office.

Janet touched up her make up, using a pencil to make her eyes just a little darker, smokier, before she hid them behind her glasses. She sprayed her hair again, keeping each follicle in place. She reapplied her fragrance.

7 p.m. Primetime. Janet watched one show after another; no point in cluttering up the DVR when she was there anyway. A cop show, a doctor show, a lawyer show, then local news, then late night. Then it was twelve. She turned the TV off. She ate an apple, drank two glasses of water. She didn't feel tired, but she didn't feel like doing anything but sleeping, either. She brushed her teeth, she washed her face. She tried to sleep and not think of the hair growing out of control, the nails rebelling against their prescribed lengths, the food turning treacherously to fat inside her—all the pollution that would have to be cleaned off the statue of her come morning. And come the next day, and the next, and the next.

ΑΨΑ

She couldn't sleep. She could not sleep. The clock at her bedside taunted her with how she couldn't sleep, sped up when she wasn't looking and then screamed how long she'd been trying to sleep, how much time she'd wasted simply lying in bed, doing nothing, contributing nothing, *being* nothing. Her eyes grew heavy but never seemed to close.

Masturbation was frustrating. She used a Hitachi to stimulate herself—a simple, reliable tool to do a job. Generate a series of impulses within her, create a sensation, allow her to shed her stress and relax. But the tool wasn't doing its job. It was like trying to resuscitate dead flesh, to carve a real woman out of a block of cold marble. The impulses vibrated between her legs, against parts of her anatomy that were in perfect working order, but the feeling didn't spread. It thudded into a wall, stayed locked in her insensate flesh, never moving to where she was locked up or clenched or needed the flow of hot blood, life, her own sexuality.

She felt broken.

With a cry of anger that was eagerly sucked into the silent walls, Janet threw the vibrator aside.

Wendy caught it.

She was dressed in a plain white tee with black letters graffitied on the front, a light flannel jacket, an oversized army jacket over that. Her jeans were ragged, but skintight from mid-thigh to a pair of boots. Firm, well-muscled legs. If they wrapped around someone, it'd be just impossible to get away.

Janet sat up, holding her bedsheet to her chest. "How'd you get in here? What are you doing here?"

Wendy brushed at her hair. It wasn't the neat, tidy ponytail it was at the office. It was free but cut short, shoulder length, tousled and windswept—freshly fucked. Locks of hair strayed like fingers down her skin, over her face. Like they had to touch her. "I'm here because you wanted me to be here. And I'm going to do what you want me to do."

She walked to a chair in the corner. Her boots were loud on the hardwood floor. They thumped, one after another, with each spindly step. Surprisingly aggressive for such long, slender legs.

"Must've hit something by accident on my Facebook page. Liked a status that you shouldn't have. Did you enjoy looking at those pictures? To think, I was always a little worried about my employer seeing them." She smiled. Bee-stung lips sharper than the teeth behind them. "Now I don't mind."

"You can't be in here," Janet said. Her heart was racing. She could hear it in her ears. It dwarfed her own voice. "It's not allowed."

"I'm allowing it. Aren't you? After all, you're not calling the cops." Wendy's eyes swiped over Janet like a touch. Her irises were the brightest thing in the dark room. "Your phone's right on the nightstand."

"You could hurt me," Janet protested. "I don't want to provoke you."

"Is that what you're worried about? That I'll hurt you?" Wendy sat down. Slouched, in fact. One leg spanning an armrest, kicky boot dangling in the air. Janet could see the toe describe little circles in the air. "Nice place for a chair, the bedroom. What, did you used to sit here and read Roberta bedtime stories? Or, no, maybe someone sat here and *watched*. Do you like to watch, Janet? Or do you like to be watched?"

Janet's throat was dry. It was all she could think of; how dry it was. "I'd like some water, please," she said, absurdly.

"Other side of the bed," Wendy replied.

Janet turned over. There, on the floor beside her bed, was a glass of water. Ice cubes floated lazily at the top. The edges weren't even rounded yet.

It was as she reached for it that Janet felt a finger of air run down her back, a burst from the air conditioning. Down her bare back.

She turned back over, careful to keep the sheet in place. It was all that separated her from Wendy.

"You always struck me as a woman who likes to do it herself." Wendy smirked, dropped back in the wingchair like it was a throne, she a royal born to power. "But I guess this explains why you aren't throwing me out. Maybe you have a few interesting tattoos you don't want me to see?"

"I'm wearing a nightie," Janet said. She drank her water. The ice cubes pushed at her lips as she upended the glass too high, following the dousing water like night-cool fingers, like the air that had lit up Janet's bare back. Her heart thundered in her chest. She felt the satin sheets against her nipples. As thorough as a caress.

Wendy was all sex, all fucking, but it wasn't something projected, something put on. It was exuded. Lazy, indolent, the heat from a furnace. It crouched inside her, not safe, but like a predator ready to pounce.

"I'm going to do something when I get up from this chair," Wendy announced. "But until then, we can talk."

"What are you going to do when you get up?" Janet asked.

"What do you want me to do?"

"Answering a question with a question is poor form."

Wendy held up a finger. "Not answering a question is worse. You didn't tell me whether you like to watch or whether you like to be watched."

Janet said nothing.

"It's okay. I get that you haven't decided yet."

"Neither," Janet said, her voice sounding loud to her own ears. It was her heart. It was settling. Not muting everything else anymore.

"Lying," Wendy mused. "What form is that?"

"I'm not lying. I enjoy my privacy."

"You enjoy your isolation. You'll enjoy other things more. Shall I get up now?"

"No."

"The great Janet Lace, always so in control." Wendy nodded to the nightstand. "You could call the cops. This is a nice neighborhood. I'm sure they wouldn't take long. And you could tell me to sit until they get here."

"Will you not get up until I tell you to?"

"I won't get up until you want me to."

"You seem to credit yourself with a great deal of knowledge regarding my wants and desires."

"I think you want the same thing everyone wants. When you sleep naked in a bed, you want someone to be in it with you."

Janet buzzed inside, having to stop her hand from tightening before she shattered the glass in it. When Wendy said she was naked, it felt like she had looked. It felt like Janet was even barer than she was. "I'm not naked."

"Shall we find out?"

"I'll scream."

"Me, I tend to moan."

"Maybe you tripped an alarm as you came in." Janet smiled at her. Politely. Speaking with the control that was the very last thing she felt. "Maybe the police are already on their way."

"So you want to see me handcuffed? You should put on your glasses then. What are they? Barton Perreira Lucky? In black, of course."

Janet reached out. Her glasses were in their case, on the nightstand. Beside her phone. She picked the case up. She opened it. She took out her glasses. Extended their earpieces. Slipped them on.

She couldn't see any farther into the darkness, but she could see more of it. With her dark hair hazing her face, Wendy seemed almost a part of it.

"So I guess we know you like to watch," Janet said. "And you make requests."

"You can't tell me you wear those glasses not knowing they make people want to fuck you."

"They let me read fine print. You find that sexy?"

"If I thought squinting was sexy, I'd date Clint Eastwood."

"Fascinating insight into what you consider a deal-breaker aside, the police could be here any minute. If you did trip an alarm."

"Then I guess I'd better hurry." Wendy leaned forward in her seat, but didn't stand up. Her hair fell in front of her face as she leaned on her knees, white shirt a deep gray in the darkness under her jacket, the black text over her breasts an alluringly different shade of shadow. She held up the Hitachi. "Like your vibe, by the way. Very classy, very…unashamed. Most women go for some cute little thing like their puppy's going to play with it or something. That or some overcompensating Bad Dragon shit, trying to punish their vajayjay for something. Which I understand, but only once every twenty-eight days."

"Are you going to use that?" Janet's breath was rushed. She hated how her control slipped, and the more she hated it the more she slipped, and the more she slipped the more she didn't hate it, couldn't hate it, had to try harder and harder just to *not like* it.

"Why should I?" Wendy asked, setting the vibrator down. "I have you."

She stood up then. There was a window between her and Janet. The moonlight from it hit Wendy like a spotlight as she stepped forward, pausing in the glow, enjoying how Janet stared. Janet imagined she could see herself, lit up all silver, in the lens of her glasses.

The light swathed Wendy, pushed against her, burned up one half of her. The other it cast into an even deeper shadow than before. But in the darkness, Janet could feel both of Wendy's eyes. They never strayed from her as Wendy shrugged off her jacket, the slow unveiling arching her back, pushing her chest into prominence. Janet could see her full breasts standing up proudly from her shirt, the strain of the fabric maybe a size too small for them, how eloquently the swell fit within the otherwise smooth, even lines of her body. The black text swimming into view like it was coming up from the very bottom of the ocean.

Fem in the Streets, Butch in the Sheets.

And Wendy smiled, as she watched herself being watched.

The jacket hit the floor. Wendy started taking off her flannel next. She glided forward, a tremor in her cleavage with every step, the striptease slow and sensual, each movement drawn out.

"Are you going to do something?" Janet asked. "Or are you just going to rethink your outfit?"

"Just trying to keep you from feeling underdressed." Wendy came to the foot of the bed, settling a hand on the bedpost. The moonlight was behind her now. It prickled in her hair, silhouetted her curves, the side of her breasts. Its light was like a slow caress that never stopped.

She finished letting her other arm out of the flannel. Then took its sleeves and wrapped them around her waist, tying them in a knot. Janet watched as she pulled the knot tight, tighter, then let it go. The sleeves falling down in a ribbon over her crotch. She looked up to Wendy's face. Wendy was smirking. Something smug in it; arrogant. Like she'd known Janet would watch.

"You know, when I was a little girl, I used to be afraid that if my leg wasn't covered by my bedsheet, that a monster would get me." Wendy looked down at the bed.

Janet's right foot poked out from under the bedsheet. The nails still red from her pedicure, almost black in the moonlight.

"Were you afraid of that?"

"Yes, I was."

"Did you stop believing in the monster? Or stop being afraid of it?"

"I got a bigger bed."

"I've noticed." Wendy's hand dangled down.

Her touch light, when it brushed against Janet's ankle through the sheet, but still unbearably tangible. Janet's mind ran away from her, tried to remember the last time she'd been touched. Just…touched.

"Should I cover you up?" Wendy asked. "Or…"

She pulled at the bedsheet. Its hem dwindled down the slopes of Janet's breasts, the contact as sweet and achingly teasing as Wendy's fingers had been.

Wendy stopped. Only teasing. She was careful to set the sheet down behind Janet's foot. Leaving it exposed. "I don't think the cops are coming," Wendy said. "I don't think I tripped any alarms."

Janet breathed. It was hard.

"Do you even have any alarms? Or did you just have another woman to keep you company?"

"I'm not afraid of you," Janet said. Her voice shook. Gasped.

"No, you're not. You're afraid of you." Wendy's body lowered. She crouched. She got down on her knees. "You're afraid of how this will feel."

You bitch, Janet thought. *You bitch, don't say that. Don't put that into words. Don't let it be true.*

Wendy's hands reached forward. They delved under the sheet to either side of Janet's foot. They touched her calf. Then they pulled back. Fingers dragging down the skin of her legs. No, not fingers. Not even fingertips. Fingernails. Short. So damn short.

Then Wendy's fingers on the bony protuberance of her ankle, the hardness of her heel. Pressure, pointed pressure, thumbs pressing into the bottom of her feet. Almost ticklish, mostly not. Mostly something else. Fingers wrapped around the tops of her feet, thumbs on the soles. Pressing, but not hard enough. Touching, but not lightly enough. Janet felt it. Nothing else. She just—felt it.

She was acutely aware of her *foot*, of all things, of the slight ache from a day in her fuck-me heels, or her don't-fuck-with-me heels. Roberta had liked to call them that. Roberta wasn't *there*.

Janet's mouth lapsed open. She didn't gasp. She wouldn't.

Thumbs, tracing down the arches of her feet, moving their pressure across them. More ticklish. Janet tried to jerk away on instinct, but Wendy had a good hold. An insistent hold. Not too tight that Janet couldn't slip away, but...

Squeezing. Her palms now. A gentle pressure, a soothing one. She could feel Wendy's fingertips pressing in. The whorls of her fingerprints. The bones providing force. Hands moving up and down, the pressure firm, dwindling on the downstroke, pressing just a little harder on the upstroke.

Janet's lips pinched inward. Tried to come together. She held her mouth open, though. Not because she wanted it to be, but because it already was, and she didn't want to react. Not to such a minor thing. Not to just being touched a little. Not to the look Wendy was giving her, darkly hooded eyes, smug smirk saying she'd known how much Janet would like it. Janet's eyelids tried to flutter shut under that stare. She kept them open.

Wendy leaned forward. Her breath was warm on Janet's toes and the room was cold. Her lips were soft, a trickle of air, and they touched where Janet hadn't known she was sensitive. She could've kicked. She could've pulled her foot away. She was holding still for Wendy. She was wanting this.

"You can touch yourself," Wendy said, "while I do this. Or do you need the vibrator?"

Janet's lips were still parted. She could feel her breath flowing through them.

"Or do you need me?"

"I...I...I could have you *fired*," Janet managed.

"You don't have to threaten me," Wendy said innocently. "I was going to do it anyway." She stood up, again.

Janet's body tensed with need, her eyes screwed shut, and when she forced them open, Wendy stood over her. At her bedside. Out of the way of the moonlight. The shirt was a white shadow on her body, her jeans a shadow on a shadow. She took them off. Slid them down her thighs, then raised one leg, then the next. Her boxers an interruption of her legs. She stooped again. In the new darkness, there was no new shadow, no white glow. Just her. Something sweet-smelling, the flannel covering her. Almost. Maybe. Not quite.

"You tasted good," Wendy said. "Just now. Does all of you taste that good? It has to taste better, right? Than your foot? Because even with that pedicure—it's still a foot."

Janet didn't know what to say.

Wendy reached out. Took her glasses, took them off, set them down nearby. "You don't need to see right now," Wendy said. "You just need to feel."

She sat down on the bed. Her flank in the light, on display, smooth, clear skin that looked like it would be perfect to the touch. As creamy and as liquid as the light itself. And behind that firm thigh, before the other one—she smelled so good. No perfume, no fragrance, just her.

"You're not very talkative now," Wendy said. "Nothing much to say?"

"Your ass is on my mattress," Janet replied. "I hope you haven't used any public toilets lately."

Wendy laughed. She moved her leg up onto the mattress, then her other one, and then she was lying down beside Janet. Just lying there, her hands behind her head, as if they were any other couple. As if they were a couple.

Janet's foot brushed against Wendy's. The breath rasped down her throat.

"I know you've wondered what it would be like," Wendy said.

"With you?"

"With a woman."

"I was married."

"You forgot," Wendy retorted. "Maybe you remember what Roberta was like, and maybe you remember what you were like with her. But you don't remember being a dyke. You don't remember women. I can tell you, Ms. Lace. I've been with women. I've fucked them. They've fucked me. I can tell you how it feels to have a woman's head between your legs, soft hair on your thighs, kissing you so good you try to squeeze your legs together just so you can breathe, but she holds you open and shows you how much more there is for you to feel. I can tell you how it feels when a finger just isn't enough, when her pussy clenches and tells you she needs more, just one more finger, just one more, until she's taken all four and she's thanking God that she's gay. I can tell you how a woman tastes, Ms. Lace. I can tell you how *I* taste—when she's done worshipping me with her tongue—when she comes up for air and kisses me just to thank me for spreading my legs. I can tell you how I taste after I come in a woman's mouth. Would you like to know that, Ms. Lace? Would you like to see how soft and smooth and gentle a woman can be…until she stops being gentle? Have you ever wondered how *hard* softness can be?"

Janet could feel how wet she was. She couldn't remember the last time she was so ready that she *needed* it, but God, she remembered it felt like this. "What would I have to do?"

"Turn over," Wendy said. "I want to see your nightie."

Janet rolled over. The sheet rolled with her, bunched and bundled beneath her, and above her, the air had such a firm touch that she could feel every stitch she wasn't wearing. Feel Wendy's eyes on every inch of her.

She was being fucked before Wendy ever touched her.

"That doesn't look like a nightie," Wendy said. "Have you been lying to me, Ms. Lace?"

Janet's buttocks quivered, exposed, so damn *visible*. God, when was Wendy going to touch her? She knew it'd be any minute… "It was," Janet said, "a bluff."

"Lying's a very naughty thing, Ms. Lace. Not as naughty as what you do at your desk, of course. After you've watched me. When you're thinking about me."

Janet could feel the bedspread shift, the eddies and currents of its fabric being pulled minutely by new pressure. Wendy's hand between Janet's legs now. Not touching her, touching the mattress beneath her.

"You open your legs so wide…" Janet could hear Wendy's fingers slide along the bedspread as they moved upward. "Then you close them, nice and tight. Clench them up." She felt the sides of Wendy's hand brush against one leg, the backs of her fingers tingle along the other. "Are you doing that for me, Ms. Lace? Are you thinking one day I'll be there?" The hardness of Wendy's knuckles along her thigh… "Well, I'm here, Ms. Lace. I'm right here."

Wendy's hand sliding under her body—sliding along her…

"I can feel the heat coming off you. God, tell me what it's like to finger-fuck yourself with that cunt of yours. Feeling the heat all around your fingers, running down your thighs…"

"Touch me…" Janet breathed into her pillow. The heat of her gasp burned against her own face. "I want you to touch me."

And suddenly Wendy had mounted her, thrown a leg over her prone body and straddled her, body pressed down atop Janet's back, flesh against her flesh, the sparse hair of her pussy tingling on the curve of Janet's ass. Now Janet gasped. Now she heard herself.

"Is that what I want?" Wendy asked, her voice, her breath right in Janet's ear. "To touch you? Because I think I want to fuck you. And not on your terms, on my terms. I wanna fuck you so hard, and so fast, and so good that you almost wanna beg me to stop, but you can't. You can't speak, you can't even breathe almost, all you can do is come. Like I want you to come. And when I've had enough—when I've fucked you so hard you can't even remember your name—I want you to thank me. Because you'll still remember *my* name. And you'll be so damn grateful I made you my bitch. Now say it. *Say it, Lace.* 'I want to be fucked.'"

Janet burned. She clenched. Her pussy was on fire and she tried to put it out by rubbing against the mattress, squirming against it like a bitch in heat, but that didn't help. Wasn't what she needed. She needed it to burn hotter. She needed to explode.

"'I want to be fucked,'" Wendy repeated. "'I want to be fucked.' 'I want to be fucked.' 'I want to be fucked.'"

Janet's eyes fluttered, her jaw clenched, her fingers gripping the bedspread tightly, gripping it until it pulled free of the mattress pad.

Wendy kept repeating herself, chanting like some orgiastic cultist, and Janet could feel her mouth forming the words, could feel their echoes beginning in the back of her throat. She just had to say it. No, she just had to *admit it*.

Then she looked up and saw Gal Gadot by her bed.

"What are you doing here?" she asked, as if she weren't the meat in a bottomless-woman-and-bed sandwich.

"I'm in everything these days," Gal Gadot said.

"Yeah, you do show up a lot. You must have a really good agent."

"Thank you," Gal Gadot said, and then Janet pointedly woke up, turning over the words 'I want to be fucked' in her mind like it was a foreign phrase she was trying to learn.

CHAPTER 5

"The problem with posting your cooking on Instagram," Wendy said as she swept through the door, "is that I know when you've made snickerdoodles. Fork 'em over, sis."

Regan sighed and plucked at her apron, as she led Wendy to a towel-covered plate in her kitchen. "You know, it would bother a lot of women that they have the same palate as my second-grader."

In the kitchen, Wendy hopped up on the counter and graciously took a snickerdoodle from the plate, before Regan equally graciously moved it away from her.

"Are you shitting me? Kids know where it's at. They eat Reese's Puffs, we eat Oat Bran. No wonder they think they're in charge." Having said her piece, Wendy bit into the snickerdoodle. She moaned approvingly.

Regan leaned against the kitchen island across from her. "So?"

"So what?"

"How's your workplace romance?" Regan demanded, arms crossed. "C'mon, Mac and Keith are at the movies, this is the perfect time to dish."

"There's nothing to dish." Wendy spoke through an angry bite. "I 'misinterpreted the relationship.'"

"Oh," Regan said. She handed Wendy another snickerdoodle. "So, she's straight?"

Wendy ate with small nibbles. "Married."

"To a woman?"

"Like it matters," Wendy growled.

"I'm just saying, you can't give up that easily."

"She's *married.*"

"But not everyone is," Regan insisted. "You just have to keep putting yourself out there. I'm really proud of you, trying to get something going there, and maybe it didn't work this time, but next time—"

"Next time, I get to go to a sexual harassment seminar." Wendy hopped down from the counter. "Let's face it, Regan, you don't have the most unbiased opinion of the dating game."

"What's that supposed to mean?"

"Regan, you have the perfect husband, okay? He looks like he's captain of a starship. Crewed by a ragtag bunch of misfits, always trying to stay one step ahead of the oppressive Universal Imperium and their psychic enforcers—"

"Not that this doesn't sound interesting, but what's your point?"

Wendy threw her hands out. "There's not someone like that out there for me! There's no perfect girl that I'll get if—" Wendy sardonically pumped her arm. "I just keep at it! You got lucky."

"And you can't?"

"Correction," Wendy said, "you got lucky and you were born with the grace and charm of a Disney princess. I'm a hot mess with the social graces of a Michael Bay movie. So if there is some perfect person out there, they're gonna have to really be into, like, sarcasm and bad dancing."

"It's not like Keith and I are made for each other, you know," Regan countered. "There are plenty of things we don't have in common."

Wendy indulged in the kind of sour face she knew Regan hated. "Name one."

"He likes his orange juice to have high pulp, and I of course prefer it pulp free…"

Wendy raised her hands to her face. "Oh my God, your marriage is doomed."

"There's no call to be snide. And my point is, maybe your person won't seem right for you, but if you're willing to work at it…"

Wendy hung her head. "Even my sister, who thinks I'm going to find my one true love on Tinder, says I'm going to have to work at it."

"What do you expect?"

"I would settle for maybe a quarter of what you have," Wendy said, bringing up her hand with the thumb and forefinger held an inch apart. "I'm not asking for, like… Okay, I assume you don't want to know my idea of a fantasy girlfriend."

"Would it cause me to lose respect for you?"

"You have respect for me?"

"Would this fantasy girlfriend own any particular kind of costume?"

"No, not exactly. See, she would actually work as—"

Regan held up a hand. "I'm good. I'm fine."

"Right. So I'm not looking for a whole list of Wendy-candy. I would just like someone who would take care of me the same way Keith takes care of you."

"I take care of him too, you know."

"Yeah, yeah. Cookie me."

Regan tossed her another snickerdoodle.

"Like I said, not going to happen, so I might as well plan on dying alone." Wendy moved to take a bite, then paused with the snickerdoodle in her face. "Hey, are there any foods you should avoid so that if you die alone and your cats eat you, they won't get sick? I would hate to poison orphaned cats with my bloated corpse."

"Is this your subtle way of wanting to be hugged and having someone pet your hair?"

Wendy pouted. "Yeah. Ya mind?"

"No, not at all." Regan went over to hug Wendy, who cuddled her right back. "Mac's getting too big to lavish affection on. You'll do until we get a dog."

"You're going to get a dog? Oh my God, can I move in?"

ÅⱯÅ

The sick thing is, Wendy thought, *Regan would lurve if I put as much effort into my life as I do into my work.* She'd just checked the clock and three hours had passed since she started on her e-mail of recommendations for Project Hawkowl Revision A114. No Facebook. No Twitter. Just cross-checking and correlation. If she could just get lesbians to send in notes on their aerodynamics, she would be married by now.

She was about to rectify the 'not checking Twitter' thing when Elizabeth Smile cleared her throat. Wendy hadn't even noticed the secretary in her doorway, and that was saying something. Maybe she was turning straight and that's why her dating life was going so bad. Now if she could just reverse-engineer the process and find a way to train it on Emily Blunt.

"Lace wants to see you," Elizabeth said, without preamble, and turned on her heel without explanation. Her skirt was just long enough for the sway of her hips to be in perfect pendulum counterpoint to the fringe of her hem, her stockings hard-pressed to stretch all the way down her endless legs.

Not that Wendy was in any mood to notice, not after hearing those five words. The boss-lady wanted to see her. *Her* boss-lady? Was she getting fired? Promoted? Janet Lace was so saturnine it could go either way. She reminded Wendy of a cat. You never knew if you were going to get to pet the kitty or if you were going to get your hand bitten.

Pet the kitty, Jesus, Cedar! Wendy thought to herself as she rose, gathering a few of her things and doing a quick spot-check of her appearance. She dusted some crumbs from lunch at her desk away from her slacks, tucked in her blouse again, tightened her belt one notch over complaints from her spine. Her hair was still in the updo she'd put it in that morning, barely, and when she powered down her monitor screen, her reflection's makeup looked presentable.

She started the long walk to her boss's office, very much looking forward to seeing Janet, no matter how much it also worried her. Being in Janet's commanding presence, she consistently felt like some moist, juicy cinnamon roll, fresh out of the oven, all warm and gooey on the inside.

So much for Emily Blunt.

Wendy tried her best to once again banish her gay thoughts as she came to Janet's door.

Elizabeth had already sat back down at her desk outside, buzzing the intercom to inside: "Ms. Cedar to see you, Jan."

The intercom clicked. Even through tinny speakers, Janet's voice was cool and controlling, a firm finger rolling down Wendy's earlobe… "Send her in."

Elizabeth gave Wendy a look and, belatedly, Wendy realized she should open the door. And go through.

Janet's office was chillingly precise. Paintings of nondescript things on the wall, unassuming furniture, a large desk whose surface held only a computer and an inbox and an outbox. The outbox's stack of papers always outnumbered the inbox's. And an altimeter wall clock, just to prove she had a personality.

Behind the desk, Janet sat flanked by the view out her floor-to-ceiling windows. Skyscrapers in the background on either side of her, like intimidating goons. Wendy gulped and heard her name in greeting. "Wendy."

"Ms. Lace," Wendy said, low-key enough. "How's tricks?"

Janet got up. She always rose like a cobra coming up from its coils, hands planted firmly on her desk, then tapering away in a supple stroke of her fingertips as she came up to her full height. Wendy didn't know if it was designed to, but it always had her *staring* at Janet's fingers.

"Assuming 'tricks' is referring to the well-being of myself and the company that supports my livelihood…"

"Always."

"Then very good." Her hands braided together, Janet walked out from behind her desk and over to her liquor cabinet. Her office was much larger than Wendy's. It had room for a liquor cabinet. It probably had room for a vineyard, if you didn't care about feng shui. "I'm very pleased to say that, while the gears may turn slowly, they do turn. We retested the new prototype, found a design flaw, and we're taking it back to the blueprint stage."

"So." Wendy paused. "The drawing board?"

"No, we already have drawings of it," Janet said, perched somewhere between oblivious and simply careless as she browsed for one particular bottle like a general inspecting her troops. Her liquor cabinet curiously resembled an art deco hotel cleaning cart to Wendy's eyes. "We're just redesigning it."

"But isn't that…bad?" Wendy asked cautiously. "I mean, it's a huge setback."

Janet came up with a bottle of brandy. "It would be, but our distinguished competition—" here Janet toasted with the bottle, before endeavoring to open it "—had a test flight of their prototype. It crashed."

"Oh my God. Is everyone all right?"

"Probably." Janet shrugged. "I didn't ask." She held the bottle out to Wendy, unopened. "Do you mind?"

"Sure," Wendy said, and worked on the cap. She wondered if Janet couldn't open it, or just couldn't open it without looking undignified.

Either way, Wendy could look undignified *and* open it.

"Thank you." Janet took the bottle back. "Now, their design flaw was the exact same scissor link problem *you* identified and that we've been taking steps to correct. So you can imagine how pleased the Old Man was to tell Senator Marston all about how our prototype is already well on its way to having that very problem licked."

"Yeah. Being licked. Cool."

"And it's all thanks to you." Janet poured for both of them into two of those pebbly, crystal glasses that Wendy was sure you weren't supposed to drink Dr Pepper out of. Of course, she tried not to drink Dr. Pepper out of anything. "You deserve a reward."

"Oh, well, I…" *Licked.* Why the hell had Janet had to enunciate it that way? *Licked.* Like it was the name of a drug or something. *Licked. Licked.* It'd been three seconds and already that sounded like complete nonsense, like fizzypuff or President Trump. "I was just doing my job."

"Ms. Cedar, there are two things you should learn from me. One, never let anyone pay you less than you're worth. Two, always take credit when it's well-deserved." Janet handed one of the glasses—tumblers, Wendy thought, then wondered why the hell they were called that—to her. "I know a glass of fine Kentucky bourbon isn't much, considering you may very well have saved lives by 'doing your job,' but it will have to do. Just know that your workmanship does not go unrecognized, or unappreciated. I'm very good at remembering employees as competent and trustworthy as you."

"Thanks." Wendy looked at the tumbler. Damn, it was dark. Like amber. "Should I drink this? I am on the clock."

"Drink," Janet said.

Wendy obeyed without thinking. It burned. Not as much as the lemonade Wendy had made as a kid without sugar, but more than Wendy thought a throat should, which was none. She coughed and sputtered, and Janet graciously took the tumbler from her.

"It's an acquired taste," she said. "Well, that'll be all. Back to work. Next time I'll see about getting you a Long Island Iced Tea—"

"Do you have a cold?" Wendy asked suddenly.

Janet froze, coiling inward into a defensive lack of affect in her speech. "Why do you ask?"

Wendy pointed to the wastebasket beside her desk. It was full of wadded-up tissues, so it was either a cold or Janet was jerking off a ton, as Wendy's scumbag brain pointed out, despite the obvious logistical issues there.

"Oh, yes, just a sniffle," Janet insisted, though she still seemed perturbed, unaccustomed to being second-guessed or however it was she'd taken Wendy's question. She knocked back what was left in Wendy's tumbler. *Well, she's good at swallowing,* Wendy's scumbag brain added, before Wendy managed to silence it for good with threats of watching Downton Abbey.

"Please go," Janet continued. "I'd hate for you to catch anything."

"Yeah. Sure," Wendy agreed, pausing nonetheless. Eyes frantically darting around, seeing if she could get Janet anything. She seemed to have plenty of napkins; a lot of fluids, even if they were largely alcoholic.

"Go, go," Janet insisted. "Make me more money. Shoo."

Wendy hurried along, reminding herself that Janet was a grown-ass woman and could buy herself all the DayQuil she needed.

ᛘᛦᛘ

Wendy did not think of her apartment as small. She thought of it as efficient. She really didn't need a couch to sit on, after all, when she had a bed, or a TV when she had a laptop, or an oven when she had a microwave, or a closet when she had a floor. Sure, it wasn't like home, where you could take a bath in water, but it was on the first floor of her building and she didn't have to work up a sweat walking her Triumph Bonneville inside and getting it up onto the kitchen table (eating would now be done on her lap, which was sadly only a single entendre).

With her Bluetooth calling Tina, she got to work on her bike as a mother would fawn over a sick child (although the Bonneville was far more expensive).

"Wendy, hey, what's up? Bike again?"

"Bike again," Wendy confirmed. "One of the cable stops disappeared, now the carbs are completely out of sync."

"You're never going to get that thing running right," Tina said between crunches.

Wendy could imagine her lying on her couch, enjoying some pita chips, while they spoke. "We're never going to get a *Terminator* movie better than *T2* either, but it doesn't mean we stop trying."

"Heh. Yeah. So I'm guessing the stop fell out?"

"Yeah, but that's impossible, there was always tension on the throttle cable."

"Betcha the cable sheath is dropping. When you turn the bars it straightens out, that puts slack in the cable and the little bastard escapes. Fuck it, tape the damn thing."

"What about a snap ring?" Wendy asked. "On the outside of the major OD?"

"As you like it. Although you'd think if your dad was going to get you a motorcycle, he'd get you one that worked. Or a penthouse apartment, for that matter."

"The bike's a birthday present," Wendy replied.

"So's being rich."

"You're talking yourself out of riding bitch this very moment."

"Hey, I always ride bitch no matter where I sit. Now, tell me you didn't call me just so I could tell you to tape a loose cable?"

Wendy cracked her neck as she went to her toolbox, situated on top of a kitchen chair, and dug out her safety glasses and needle-nose pliers. "You know any homeopathic cold remedies? You know, tea leaves or whatever?"

"You mean from Vietnam, where I was born, or from Cleveland, where I actually grew up?"

"Either's fine," Wendy said, pouring an añejo into a tequila glass. The most important safety equipment of all.

"Because if we can't figure out how to win the World Series, we definitely can't cure the common cold."

Wendy got a sangrita from the freezer, carrying the shot glass in the same hand as the añejo. She was a professional. "Okay, but you guys have noodles, right? You eat noodles when you have a cold? That's like a universal—universally acknowledged treatment for—"

"Don't."

"What?" Wendy asked, getting a snap ring out of the parts shelf on the wall.

"You're planning something. Don't do it."

"I'm trying to do something nice for a friend who is down with the cold."

"I'm your only friend, remember? Who's this skanky other friend? Is she younger than me?"

Wendy paused, finding the new cable stop that she'd already put in. This one she wasn't losing. "She…might be Janet Lace."

"Don't," Tina said, one note higher than before.

"It's not—"

"No."

"I'm just—"

"Nooooo."

Gritting her teeth, Wendy jammed the tips of the pliers into the holes at the end of the snap ring. It took her a moment to get them through. "It's just a little care package to let her know I'm thinking of her. It's barely even romantic."

"It's your boss! She can fire you!"

"I've thought of that."

"And?"

Wendy opened the pliers, forcing the arms of the snap ring to open. "She's not going to. Listen, men have been seducing women for hundreds of years at least. I think I can pull it off."

"Remember the last time you tried to seduce someone?"

Her hands occupied with the pliers and snap ring, Wendy bit down on the rim of her tequila, eased the glass over, and sucked up what she could. "That lawsuit was dropped."

Tina took a breath deep enough for a spiel as Wendy slipped the widened snap ring over the cable stop and the groove where she wanted it to stay. "Listen—if this Lace person is so nice, why don't you just ask her out on a date? The worst thing she can do is say no, and then at least you can forget the whole thing like I'm telling you to do right now."

"I would," Wendy protested, closing the pliers gently. "I absolutely would, but, she might be, and this is just a possibility—she could be married."

"*Could* be married? What, was he shot down over German lines or something?"

Wendy pulled the pliers away, letting the ring snap closed. "She wears a wedding ring… It could just be so that men don't see her as an object of desire and sexually harass her."

"Yes, that wedding ring is clearly discouraging people from obsessing over her."

Wendy heard a crunch of pita chips over the line. She'd driven Tina to stress eating.

With a heaving sigh, Wendy tossed the pliers back into her toolbox. "Okay, you think I don't know it's not going to happen? I get it, it's me, it's not going to happen. But I can at least be nice to her! And she can smile at me! And I can have these really nice sex dreams where she asks me to work late and—sorry. Private thought."

"No, keep going, this is like watching a true crime show for lesbians. My best friend is O.J. Simpson with a vagina."

Wendy tapped at the snap ring with a thumb ring on her right hand, making sure it was properly seated. It didn't budge. "Tina, my ovaries are begging me here. She has a cold and I can take care of her a little bit. This is the only workout my libido gets. At least you can watch Ryan Gosling movies."

"God, I'm starting to see why my parents had an arranged marriage. Okay, go ahead and pick her up some tissues, in case she runs out. That won't be too creepy. Just for God's sake, be subtle about it. Try to conceal your raging les-boner?"

Wendy whipped her safety glasses off and snatched up her sangrita. "I will just ask how she's doing on tissues because I happen to have some extras in my desk. She won't even be able to tell I'm gay."

"Oh, she'll know, but maybe she'll think you're interested in an age-appropriate relationship."

"Okay, yeah, I can totally get away with that one." Wendy took a sip of sangrita, then immediately back to the good stuff. The tequila was tasting better already. "I should get her some DayQuil too, right? In case she had some at home but didn't bring any to the office with her?"

"It's like Hollywood made a prequel to Single White Female, I swear to God…"

She hung up.

Wendy went to stir the chicken broth she had going on her stove.

ΔⱯꝊ

Janet tried to focus on *Hunting Warbirds*, let herself be pulled in by the first few pages until her imagination was well and truly fired, but her attention refused to be so easily assigned. She couldn't relegate it away from the last words Roberta had spoken to her, or the dream of Wendy that stayed as stubbornly fresh as if she were waking up from it every second.

She closed the book on its first page as Elizabeth came in, bearing papers for her signature. Intuiting Janet's mood, she left without a word, but with a consoling smile. Janet was signing them when her intercom buzzed—a smooth tone reminiscent of a Tibetan singing bowl. It only disturbed her in so much as she paused in the middle of a pen stroke, taking the time to use her free hand to toggle the intercom, then finishing her signature. "Yes, Elizabeth, what is it?"

"Wendy Cedar here to see you, boss."

Janet quirked an eyebrow and lifted the contract to double-check if her signature was required on the next page. "Does she have an appointment?"

"Nope."

"Oh well. Send her in."

Wendy entered, dressed tolerably, carrying what looked to Janet like a quite undersized briefcase.

"Is that a lunchbox?" Janet asked.

"Yeah."

"I didn't know you were a parent."

"Oh, I'm not." Wendy pulled up a chair before Janet's desk, set the lunchbox down on it, paused to get it just so for Janet's benefit, then opened it up. The first thing she pulled out was a large Tupperware container. "Chicken noodle soup, old family recipe. Not my family, I found it on the internet, at the end of like a five-thousand-word short story on the emasculation of the American male after Vietnam, it was like out of a cookbook that Hemingway would write, but I tried the recipe and it was actually pretty good, and it is homemade, and it could be vegan, well, the noodles aren't vegan, but I'm pretty sure the broth doesn't have a face."

Janet blinked. "Did I…ask you to bring me chicken soup? And forget about it?"

"No, it's for your cold." Wendy explained, sounding briskly sure of herself.

It was her confidence that Janet found most off-putting. She seemed a hundred percent convinced that Janet required chicken soup.

"And here's a bottle of Sprite, diet, straight from the vending machine so it's still cold. Although the prices are ridiculous. Like, a buck for this bottle. I could get at least a liter of this at any convenience store. It'd be warm, yeah, but are we really charging seventy-five cents for the equivalent of a couple ice cubes? What is this, Tito's Yugoslavia?" She gleaned Janet's bewilderment quickly. "Or a more relatable metaphor? Here's a cookie." Wendy brought out a cookie. It was the size of a piece of bread and emblazoned with chocolate chips. "Don't worry, they're not raisins."

"And this is for my cold?"

"Yeah, I mean, I know how hard you work, you always take your lunch in here, send Lizzie—" Wendy jerked her thumb back to Elizabeth's desk "—out to get you lunch, if you even have lunch, but c'mon, there's Chinese food and then there's food that's good for fighting a cold."

"This is a very considerate gesture." This time, Janet didn't blink, but fully closed her eyes for a few seconds before opening them again. "Would you like me to pay you back for the ingredients?"

"No, no no no, it's just a friendly—an act of friendship. 'Cause we're friends." Wendy quickly amended her statement. "Or friendly. We're friendly. Like a mentor or a…an employer." Wendy cocked her head. "Kind of warm acquaintances, is how I would like to think of us."

"Did you bring a spoon?"

"Yes!" Wendy said, managing to sound remarkably like she was agreeing to something. She pulled out an actual metal spoon, wrapped in a napkin, from the bottom of the lunchbox.

"Because I have some plastic utensils in my desk," Janet finished. "Metal is nice, though. Very sturdy. Thank you for the gesture of…" Janet sought out a word. "Goodwill?"

Wendy made an elaborate gesture that amounted to 'let's call it that.'

Janet reached for the Sprite.

"Wait!"

"What? You already said it was diet."

Wendy felt around in the lunchbox. "I got you some extra DayQuil too, in case you ran out. So you should probably take that before the Sprite, so you have something to wash it down—" Wendy then looked inside the lunchbox. "And I left it in my car. This is a very small lunchbox, there wasn't a lot of room, and I was pretty worried about smashing the cookie."

"Would you like to go and get it?" Janet asked solicitously.

"Yes I would," Wendy agreed, as unfailingly conciliatory as before. "I will be right back—friend."

Wendy came out of the subbasement parking lot humming to herself, DayQuil firmly gripped in hand. She got onto the elevator with two middle management types, sliding neatly out of their minds once they'd gotten her floor for her. Their conversation passed in front of her like the ball at a tennis match.

"So I checked the obituaries—no mention of a Lace."

"Maybe he was living abroad. Maybe she didn't take his name."

"Face it, man, her husband didn't die, he left her, that's why she's not wearing the ring anymore."

"Who would leave *that*?"

"Like the man said, show me a beautiful woman and I'll show you a man who's tired of fucking her."

"Yeah, no shit, but I mean leaving Janet Lace sounds like leaving the Mafia. Ya just *don't do it*. Her husband died. That's why she's wearing black."

"She *always* wears black."

"Black and gray."

"Yeah, very dark gray. Like Batman."

"Batman sometimes does yellow, though."

"Yeah, and blue."

The elevator stopped. Wendy got off, feeling like her head was about to explode. She pitched the DayQuil into the nearest trash can.

ÅＶＡ

"You know what?" Wendy said, taking advantage of Elizabeth's lunch break to slide right into Janet's office. Janet was already eating the soup. Shit. "It just occurs to me that you have a very strong constitution, you're probably over your cold already, it was really overstepping my bounds to think you needed chicken soup or chicken noodle soup or any soup, really—"

She started lifting the Tupperware bowl away from Janet, Janet precariously lifting her spoon with the bowl.

"What are you doing?"

"I'll just take this," Wendy said. "Yeah, I'll just get it out of your way, you probably already have lunch arrangements—"

"Set that back down. I was eating that."

"Yeah, okay, yeah—"

Janet looked at the bowl as Wendy placed it back on her desk. "Is this poisoned?"

Wendy was now completely taken aback. "I don't know, is it? I mean, why would it be poisoned?"

"A bit of laxative or something else slipped into it as some sort of prank," Janet said, folding her hands together and staring at the soup as if she could intimidate it into giving up its secrets. "Well, that may seem like a harmless gag to you, but you should know it's still a very serious crime."

"No! No no no, no laxatives, no…" Wendy stooped to the bowl and began ladling soup into her mouth, swallowing as many mouthfuls as she could. "See? Harmless! Nothing in the soup—"

"Stop eating my soup."

Wendy stood bolt upright. "Yeah, okay."

"I was really enjoying that soup," Janet said. She opened a drawer and got out a plastic spoon in a cellophane wrapper. "And now you've gotten your germs on the spoon."

"Sorry."

"Please take the spoon. I was going to have to give it back to you anyway."

"Yeah." Wendy snatched it up, putting it into her breast pocket, and was then quite aware of the moisture in it seeping into her shirt. "So this is maybe a little not my business, but I noticed you're not wearing your wedding ring."

"You did, did you?" Janet asked, stirring her new spoon into the soup.

Wendy put her hands on her hips. "Yeah, I'm perceptive like that."

"I haven't worn it for a week."

Wendy paused. "I thought you might've lost it."

"No, that would be my wife…in Cancun."

Wendy tried very hard to, for once in her life, be straight. This was not the time to beg for Janet's services as life coach, to ask for tales of nineties lesbian intrigue, to reminisce about Missy Peregrym's abs in *Stick It*. Even if she could hear her mental-Regan telling her to throw some dumb nugget of her own gaydom out there—'I'd have a wife too, if I were married, which I can do since the law changed, from not allowing lesbians to marry to allowing lesbians to marry, which you would know, since you are a previously married lesbian and could be a married lesbian again with my help'—as if Janet couldn't tell. Hadn't told, with that 'I think you've misunderstood our relationship' open-heart surgery.

Janet took a mouthful of soup. "This is very good, by the way. Thank you for making it."

"Any time!" Wendy put her hands together. Took a deep breath. *Say something supportive, say something supportive, you're a supportive person, you just have to say something and it'll be nice and she'll feel better.* "Ms. Lace… Janet…"

"Mm," Janet replied. "You can go, if you want. I'll get the accoutrements back to you."

"Accoutre—oh, the Tupperware, no, you can keep it." Wendy forced herself into motion, speech, reaching out and gripping Janet's shoulder. She felt tensed muscle beneath the lining of her jacket, like bedrock under the smooth sand of the desert. *Christ, have they invented Super-Pilates?* "I just wanted to say that you're a really good boss. You're patient, understanding— maybe a little prickly, but you never seem to ask more of us than you do of yourself. And maybe we don't say so, but we all appreciate working for someone who trusts us and respects us, like a family, you might say."

"Are we having a moment?" Janet asked suddenly.

"N-no?" Wendy took her hand away.

"Are you trying to have a moment?"

"Nope!" Wendy sounded certain.

Janet stood up. She wasn't taller than Wendy, but her high heels made Wendy's heels their bitch. Wendy swallowed nothing, and a lot of it.

Standing across from Wendy, Janet reached out and placed her hand on Wendy's cheek. Wendy could feel every downy little hair on her face touch the hand as it came in, feel the air give way, feel every softened molecule of Janet's palm as it touched itself to Wendy's face. Janet's thumb swiped out, rolling with careful slowness over Wendy's lip, and the tip of Janet's forefinger tickled at the fringe of Wendy's hair. Her face was burning. Janet's hand was cool, and soft as velvet. Wendy wondered how long she should stand there, letting Janet touch her face like a very sensual blind person, and then locked her legs in place, determined to stand there as long as she could.

"Wendy," Janet said quietly. "Does this strike you as an appropriate gesture for an office environment?"

"Yes. Absolutely. Fine by me."

"It's not," Janet corrected ruthlessly. "While pleasant, perhaps even pleasurable—" (Wendy resisted the urge to squeak) "—within the workplace, it also distorts the boundaries of a supervisor-slash-subordinate relationship."

Wendy tried to nod while not dislodging Janet's hand. "I understand."

A bead of sweat rolled down Wendy's forehead, between Janet's fingers. Janet moved one digit, spearing it on the end of a short fingernail, and watching curiously as the dollop of saltwater spread out to bridge Wendy's skin to her enamel. Brusquely satisfied, Janet took her hand away. "I think you had best get back to work."

"Yeah. Absolutely. Yes." Wendy ran a hand through her hair. Walked backwards. "But, you know, if you ever want more chicken soup, I make a lot, so…I have lots of leftovers…or fresh soup, I could make you fresh soup, I have a lot of ingredients…wouldn't want them to expire. Not that they're going to expire anytime soon…" Wendy collided with the door to Janet's office.

Through the window, Elizabeth looked at her.

Wendy gave her a quick, panicked look, then was back to Janet. Janet had sat back down.

"I buy very long-lasting ingredients," Wendy said, and rushed out of the room.

ΑΨΑ

"How do you accidentally hit on your boss?" Tina asked.

"Very badly," Wendy replied, looking around the small outdoor café where she'd met her friend after work. The place was still largely undiscovered, if not uncharted, but the soup of the day was chicken noodle and that gave her flashbacks to wanting to spend the last week with her head in her hands. "I was just trying to do something nice for her while she was sick, but then she wasn't sick, and it just got taken the wrong way."

"Well, that's what you get for being a kiss-ass." Tina studied her menu. "You know, anyone allergic to kale would not have a good time here."

"I was not being a kiss-ass," Wendy insisted. "It's not that she's my boss, it's that she's kinda cool and withholding, but then also a little nice and gentle from time to time? And her hair is really nice and she wears glasses."

"Ah yes, nothing sexier than not being able to watch movies in 3D."

"I've had dreams about her nibbling on the earpiece. Every time she takes them off to clean them I have a little moment when I think she's going to do the thing and—" Wendy paused. "It's a good moment."

"I've always wondered what lesbians fantasize about. I thought it was adopting cats."

"Ha ha," Wendy said sardonically. "I already have a cat." She picked up her menu. Then set it back down. "So Janet has a puppy and it keeps running around Godzilla, trying to get him to play, and Godzilla is just like so annoyed, but in that cat way that cats do where it's sorta cute, and eventually they start falling asleep on each other, and also they can talk…"

"I'm starting to see why the seduction didn't go as planned."

"I didn't plan it!" Wendy protested. "I was just trying to do something nice for a friend. Acquaintance."

"You've never brought me artisanal chicken soup when I was sick. Do I need to get a dog?"

Wendy fell back in her seat. "I'm going to die alone. I can't crush on someone who lives across the hall, I can't even crush on a celebrity, I have to crush on the most unobtainable person on the planet."

"Oh, c'mon, I'm pretty sure Jennifer Lawrence is more unobtainable."

"No, no, I haven't met J-Law. If I met her, she might be into me. I've met Janet and she isn't into me. Or a goodly portion of the emotional spectrum. So why am I having dreams about her?"

"What dreams?" Tina asked. "I still need to know what lesbian wet dreams are like."

"I'm not telling you that."

"I've gotta know."

"I'll send you an e-mail."

"Subject: my big gay sex dream about my lesbian crush on my boss."

"Any crush I have is a lesbian crush, so now you're just being redundant."

"I mean, haven't you ever wondered what straight women fantasize about?"

"I saw Twilight *and* Fifty Shades of Grey. I know way too much about what straight women fantasize about."

"Also sometimes Kylo Ren."

"Jesus Christ."

"Yeah, I know. Hey, look at it this way, even if you're not getting laid, you're still working at your dream job with a hot boss. I can't even work in the aerospace industry, because I'm from fucking Vietnam and I can't get a security clearance. Engineering degree, graduated with honors, and now I build model planes. You know who else builds model planes? Children. Children with pieces of paper."

"It's bullshit, yeah. But think of it this way. Can you put a G.I. Joe in the cockpit of one of the planes you design?"

"Yes."

"I can't do it. Might have a spy camera in it. So there you go."

ÅⱯÅ

Elizabeth came over right on time, buzzing to be let in just as Janet was taking out the steak she'd cooked. As soon as her oven mitts were off, she rushed to buzz Elizabeth up before Elizabeth could try her cell phone.

"I come bearing gifts," Elizabeth said, referring to the 2005 Bricco dell'Uccellone with a ribbon tied about it. She held it out to Janet, then snatched it back. "Wait, is this good for a cold?"

Janet gave her a dead-eyed look. "You're very funny."

"Should I even be here? I'd hate to catch what you've got."

Janet snatched the wine from her. "You know, if some man came in and tried to coddle me the way she did—"

Elizabeth affected abject shock at Janet's effrontery as she let herself in. "It's cute! And she didn't mean anything by it. And honestly, you're not going to have twentysomething hotties fawning over you forever. Not unless you're secretly Sean Connery." She glanced at Janet suspiciously. "Say something with an 's' in it—but not an 'h' after the 's'."

"The food's getting cold," Janet advised her, politely ignoring that Elizabeth had slipped out of her heels.

The meal was filling. The taste decent.

"You're holding up well," Elizabeth said, stepping in just before the silence could get unbearable.

"I am?" Janet replied absently.

"Yeah. No empty beer cans strewn around or anything."

Janet got into the spirit of things. "I swept them under the rug," she said, smiling in dim thanks to Elizabeth for trying to cheer her up.

Elizabeth laughed suddenly. "I just pictured you dying of consumption and Wendy Cedar nursing you back to health."

"Consumption is fatal half the time," Janet said.

Her salad was dry, she realized. She reached for the dressing and noticed it was out of reach just before Elizabeth passed it to her.

They drank Elizabeth's wine and listened to Janet's records. Karen O, Janet thought. At least Elizabeth couldn't complain about her musical tastes being out of date. Although perhaps listening to Ms. O sing torch songs to her loneliness wasn't the best way to reassure Elizabeth about her state of mind.

"Elizabeth?"

"Yeah, Jan?"

"What was I like with Roberta?"

Janet hadn't seen such a quizzical expression on Elizabeth's face in a long time. "What do you mean?"

"How did I seem? Compared to how I am now?"

"What, you mean did she rip your heart out, are you a shadow of the woman you once were, was she your better half—no, bullshit, you're fine. You're great."

Janet nodded. "Because if I was happy then, I should be sad now. That stands to reason."

"Oh, we're reasoning now," Elizabeth said, holding out her glass to have it filled. Janet did so and she slumped back in her seat. "It's okay, Jan. I get it, you're hurting. It's not some big mystery that has to be solved."

"But I don't feel any different." Janet couldn't take the sympathetic concern that Elizabeth sent her way, so she stared at her pristine wineglass. The blood-red Barbera overlaid her reflection. "I feel exactly the way I did when she was here."

"So you feel numb. Big deal. There's no right way to get divorced. As long as you're not hiring a hitman, who cares if you're not throwing glasses of whiskey into a blazing fireplace?" Elizabeth sipped her wine. "We can try that, though, if you want. I'm not a whiskey girl."

Janet almost could've smiled. Almost. "Do you think someone can be sad without realizing it?"

"I think there are a lot of things people cannot realize. I also think the way you're feeling now can color everything. If I took you back a year and showed you us laughing together, would you say you were crying on the inside?"

Janet drained her glass instead of answering. When she looked at it again, her reflection was waning. Barely there at all.

"Would you like me to spend the night?" Elizabeth asked. "It'll be fun, we can braid each other's hair and talk about boys."

"I think I'll pass. I'd hate for you to show up at work tomorrow in yesterday's clothes."

"Well, if you think I don't know how to look good in yesterday's clothes, you are delusional." Elizabeth got up, wineglass hooked on her finger, and took the bottle to give Janet a refill. "I'll go put the cork back in."

Janet waved her wineglass slow-motion in the air, picturing herself flinging it into a roaring fireplace with a dramatic burst of answering flames, cathartic and cleansing. She preferred to drink it, though.

"It would be interesting, wouldn't it?" she called.

Elizabeth was putting her shoes back on. "What?"

"Someone nursing you back to health. That never happens after you're a child, with your parents all over you. You go to hospitals, but it isn't the same." She shrugged. "I suppose it'd probably get irritating, being hovered over like that."

"You never got sick?" Elizabeth asked. "Roberta never made you Jello or anything?"

"I got sick. I just didn't want to bother her."

ÅⱯÅ

Janet stayed at work late the next night, waiting for a memo from Testing. It would need her notes as soon as possible. As she waited—the office closing down around her, windows going dark one by one—she started on her new book.

She wasn't four pages in when she read it; if it was a snake, it would've bitten her. She was struck by the same image the author, Carl Hoffman, had been: the *Kee Bird* lying on the frozen lake where it had crashed, silver as a dollar coin lying on the sidewalk, a grand old dame who hadn't aged a day save for her bent props and missing rudder. Its dodo bird-like mascot straddling the nose beside her title in crooked yellow letters. The panes of glass still intact. The tail a bright red, like a bloody hand reaching up for help.

> *We banked hard to the left, and swung around for another look in stunned silence. "You know," said the pilot finally over the intercom, as he swept eighty-five feet above the Kee Bird, "I heard that some guys came to the plane last summer and actually got an engine started."*
>
> *"No way," I said, mesmerized by the ghost of an airplane I had worshiped for years and which, as far as I could remember, I had never seen in real life.*
>
> *The pilot circled for another low pass. "Apparently they changed the spark plugs in one of the engines, connected it to a battery, and it fired right up. And they're coming back this summer to fly it out."*
>
> *The Kee Bird touched a powerful nerve, like hearing a song or smelling a scent that instantly returned me to the wonder of childhood. I couldn't shake the image of it sitting there on the snow, a talisman from an age that seemed more exciting and romantic than my own. I wanted to see it fly, to hear its engines roar.*

Janet had to put the book down just to think of it: to take a team out there, put up some tents, and start in on the old girl. After seventy years, it would need work. Some parts fixed, others replaced, but if she could hand-pick a few guys, a few good guys, and get herself an expense account—rig some ski-wheels on the landing gear...

It was impossible, she knew it was impossible, but she'd thought it, Hoffman had thought it; she couldn't imagine anyone who'd so much as thrown a paper airplane could not think it. Clear a runway, tinker with the engine, gas her up, and just *go*. Fly the last of the Super fortresses.

Some unpoetic part of Janet's soul pointed out how frustrating it would no doubt be, since she was used to the more precise, computerized airplane, some of which she had worked on. What kind of idiot would want to give that up for an oversized crop duster?

But there was something about that generation of planes: the P-38 Lightning, the P-51 Mustang, the F4U Corsair—all the hanging models of her childhood that she'd only seen fly in a stiff breeze. They had an elegance, an indomitable spirit, an endurance where the modern jet fighter so often seemed fragile and temperamental, fussy as hell when they weren't ingratiatingly smooth and responsive and soulless.

But a bird like the B-29…that had hot blood in its veins. It was the difference between riding a horse and a motorcycle. The bike might not fight you, might not buck you, but it was a slave. A horse, you had to fight a bit, give a bit of slack to—you had to respect her and get her to respect you. And when you did? When you put yourself into the horse and let the horse into you?

Janet remembered visiting her uncle's stable growing up, the first time he'd let her cut loose and bring Humphrey Bogart the Pony to a gallop. It'd felt like they were flying.

How could you only want to fly once?

Wendy finished late, stepping out of her partitioned office and into a half-lit world of janitors gossiping. She almost felt like apologizing to them as she stepped on the neat lines of the vacuumed carpet, into the elevator, and descended to the lobby, where the night watchman was waiting to monitor her journey down the walkway to the parking garage next door.

That actually required another elevator ride, as Wendy's parking space was on the fifth floor, and she was just too damn tired to take the stairs like Michelle Obama would want her to. She could hear her bed calling to her, an exciting evening for the career woman on the go. *First up, we actually get home, waking us up all over again since you can't find a commute to go with your new posting. Then we wash up again so tomorrow morning you don't look like something trying to kill Jamie Lee Curtis. Then we lie in bed and try to watch something boring enough to put us to sleep, but not so boring that we'll turn it off and be alone with our thoughts. Thank God for network television.*

Then Wendy froze, all of a sudden woken right the hell up, no shower or motorcycle ride required. Janet Lace was around the corner.

She looked absolutely stunning. A very dark blouse, slightly maroon, accentuated her figure, with the gray jacket of the day off to allow the lines of her body to become apparent in the loose fabric. Good. Hell with it. Wendy hated that jacket in retrospect for reducing Peak Janet Lace to Edited-for-TV Janet Lace.

But the skirt that went with it was nice—a crisply gray, woolen thing that straddled her knees, somehow thrilling in how it left the smooth motion of her thighs unobstructed but invisible as she walked virtually in place, pacing the length of her car doors. Her cell phone was in her hands. She looked at it once, like a bad hand of cards, then stopped and planted her fists on her hips and almost *blurred* with the energy inside her. Wendy had never seen someone *that* frustrated concealing it *that* hard.

She turned abruptly.

Wendy was a deer in the headlights. She was sure Janet had never seen someone this frustrated not concealing it at all.

"Ms. Cedar," Janet greeted, forcing cordiality to a point where it was almost polite.

It was hot, even at night, the parking garage cut out the cooling breezes, letting the air stifle. You wouldn't know it from looking at Janet, though. Her skin didn't sweat, it glimmered, a dewy layer of perspiration that struggled to pull one hair out of place. If she strained her eyes, Wendy could see a droplet of sweat caressing the line of her jaw…

"Ms. Lace." Wendy shoved her hands in her pockets. "What's up?"

Great pick-up line, her inner Professor Snape said. *And how will we seal the deal? Going for a high-five?*

With her hands in her pockets, her backpack started sliding from her shoulders. Wendy moved hurriedly to steady it. Then—and even her inner Professor Snape sighed in disbelief—she gave an anxious smile.

Janet mirrored Wendy, shoving her phone into her pocket. *Holy shit, her skirt even has pockets.* "A flat tire. I must've punctured it on the way over and now it's completely flat."

Wendy automatically moved forward to look at it. "You call a tow truck?"

"I *tried,*" Janet said, putting an aggravated emphasis on the word. She clenched her fists so tightly for a beat that her black leather gloves squelched together.

Wendy looked at her, but her ire seemed entirely self-directed, not coming her way at all.

"I had researched a very highly reviewed towing service, one which operates at night, but in the four years since I saved their number to my phone, they have gone out of business. I can't find another towing service that works at night, so it seems I'll just have to call a taxi, leave my vehicle unattended all night long, and negotiate its rescue tomorrow morning, amidst all the other things I must attend to!" Janet followed all that with a deep breath, as if further frustrated by how she'd vented. She flashed Wendy a look that seemed both unintended and apologetic.

"I could wait with you, if you wanted. I mean, if you're worried about leaving your car here."

"Thank you, that won't be necessary." Janet's lips pinched together slightly. Another bead of sweat touched the little bow of her lips, and she automatically licked it away.

Wendy felt as if she'd suddenly developed telescopic eyes just to see that.

"But if that's what you want?"

"It is," Wendy said. Sliding her backpack off and onto the ground, she regarded the car. Gave the flat tire a kick, just because how often did you literally get to kick a tire? She felt a slick of sweat between her shoulder blades, drawn by the lack of air conditioning. "Have you tried changing it?"

Janet scoffed, and again it seemed directly more inward than outward, as if she were more frustrated with herself than anything else. "Even if I knew how, this is a six thousand dollar ensemble and half my assets just ran off with a yoga instructor. I literally can't afford to replace it."

"Well, lucky for you, I dress like a hobo," Wendy said, beaming a grin at her. "Pop the trunk." *Don't smile!* her inner Snape screamed. *That wasn't charming!*

An eyebrow raised, Janet reached into her pocket and clicked a button on her key fob, resulting in her maimed car beeping and opening up its trunk. Trust Janet Lace to have everything she needed to change a tire, and in pristine condition. Hell, even as she tossed her jacket into the ample trunk space, it looked like Janet had enough to survive traveling back in time. A first-aid kit, road flares—was that a flare gun?

Don't snoop, Cedar, she told herself, selecting the jack and a lug wrench that looked large enough to teach a Roman centurion a thing or two. "Hold this," she said, handing the wrench to Janet, whose eyebrows oozed shock from halfway to her hairline. *Oh yeah, and tell her what to do, she'll love that.* She laid the jack on the ground by the tire and went to get the spare tire next.

But first, Wendy shrugged off her jacket. It'd been casual Friday at Savin Aerospace, and she'd dressed like it, wearing a fleece jacket zipped up over a black tank top. It was really only after she felt the air on her breasts that Wendy realized how low-cut the tank was. And her jeans weren't exactly baggy. Hell, you could see her belly button. *And now she thinks I'm a hooker. Great.*

Janet offered her hand, taking the jacket from Wendy, and with her sleeves metaphorically rolled up, Wendy got the tire. She lugged it out of the trunk with a grunt of effort—*oh so feminine*—and rolled it to a stop beside the jacket. Then she wiped at her forehead with the back of her hand, realizing she'd started to sweat. *Now let's see if there's some mud we can roll around in to really complete the look, shall we?*

Wendy took the wrench from Janet, who immediately crossed her arms over her chest in abject disapproval. *Yeah, I know, I know.* She removed the cover from the wheel rim, then loosened the lug nuts in a star motion. She left the wrench by the cover on the ground as she inserted the jack.

"So I heard about your divorce," Wendy said, her voice strained as she pumped the lever with all her might, raising the car in smooth degrees.

"Oh?" Janet asked, her arms tightened around herself.

"Yeah. I was real sorry to hear about that."

"Really?" Janet asked, sounding even more *Janet.* "You're sorry to hear that I'm single? You'd prefer I be in a loveless marriage?"

Wendy took her wrench to the lugs again, grunting as she twisted them off one by one, feeling about as ladylike as Stone Cold Steve Austin. "I'm sorry—" she strained, working on a particularly stubborn one. "That you're going through a—" Wendy was interrupted by a noise deep in her chest as the lug nut gave. "Tough time." She set the lug nut down on the parking garage's concrete with a clink and started on the next one.

"I appreciate that," Janet said formally.

Move on, move on, abandon conversation! "So, how 'bout dem Yankees?" Wendy asked as she began prying the flat tire out, her biceps swelling in a way that would look great on Instagram, not so great when her crush could actually smell her.

"I don't watch baseball. I prefer hockey."

"What? Shut up, me too!"

"So why do you want me to shut up?"

Wendy paused as she reached for the spare. "It's a…it's a figure of…"

"I know, Wendy. I'm just playing with you. I'm not *that* old."

Tell me about it. Janet looked like at some point in her thirties, she'd told the aging process 'let's not have any of that.'

Wendy shoved the new tire into place, now feeling her tank top clinging to her, waterlogged with sweat. *Shouldn't have taken the jacket off.* She twisted the lug nuts back into place with her hands. Out of the corner of her eye, she saw Janet raise the jacket to her nostrils. *Definitely shouldn't have taken the jacket off. Shit, did I wear deodorant today? Perfume? Scented shampoo? Spill some tea on me that smelled nice?*

Wendy stood, swiping her hands on her jeans, leaving *most* attractive swaths of damp sweat and grease on them. Her hair was probably a mess too. Dark with sweat, completely disheveled—some of it was already hanging in her eyes. She took her jacket back from Janet, throwing it on, noticing that Janet crossed her arms as soon as her hands were free.

"So, uh, that's how you change a tire," Wendy said. She went to get the flat tire, although her eyes kept darting back to Janet as if she'd stop crossing her arms in disapproval. She did not. "Now you know, in case you drive over any more pikes…maces…morning stars…" *Stop naming medieval weaponry.*

"I could just call you," Janet said. Brutal, brutal sarcasm.

Wendy tossed the flat tire into the trunk along with the jack and lug wrench. She gave a friendly nod to Janet, who nodded back to her with great tolerance, and nearly ran to her motorcycle. It was parked in the same damn row, so Janet got to watch as she straddled it like a Level 9000 Gay. Wendy put on her helmet and instantly went blind. *Backwards.* She took it off, turned it around, put it on again. When she started the Triumph, the engine roared like it was the fucking Batmobile. Cool at any other time, not so much while Janet was still staring at her with her arms crossed.

Probably worried I'll try to mug her, driving around like I'm in a biker gang. Wendy ripped the throttle, and even if the tires squealed as she took off, it was worth it to get out of there as soon as possible. It didn't take her long to realize she could've offered Janet a ride. Janet Lace, pressed into her back, arms around her waist, the wind in their hair…might've been slightly more romantic than watching Mrs. Arnold Schwarzenegger butch up.

Wendy Cedar: Master of Seduction. Classes at 7 and 10. Learn how to utterly repulse women without saying more than six syllables! And she was pretty sure she *had* forgotten to wear deodorant, too.

Janet waited until the motorcycle had screamed off into the night, the echoing throb of its engine lost in the distance, before she uncrossed her arms. Even that simple motion made her nipples feel as if they were shredding through her bra. Christ, they could've been about to fucking explode.

CHAPTER 6

Elizabeth took off her bra, then her high heels. It was quite a show, even in the dark. Even with her clothes still on.

"Please don't tell me I'm still paying you," Janet said as Elizabeth came into her office, heels in one hand, bra in the other.

"Clocked out five minutes ago."

"Good. Brandy's in the usual place."

Elizabeth went to the liquor cabinet—a retired airline drink trolley from back when flying commercial was a luxury, not a curse. She brought out two sniffers and a bottle. "So do you need a reason to work late or is this just force of habit?"

"Someone, somewhere, who makes more than me thinks we have a security leak. Obviously, they don't want to involve the authorities, so we're going through e-mails."

"You can do that?"

"It's in their contracts."

"Eh. Mind if I pay homage to our dark master?"

"Go right ahead."

Elizabeth opened a file folder on one of Janet's cabinets, revealing a pair of speakers and an iPod dock. She dropped her iPod in and the empty office was filled with Dio.

"You know men listen to this, right?" Janet asked.

"What?"

"Obviously, we're not reviewing our own employees—that's just asking for trouble—so I'm looking at Donnie's department. Someone must've made a mistake. Since Wendy used to be on his team, I've gotten her e-mails. Blame HR for taking epochs to update anyone's file."

"The deuce you say!" Elizabeth rushed around Janet's desk. "What's she say about me?"

"I'm not looking for something like that."

Elizabeth gasped. "C'mon. Does she think I'm pretty? You could be keeping me from my future wife."

"Please go enjoy your drink," Janet insisted stridently. "If you're not working, at least try not to interfere with my duties."

Elizabeth left Janet's filled sniffer on the desk and retreated to a sofa along the wall, making herself comfortable, picking up her bra and putting it in her pocket. "No need to be a grump about it—wait a minute."

Janet resoundingly minimized the window. "What am I thinking, obviously it can't be Wendy, she was an intern, what does she know?"

"You're a little too defensive," Elizabeth opined, sipping away. "You *like* her!"

Janet looked away from her screen sharply. "Get serious. I don't like anyone."

"You have a crush! You're all flustered, it's adorable!"

"You're right," Janet agreed, after a moment. Then she resoundingly resumed typing. "I'll just have to transfer her."

"Whoa, what? That's kind of gross. Kicking someone to the curb because you think they're hot and totally want to snuggle with them?"

Janet scowled at her. "It's not as if I'm firing her. I'll transfer her somewhere nice. It'll be something of a promotion."

"Oh, yes, promoting someone because you want to bang them, that's much better."

"And your suggestion?"

"Bang her. Not like you'd be the first executive to do it. Although you may be her first..." Elizabeth finger-gunned Janet, to which Janet enthusiastically did not consent.

"I'm sure a young woman as engaging and alluring as Wendy Cedar has far better prospects than—it doesn't matter. I'll find some way to deal with the situation. A *realistic* way."

"Maybe you'll be lucky and she'll end up being the spy."

"Ha!" Janet stopped laughing quickly. Then she reopened Wendy's window. "Then again, that would resolve everything..."

"And now you're dealing with your feelings by accusing others of espionage. Have you learned nothing from me?"

"'Beer before liquor, never been sicker,'" Janet quoted, somewhat frantically paging through Wendy's messages. The woman was infuriatingly business-like when it came to her correspondence on company time. She actually used her work e-mail for work, the freak.

"Let's think about this rationally, though," Elizabeth said, hopping up on one of Janet's shorter filing cabinets and crossing her legs under her. "You're you, Janet Lace, who has needed to get laid since before you legally could get laid."

"That's a very creepy thing to say," Janet replied.

"And you were married for a bit, which at least presented the possibility of sex—mostly since single women are irresistibly attracted to marrieds."

"I've never been attracted to a married person in my life."

"Okay, it's just me, I'm sick. But now—now you are divorced. So what are your options for replacing the stick in your ass with—"

"Are you endeavoring to outdo the pedophilia comment?"

Elizabeth groaned as the iPod went over to the next song, a slow ballad. She jumped down, stomped over to it, and skipped to a bop. "Show a little gratitude, I'm trying to get you laid here. So what are your options? There're hookers…"

Janet shook her head in quite involuntary amusement. "Oh, that's my first option?"

"Hey, they're sex workers, let them go first for once. The problem being, most of them are straight. Have you *ever* been eaten out by a straight woman?"

"By definition, no."

"It's like your pussy is the cockroaches on an episode of Fear Factor. Very bad for your self-esteem."

Janet took off her glasses and kneaded her sinuses. "Well, you have thoroughly shot down my plan to debase myself with lesbian prostitutes. How should I repay your words of wisdom?"

"Wear tighter skirts," Elizabeth replied without missing a beat. "Then there's dating—"

"Sure you don't want to go arranged marriage first? Mail-order bride?"

"Not in this economy. Now, I assume you've absorbed enough of *me* talking about *my* dating life to know you wouldn't stand a chance. You'd be like a seal on Shark Week. At best, you manage to jump through the air in HD slow-motion before a Great White jumps after you and bites you out of the air. Because, I love you, but you are not as good a date as me."

"So I don't put out?"

"Exactly." Elizabeth wound her hands together. "Which leaves this young, impressionable, eager-to-please girl with a huge crush on you that just wants to have a clandestine office affair before Donald Trump starts World War 3."

"Office romances never work out."

Elizabeth flailed her hands by her ears. "I'm not saying you have to introduce her to your father—I don't hate her or anything—I'm saying she so *clearly wants to eat you.* Just let her. Lie back and think of spreadsheets or whatever. Let your skin clear up and your pores open and your hair get that bounce in it again."

"So she's taking me to a spa at some point?"

"Excess sarcasm is a symptom of chastity." Elizabeth waved a finger at her. "You'd be doing her a favor! She'll be able to tell her grandkids about how when she was their age, she had a great fuck with a hot older woman, they'll discover the love letters the two of you wrote, back and forth, they'll turn it into a book, and then into a movie, older women will become sexy, by then I'll be old, but then there'll be all these new hot twentysomethings who want to have their own May/December romance."

"I hardly think I'm a December."

"August?" Elizabeth bargained.

"I'll take it."

"Where was I?"

"You were shutting up and letting me work."

"I'm just saying, you remember what a big deal it was when *Bound* came out? She grew up on *Bound*! That's her starting point."

"I'm actually going through her e-mails and, believe it or not, there's nothing in here about her being in treatment for nymphomania, so I think this obsession you've assigned her about me is sexualizing something entirely innocent—OH GOD!"

"What?" Elizabeth demanded, the smell of gossip propelling her next to Janet almost in a single bound. Janet was too stunned to close the window before Elizabeth could see.

Elizabeth saw. And laughed. "Ho, shit!"

Wendy's phone rang. She stopped, staring at her computer screen, wondering whether to finish her thought or silence the most incessantly Pavlovian sound in the world, but then she realized she'd completely lost her train of thought and the e-mail was ruined anyway. And the phone was on its third ring. She picked it up. "Wendy Cedar."

"Wendy. Smile."

Wendy thought *don't tell me what to do* before realizing it was Elizabeth introducing herself. "Yeah?"

"Janet wants to see you."

"She really pays you just to make phone calls for her?"

"If you had the money, wouldn't you?" Then Elizabeth hung up.

Wendy stared at her screen, trying to summon up however she'd been hoping to 'end the e-mail, but it was hopeless. She saved the draft and resolved to think on it over lunch. Or maybe the come-to-Jesus with Janet would jog something loose.

After a brisk walk from her end of the hall to Janet's, she came to Elizabeth's little cubby, was waved in, and finally arrived in Janet's presence.

"Ms. Lace, hi," Wendy opened. "Finally getting that Tupperware back to me, huh? I was totally okay with you keeping it, but yeah, super-considerate to be giving it back."

Janet steamrolled over her attempts at sociability. "Do you recall subsection B, paragraph twelve, of your employment contract?"

"Hold on, I know this one, was just thinking of it five minutes ago—" Wendy didn't know why she made lame jokes around Janet. She never laughed…well, sometimes she smiled.

"The contract that you signed, in the wake of the Patriot Act, designates this company as a defense contractor and you as a government employee with a corresponding security clearance. That being the case, in the event of a credible breach of corporate secrecy, we retain the right to go through private communications."

"Excuse me?"

"We can read your e-mails," Janet said, barely mustering a sigh over Wendy once more driving outside the fast lane.

"Read my—I have never, not once—I wouldn't leak information, Janet, you *know me*. Who would I even leak it to?"

"Foreign powers. Corporate rivals. Stephen Colbert. How am I supposed to know?"

"Are you calling me a traitor? *Are you sending me to Guantanamo Bay?*" This seemed like the worst possible way to combine Janet and bondage. She was tempted to throw off a 'do you know who my father is?' as if that wouldn't make her the bad guy in every eighties movie.

Janet picked up a file from her inbox, looking it over while Wendy's outburst wrapped up. "No. Of course not. Honestly, Ms. Cedar, show some decorum."

"You're the one talking about…the Patriot Act and stuff!"

"Now, the leak has been found and it's not you or anyone you know. But, in the course of investigating this security breach, I have seen your private files from the time of the incident. Do you recall sending an e-mail on the fifteenth of last month?"

Wendy rolled her eyes, a bit peeved at Janet for getting so heavy-handed with her just for entering a Fandango contest or whatever on company time. "Let me think—were there a lot of naked pictures of Jennifer Lawrence in it?"

Janet smirked—Wendy remembered how she had once thought of herself as a cinnamon roll, only now Janet was snitching some frosting off her.

Resetting her glasses on the bridge of her nose, she examined the document from the inbox once more. "From: WCedar@gmail.com. To: tinatee@gmail.com. Subject: Heatwave." Janet cleared her throat. "'Hey Tina, I took nutmeg before bed and it did *nothing.* I had insomnia all night, barely got four hours' sleep, napped on the subway train like a tourist— horrible place to have the Dream. I'm not even sure I should tell you about it, you huge perv, after you promised me your dumb fad diet would have me dreaming about puppies and kittens and shit.'"

"Ummmmm," said Wendy, who was now sure no, this was the worst possible combination of Janet and bondage, give her Gitmo any day. "That's private and I don't see what it has to do with the aerospace industry and you already said I wasn't the mole, Jesus."

Janet paused a moment, staring at Wendy as if trying to squeeze more words out of her suddenly parched throat, then continued. "'Okay, so I'm dreaming that I'm working late in the office. Everything's dark, it's just me and Janet. I can see the lights of her office are on, but that's the only light except for my computer. Suddenly, I get an e-mail from her.'"

"I remember it, okay!" Wendy cried, surprising herself at how strident she suddenly was. "And I'm absolutely sure I wrote that on my lunch break, so that's not even a little bit company business!"

"Really?" Janet asked, setting the paper mercifully down. "Is this the kind of fixation you think one employee should have on another employee?"

"It wasn't a—it was just a weird dream!"

"One of several."

"They made a lot of Transformers movies too, so what!?"

"I'm going to have to make a record of this."

That was like biting into an ice cube. Wendy's co-workers didn't even know she was gay. "Janet, please. C'mon. It was just a stupid dream I had that I told a friend about. It's nothing, nothing—"

"I would like you to conclusively identify the contents of this electronic communication, and then go on record assuring this company that the events relayed were absolutely false and had no bearing on reality."

And just like that, Wendy snapped back into peevishness. It *figured.* "This is all because you don't want people to think you're having an office romance? Fuck, why'd you hire Elizabeth then?"

She shouldn't have said that. She should not have said that. But people tended to notice when someone as *L Word* as Janet hired a thirty-something Instagram model to be her secretary.

"Are you willing to refute these—" Janet held up the paper with a huff of disapproval "—*allegations,* or not?"

"I'll do it." Wendy laughed harshly, out of nowhere. "You want me to write 'Janet Lace is straight' fifty times on the blackboard, too?"

Janet stood up from her desk. "I'll thank you not to presume my sexual orientation."

"Oh, you mean you have one?" Despite her looks, or maybe a little bit because of them, Janet was just about the most dead-below-the-waist woman Wendy had ever met. For a woman so achingly lovely, she was as withholding and tightly wound as a submarine hatch.

Janet's reply was to open another, bigger drawer in her desk. She took out a video camera, the kind that fit neatly on one hand. She opened up the little viewfinder window and aimed it at Wendy before setting it down on her desktop. "Identify yourself for the record."

Wendy heaved a sigh. "Wendy Augustine Cedar."

"Augustine," Janet repeated ponderously.

"It means 'beloved of God'."

"No, it doesn't. Read now."

Wendy shied away from the sight of her reflection in the camera lens, picking up the document and making an effort not to crush it in her grip. "'From: WCedar@gmail.com—'"

"Skip to where I left off," Janet instructed. "You'd received an e-mail…"

And then she did a funny thing.

She unbuttoned the first button on her blouse.

For Janet, that was a lot of button.

It was a lot of button for Wendy, too.

"Read," Janet said, and Wendy scanned the document to find her place, wondering how in the hell she was going to survive reading this out loud, with Janet watching her, *with her button unbuttoned*.

Wendy cleared her throat. She could feel Janet's eyes on her—all over her, in fact—searching for the slightest hint of weakness, probably. Well, she wouldn't be disappointed. Wendy could feel sweat like acupuncture needles, on her brow, the nape of her neck, under her arms, behind her knees. How could she suddenly be doing this at the end of the work-day, right when she should be wrapping up to go home? She should've been given advance notice, like for a meeting. A chance to freshen up. What she wouldn't give for a hobo shower right about now.

"'The e-mail tells me to go to Janet's office,'" Wendy read, forcing her voice to be as strong and strident as it could be. She wouldn't be intimidated. She'd read the goddamn e-mail like it was King Lear. "So I get up and I go. It feels like a mile, going through the dark office with all the darkened computer screens, the only light coming from Janet's waiting office. Finally, I get there and I'm feeling this burning in my legs, like I've had a really good jog…yes, Tina, such a thing exists—'"

"Speak up, please," Janet said.

Janet's comment jerked Wendy back to reality. Not letting her lose herself in her recital, the bitch, her voice was perfectly audible. Wendy raised her voice. "'I open the door. Or I try to, because just as I'm reaching it, it flies open, and who should be coming out but Elizabeth, bare-ass naked. Thank you, subconscious.'" Wendy deliberately met Janet's eyes to dryly enunciate "'Smiley face.'"

Janet offered her a thin smile as she paused the recording. Then pressed her intercom button. "Elizabeth, would you join us for a moment?"

"Yeah, boss," Elizabeth replied, and Wendy's heart skipped a beat.

Goddamn, but Janet knew every trick in the book. That confidence was part of what made her so appealing, but it was a bitch to have it turned on you. As hot—Wendy meant to think 'empowering,' she immediately corrected herself—as it was to see Janet demolish some jackass who doubted her credentials or criticized her because of her personal life rather than her work—and as fun as it was to imagine what *else* Janet might be a master of—at the moment, Wendy wished Janet was at least a little bit *human*, feeling at least a little bit of the vulnerability she felt.

Elizabeth came in, still looking like she and Janet were role-playing some sort of Mad Men sex scene.

Janet greeted her with a warm smile, in marked contrast to the decidedly more pinched one she had given Wendy. At the moment, Wendy would've given anything to be on Janet's grin list.

"Wendy here," Janet said, "is under the impression that we're lovers."

"I didn't say that," Wendy said quickly.

"You implied it."

"I did not!"

Janet rewound the camcorder. Played the last few seconds. The audio quality was excellent. Wendy had bought a digital camera and somehow it only managed pictures in sepia tones. Of course Janet would practically have her own Q Branch in comparison.

"I think that's a very clear implication," Janet said, while Wendy looked around for a fire extinguisher that could handle her burning cheeks. "Now, Elizabeth," Janet continued, "*are* we dating?"

"No, ma'am."

"Are you single?"

"No. There's this chick in security, she's great, *tightest* ass you've ever seen—"

"Katie?" Wendy guessed, and Elizabeth nodded enthusiastically.

"*Thank you*, Elizabeth," Janet said with a note of finality. "And am I single?"

"Yes, ma'am."

"Thanks. That will be all."

Dismissed, Elizabeth turned on her heel and left the room. She closed the door behind her.

"You may resume," Janet said, pressing the record button again.

Wendy gave her a fixed look, barely glancing at the paper. She remembered the dream all too clearly. "'I go into the office and there Janet is. Behind her desk.'"

Wendy paused, noting Janet's current position with dark irony. As if in response—and there was definitely a wan acknowledgment in how Janet's eyebrows jostled curiously—Janet got up from her perch, came around her desk, and now leaned against it, facing Wendy. She looked even more unbelievable in full, her pencil skirt gracing her legs like dark leaves after a brisk spring rain, her white silk blouse tight to her body. It'd fallen lower with her motion, the unbuttoned portion gaping wide over the beginnings of the black lace camisole underneath.

Wendy felt absurdly tempted by that glimpse, like Janet had set out bait for her and was ready to spring a trap when she went for it. There was the slightest of upticks at the corner of Janet's mouth; a smirking smile waiting to be born when Wendy accepted the challenge. Wendy didn't know if she should ignore it or... There was no way Janet *wanted* her to make a move, was there?

Of course not. Absolutely not. She was just trying to fluster Wendy and Wendy had to be unflusterable. Or, you know, an actual word.

Damn, Janet's necklace... Wendy would give a lot to spend five minutes as that necklace. Be close to that cleavage and be wrapped around Janet's throat? Wasn't that the American Dream?

"'She starts riding me—'" Here Wendy paused, giving Janet her own impish look. She might not've been able to keep a relationship going for so much as three dates, but she could sure as hell get one started, and looks like the one she gave Janet were a big reason why. In terms of eye-fucking, her dick was bomb.

"'As usual,'" Wendy continued, gratified to see Janet blink a few times. "'I don't know what it is—no one *likes* getting read the riot act. But when Janet does it, it's like I'm a teenager again. My palms are sweaty and my throat is dry and my knees are weak. All that...'"

Wendy paused again, unconsciously this time. Christ, this really was embarrassing. Was Janet really doing it for some sort of ego trip or was she trying to cover her ass against some sort of lawsuit?

"'All that intelligence and intensity focused on me, even castigating me, it's intoxicating. I almost want her to make me cry. Slap me. Hug me and tell me she knows I'm doing my best. I don't even know. All I know is, in the dream I don't have to know. I don't have to worry about doing the right thing, because Janet takes control. She tells me I've been slacking off, being inefficient, the usual—and that if I'm not getting paid to work, maybe I should be doing something else…'"

Wendy's voice trailed off. Her eyes had been locked on the page, going over the crisp black letters. There was not a single dot of blotted ink. Janet's printer had put it all down perfectly, making it look realer than real. On her computer, the words had been minutely distorted by her old monitor with its lightly-smeared screen, but on paper, they might as well have been carved in stone.

She couldn't bear to look up, to see Janet waiting expectantly. Her hands gripping the edge of her desk. Those long fingers curling into the darkness underneath…

"Is this what you want?" Wendy asked in a low voice, wondering if Janet would call the whole thing off, say it was all a prank, that she just wanted to know how far Wendy would go before sniffing bullshit.

But Janet stared back at her. Her blouse seemed to have lost another button. Wendy could see more of the curves of her breasts, the darkness inside her half-closed blouse, where the lace camisole tattooed her bare body. Just one brushing touch to make that unbuttoned blouse fall open, to see Janet's plunging cleavage in more detail than ever before—to know if that look in her eyes was desire or disdain.

"Keep going," Janet said, her voice husky. Almost hoarse.

Wendy didn't look at the paper again. "'Her legs are crossed, but when she uncrosses them, I can see into her skirt. She's not wearing any panties. Her cunt is beautiful.'" The word, crude and overwhelming, sounded bizarrely loud in the office. Like someone could overhear.

Janet shifted her legs. Her skirt moved a scant half-inch up her thigh.

Wendy could see smooth skin, firm muscle; *tense* muscle. She looked back up into Janet's eyes. It was getting hard to look away from them for too long.

"'I start to go to her. She says no: I'm her employee. She's the boss. I should show my…'" Wendy had to swallow "'…my respect. I get down on my knees. Then I put my hands on the floor. I swear, I could feel every fiber of the carpet. Like I was really touching it. And, on all fours, I cross the office, convinced I wasn't dreaming, feeling the carpet under my knees and my hands and feeling Janet look at me like she's looking through me into that hot pit in my stomach, just like when I'm at work and I catch her staring at me from across the room. I crawl underneath her desk."

Wendy was acutely aware of her breathing. Every breath granting her a reprieve from having to read this, and frustratingly putting more distance between seeing what Janet's reaction would be.

"'I kiss her knee and she spreads her legs and I can *smell* her, really smell her, you know how long it's been since I've smelled a woman there? And I could've sworn that was how Janet's cunt would smell, I woke up almost wanting to sniff her panties so I could know for...for...'"

"For sure?" Janet ventured. Her hands weren't on the desk anymore. They were delicately poised on the hem of her skirt, thumb and forefinger alone, skimming its length up her knees, up her thighs...

"For sure," Wendy confirmed numbly. This wasn't some game. Janet was way too dignified to be so brazen for a joke. This was actually—she was actually *propositioning* her. Her gaze fled from Janet, like she'd been staring into the sun—finding no solace in the stark, sexual words of the document. "'I bow my head, feeling my ears rub against her inner thighs as I move closer and closer to her cunt. I knew from the beginning it was wet, but the closer I get, the more I learn just *how* wet she is. How much she wants me. I decide to try something different, something I think will please her. Closing my eyes, I—'"

That was the end of the page. Wendy moved to shift through the sheaf of papers to the one below it, but her fingers were clumsy, and she sort of crumpled the page on top and dropped a few and, worst of all, said "Oopsie!"

Janet cocked her head. "I think that's enough."

She stopped the recording. She'd been sitting parallel to the camera—it'd caught none of what she'd been doing.

"I can keep going if you want," Wendy said through the lump in her throat. Then—either because she wanted to show Janet up or just wanted to spend more time in Janet's presence on the off-chance Janet's hands could do more things with her skirt—she went a step further. "You can leave the camera off."

89

There. That was about as open an invitation as Wendy could make without combusting on the spot. Her anxiety was screaming at her to jump through the nearest window (fastest way to leave the building), her pussy was demanding she take off some underwear (her nipples concurred), and her stomach was standing by to reintroduce last night's peach cobbler if Janet did the sensible thing and told her to fuck off.

"I like having the camera on." Janet smiled jauntily. "Do you know why?"

Wendy felt faint. Was this what being hypnotized felt like? *Stop looking at Janet's skirt, she is definitely still wearing it!* "Why?"

"Because when it's late at night, and I'm bored, I can watch this recording. I have a very nice TV, Wendy. Great sound system, too."

"I bet," Wendy said, sounding vaguely like she was having a stroke.

"And while I watch it, in the privacy of my own home, I can touch myself. My womanhood. My breasts. My clit."

Hearing Janet Lace say the word 'clit'; Wendy thought she came a little.

Janet's smile widened, like she had some radar for Lace-induced orgasms. "Whatever I want, really. I'm sure you've thought about touching me, so you can understand how much I would enjoy it."

Wendy just nodded. Had she died? Was this Purgatory? *Please, Demon Janet, show me some more of your gams before poking me with a pitchfork.*

Janet nodded to herself, like she was more mentally setting plans aloud than communicating with Wendy. "And watching you, listening to you—I think I'll most definitely come. While I imagine you under my desk. Eating me out." She clapped her hands together in the self-congratulatory manner of all office bosses.

Wendy jumped.

"I just have that same fantasy, you know. What're the odds? Having you service me while I take a phone call or compose an e-mail. It's the kind of thing I'd really enjoy."

Sheer need drove Wendy's thighs together, squeezed them so tightly she'd need a crowbar to get them apart. "Uh-huh," she said, unable to fully close her mouth after that utterance.

Janet scooped up the camera. "Well. Thank you for helping me get this out of the way so quickly and painlessly. I was hoping to have this wrapped up by the end of the business day. I think you should be able to beat rush hour and I might be able to catch the subway, which is a great relief. Don't you find it hard to unwind when you leave unfinished business at the office?"

This time, Wendy didn't answer. The capacity for speech had deserted her. All she could think of was the sensation of afterglow in her groin— the wet, leaden warmth of the voluptuous pleasure she'd felt. Janet had done that. Without even touching her. Without taking off a single item of clothing.

Janet looked Wendy over, looking faintly embarrassed by the state she'd reduced her to. Then she shrugged and moved for the door. "I think I'll give you a raise," she said in passing.

Wendy grabbed her arm.

Janet looked at her as usual. Warningly. Chidingly. Challengingly. "Miss Cedar—"

"Wendy," she corrected, and kissed Janet as hard as she could.

Well, that was her tongue down Janet's throat.

Wendy had forgotten for a moment. Because it was a good kiss. A really, really good kiss. Janet's mouth just fit to hers, lips moving in sudden harmony, moving against hers, under hers, her tongue pushing against Wendy's in a way seemingly designed to elicit the outright pornographic moan that Wendy felt rise up in her throat. So for a good twenty seconds, Wendy's mind was blank and all she could think was:

A. she was kissing the fuck out of someone, and

B. they were kissing the fuck out of her right back.

Then she stopped and oh God, oh God, she was kissing Janet. Her boss Janet. Another woman Janet. Boss-lady Janet. Janet Lace.

Her

Fucking

Boss.

Wendy pulled away, seeing the exact same storm of indecision on Janet's face that must've been on her own. Almost confusion over what had happened, the sudden passion that had seized them. The fact of how pleasurable it had been, how heated it had been, and the fact of who it had been with, and how, and why.

She'd kissed her fucking boss and her fucking boss had liked it.

Just in Wendy's opinion.

Because just like that, Janet snapped shut again, her face blank except for the slightest pursing of her lips, reddened as they were by a trace of Wendy's lipstick. Wendy's eyes were drawn to it; Janet seemed to be on the verge of sucking on her lower lip, maybe? But she restrained herself.

Janet's teeth showed a sharp, ivory white as she spoke. "I think you should go."

Wendy said, in a voice about as small as it could get without consciously being a whisper, "Oh."

She felt numb, and a strong sense of curiosity at her own numbness. She really hadn't known her own heart could just flatline like that. She wasn't in high school anymore. She didn't crush on people that hard. Only apparently she had been crushing on Janet *exactly* that hard, and apparently she'd actually hoped there could be something there on second ten of the twenty-second kiss, thinking this could be a heavily censored story for the grandkids one day. And then…nope. Flat-out denial, everything burnt to cinders in a second. She felt like gagging on sobs, vomiting as she cried, but, dead-faced, she turned around and went for the door.

Jesus. Her fucking boss.

ᛝᛉᛝ

Wendy didn't bother going back to her desk. She went straight to the elevator. She was probably fired, and if she was operating on more than a fifth-grade reading level, she might've thought to collect some things from her desk. No, no, not under Janet's watchful eye; tail between her legs, gathering up her things like she was looting a corpse. She didn't care if it took ten hours, she'd wait for Janet to leave, *then* get her things. The security guards all liked her, they'd let her in for a few minutes, believe her when she said she wouldn't drop a deuce on anything. Right now, she just had to go. Just *go*. See if there was anywhere she could scream her lungs out without getting the police called.

She was walking through the lobby with vague plans of ducking into an alley, crying her eyes out, and maybe getting stabbed by a mugger for good measure, when suddenly Elizabeth was in front of her. She held a box.

"Janet wanted me to give you this," she said. "You really thought we were dating?"

"I don't know what I thought," Wendy replied, stiffly taking the box as Elizabeth passed it to her. Her severance papers, probably. Hell, maybe all of her personal stuff. Janet wouldn't even let her sulk back to box it up herself. Maybe she'd had it cleaned out while they were talking. Maybe she was some kind of psycho who got off on humiliating her employees before she fired them. *Maybe you shouldn't have kissed your fucking boss, Wendy.*

"Hey," Elizabeth said, suddenly sounding as concerned as a well-paid psychologist. "Everything okay?"

"It's fine. I'm fine. Go, go, get out of here. Mistress Janet probably wants a latte."

"All right," Elizabeth agreed, looking like she'd much rather soothe and comfort Wendy by any means necessary. On any other day, Wendy would've loved that. "Call me if you need anything?"

"Yeah." Wendy would not sniffle. She *would not*. "Of course."

With a nod and a final sympathetic look, Elizabeth headed back.

It occurred to Wendy that she'd just seen Elizabeth for the last time. She'd just seen *everyone* for the last time.

She couldn't think about that. The box in her hands was solid, one of those Amazon jobs, a block of cardboard taped shut at the top. Wendy got out her keys and dragged them along the taped opening, and was jostling her keys back into her pocket when her phone rang.

Like another ball had just been added to her juggling act, Wendy mixed up tucking the box under her arm and switching the keys for her phone, finally stopping to put her keys firmly in her pocket (the phone maddeningly, insistently ringing) and *then* drawing the phone out. She answered it in a huff. "What?"

"Don't open the box here," Janet said.

Wendy looked around. On the second floor, overlooking the first floor lobby, Janet was leaning on the baluster, staring down at her. It was too far for them to really hear each other without phones, mollifying the ridiculousness of the situation somewhat, but Wendy still felt like shouting across the thirty or forty feet between them. Preferably something rude.

"What do you care?" Wendy asked. "What is it, anyway? *Seven Habits of Highly Efficient People Who Don't Get Fired For Sexual Harassment*?"

Even from a distance, Wendy could see Janet's brows knit together. "Who fired you?"

"You did!"

"You're not fired."

"Yes, I am!"

"Wendy, who would know better, you or me?"

Wendy realized, familiarly enough, that she was being ridiculous. She took a deep, calming breath and tried to force her brain out of sleep mode. "So what's in the box?"

"Go home. Then open it."

"Oh, so the bomb only takes me out?"

Forty feet between them and Janet managed to fill it all with confused indignation. "It's not a bomb!"

"Office supplies, then? You gonna frame me for stealing office supplies?" Wendy shook the box. "Maybe a tablet…"

"If it is a bomb, I'm sure shaking it's a good idea."

"You said it wasn't a bomb."

"You said it was!"

"Well, I say things, okay, I think out loud!"

"Good to know you do your thinking some way."

Wendy harrumphed. Maybe the kiss had just been so good because Janet hadn't been *talking*. "What is it?"

"Go home and find out. I gave you the rest of the day off for a reason."

"Tell me or I'll open it."

"I *said* not to open it!"

Wendy peeled the tape back. "Janet?"

"Don't open it in public, dummy, it's a vibrator!"

Oh. Well then.

Janet took her own calming breath—more affected by their *whatever* than Wendy had figured—and then lowered her voice from the shrill hiss that had just gone into Wendy's ear. Resuming the seductive timbre it'd had in her office, Janet said, "I would really like it if you were *inspired* by me. The same way I am by you. Especially if you could send me…proof, shall we say?"

All the air had left Wendy's lungs, never to return. "Proof. Okay," she wheezed.

"You have my phone number," Janet finished, and hung up her phone. Without a second look, she turned around and walked.

Well, that ass *was* inspiring.

Her legs decidedly unsteady, Wendy put one foot in front of the other, the lobby stretching before her for an eternity, each of them determined to outlast the other.

She wasn't fired.

She was going to masturbate while thinking about Janet Lace.

While filming herself doing it.

For Janet Lace.

She wondered how this would affect the bonus situation…

Well, it was a vibrator, Wendy could say that with some confidence. What it was supposed to vibrate, she had no idea. Oil derricks? Small naval ships? Kinky elephants? Jesus, it looked like a suppository for Optimus Prime. It looked like a baby redesigned by H.R. Giger. It looked like the little dangling thing at the back of your throat if you were a monster truck.

Wendy definitely didn't have enough lubricant for this. Maybe she was supposed to ride it? Had it come with a saddle? She checked the box. No saddle.

"Maybe she forgot the saddle." Wendy took a drag from the bottle. She'd been saving the tequila for a special occasion, it being a gift and her not really liking tequila, but if there was one way to describe having your boss sexually proposition you, getting a vibrator from her, and then not being able to figure out the mechanics of clitoral stimulation like she was a guy or something, she supposed 'special' was on the list.

Maybe it was literally a massager. Like, for your back. If she laid down on it, it would work the kinks out of her back, and that was Janet's fetish.

Only it looked like it would roll around, like a medicine ball. A medicine ball that had also tried to kill Sarah Connor.

She swigged some more tequila. It was getting better the more she had of it. Maybe that was the design principle behind the vibrator. Sure, the first foot or so would hurt, but then, like, by the metric system…

E-mail. Wendy happily abandoned the vibrator-slash-possible-Roswell-artifact to get on her laptop. She would send Janet a nice e-mail saying that, while she was very excited about the prospect of kinky sex with her—preferably kinky in the sense of Miley Cyrus trying to be shocking, not the backroom of a sex shop—she would prefer something that had less mental association with a C-section for her. Maybe, it being their first date and all, Janet could just pee on her?

Wendy quickly hit backspace. Don't suggest peeing, obviously. Handcuffs? Probably give her a cramp. Whips? Riding crops? Painful. She didn't get the appeal. If she wanted sex to hurt, she would date a woman with long nails.

"I was born in the wrong decade," Wendy lamented to her computer. "I managed to be prepubescent through the years when just being a lesbian was kinky enough, and now that I'm in my twenties, I have to pretend I like strap-ons."

Maybe a dog collar. That wasn't so bad. A little demeaning, but hell, she rode the subway. Of course, a collar also meant she'd have to let Janet put a leash on her, right? Again, not so bad, but it definitely seemed like there should be a hard NO in there somewhere.

Wendy counted off on her fingers. "Barking like a dog. Walking around on all fours… I should probably only be called a bitch once or twice. I'm not that hip, that's not a friendly thing for me."

She jotted that down. This was coming together nicely. What else, what else was kinky—blindfolds. She would totally let Janet blindfold her. And ice cubes. She didn't really get the appeal of rubbing ice cubes all over someone, but if Janet was into that, she could meet her halfway. And leather clothes—she could do that, as long as it wasn't summer. Leather didn't breathe, after all.

Wendy took another swig. She could absolutely be kinky. It wasn't a problem at all. Not like she'd never had a weird sexual fantasy in her life.

ÅⱯÅ

Going into work the next morning, Wendy felt a sense of relief that was almost giddy; Janet liked her. She felt a sense of nervousness that would've given Larry King three heart attacks. She'd actually admitted some of the things she wanted to do with Janet. They could actually happen. Or Janet could think she was a sick freak, or a wussy sick freak who wasn't even sure about being peed on, or just…not enough. Not pretty enough, not experienced enough, not old enough. Whatever she wanted to give Janet, it didn't tip the scales; too bad, so sad, go to the back of the line.

It was no small wonder that Wendy tried assiduously to feel nothing at all. *Just get it over with, Janet, and tell me you want to fuzzy handcuff someone else.* Or Janet could bend her over that desk, giving Wendy a once-in-a-lifetime enjoyment of a sex act involving hardwood. That was a good possibility. Wendy could get high on that possibility. It was a possibility so good, she almost wanted to wait on it happening so she could keep anticipating it. If only she could rule out the possibility of Janet doing the other thing, the thing with no sex!

Wendy entered Janet's office clutching her purse like she was doing a drug deal. "Is it true bread helps with hangovers?"

"Does bread help with…" Janet paused. "Are you on lunch break?"

"I think I've been on lunch break since I drank the worm." Wendy limped over to Janet's desk, helped herself to a chair, and slumped down in it. "Why?"

"I just don't like to be conducting personal business on company time."

Wendy smiled. This definitely didn't seem to be going in a 'let's *not* have sex' direction. "So we're having lunch together?"

"I suppose, technically—"

"You order pizza? I think I could stomach some pizza."

Brow furrowed, Janet reached down to open a drawer. "I have some power bars. And a bottle of water."

"That'll do," Wendy said. "I suppose I should pack a lunch. Then I can just bring it in here and we can do lunch that way."

"Or we could eat out," Janet said.

There was a slight pause.

"Should I wink?" Wendy asked.

"I think you should've winked."

"Sorry, I might still be a little drunk."

Janet handed her a water bottle and two power bars.

Wendy took the bottle, uncapped it, gulped down water, then paused to say, "So, get any good e-mails lately?" Then drank more.

"I did," Janet announced evenly. She turned to her laptop. "'Dear Boss MILF, have you ever seen the movie *Ella Enchanted*? In it, Ella, played by Anne Hathaway, is under a spell where she has to do whatever anyone tells her to do, no matter how embarrassed it makes her. I think it'd be kinda hot if I dressed up as Ella and you told me to do stuff and maybe I cried a little and then we did sex.'" Janet paused a moment. "And this next line is either a typo or a saying in Swahili."

Wendy pursed her lips. "Probably a typo."

"Yes. Moving on. 'P.S. no butt stuff.'" Janet resolutely tapped on her keyboard to close the e-mail, then just stared at Wendy, as unimpressed as a *Downton Abbey* character would be with the poor.

"I was drunk," Wendy said. "We can negotiate on the butt stuff. Wait, who would be doing the butt stuff and who would be receiving?"

"Is this you making fun of me?"

Wendy held her hands up. "No, *Ella Enchanted* is actually a pretty good movie. I mean, it's no Princess Bride, what is? But it's a pretty good-faith effort. It has Hugh Dancy from Hannibal, which gives the whole thing an added layer of hilarity if you're a Hannibal fan, *which you should be*, and they also got Eric Idle, and Anne Hathaway is great in it, I really don't understand the backlash, she's talented, she's charming—"

"Wendy!"

"—willing to do nude scenes." Wendy stopped and held her head. "I promise, I'm not making fun of you."

"What does MILF mean?"

"Mother I'd Like to…Friend."

Janet nodded, as if that made sense. "I thought we were going to have an…an intimacy. I told you what I wanted you to do and you seemed fine with it."

"I was! I am! But Janet, look at this thing." Wendy plonked her purse down on Janet's desk and wrestled the supposed vibrator out of it. "I mean, come *on*! If I ran an auto shop, I wouldn't have enough lube for that! Who do you think I've been dating, the Expendables?"

"It has a very high user rating on Amazon!" Janet objected, trying hard to look Wendy in the eye as Wendy waved the thing in front of her face.

"Well, then the company had to have paid for good reviews, because there is no way *that* many women have a fantasy of being fucked by Ultron."

Elizabeth chose then to poke her head in the door. "Jan, Mr. Marlowe needs an answer on the conference, ASAP." She didn't actually raise an eyebrow at the sight of a vibrator being waved in her boss's face, but managed to convey one entirely through voice. "Didn't Indiana Jones find that in his last movie?"

Wendy stuffed it back in her purse. Naturally, it didn't quite fit.

Janet leaned to one side of her. "Tell Marlowe I'm reviewing the options right now."

Elizabeth closed the door behind her.

Wendy successfully got her purse to do a sword-swallowing act. "I mean, I get that *that* part is to stimulate my clit, but what are all these for? How many clits do you think I have?" She looked up to see Janet jotting out a quick e-mail. "Seriously?"

Janet stopped, slapping her hands down on the keyboard with a crunch of keys. Then she took her hands away and backspaced through all the gibberish she'd just made. "This was a mistake."

"It's okay, you can just press Ctrl-Z."

"No, *this*." Janet slammed the laptop shut. "I gave you a simple instruction to gauge your willingness to enter into an arrangement, and the next day, all you're interested in is immature jokes and excuses."

"Willingness?" Wendy asked, not giving an inch. "I think I proved how willing I was when I came into your office and let you fuck me."

"I didn't lay a finger—"

"I didn't say you touched me, I said you *fucked* me." Wendy's lips curled around the word, relishing the slight emphasis she put into it, the quiver she saw go through Janet. Not much—the radio mast on a skyscraper in a high wind—but she *saw* it. "You asked me into your office and you. Fucked. Me."

Janet stood up slowly, like a rattlesnake uncoiling its head, and Wendy thought maybe this hadn't been exactly the best tack to take. "You should leave this office right now."

"Or what?" Wendy asked, marshaling her willpower. It didn't hurt that Janet with her arms steepled on her desk, glaring at Wendy with all kinds of power, inspiring the kind of awe most people only got from religion, was actually kinda hot. "You'll spank me?"

"I ought to," Janet snapped. "I should bend you over this desk and paddle your ass until you're begging me to stop." The very tip of the left side of Janet's lip hooked upward. "Or to keep going. As long as you beg."

God, she could be a smug bitch. "Is that supposed to scare me? Do it. You have my permission or safe word or whatever. Get on with it. Punish me already."

And as Janet stared at her, her lips looking as dry as Wendy's felt, her gaze *raking* over Wendy's body like fingernails down her back, like warm water over her skin, Wendy realized something.

Janet was *into* her. She was attracted to her. Janet Lace had a big fucking girl-crush—scratch that, *regular* crush, *sexy* crush—on her. Wendy Cedar. After all, Janet had seen her go-sign and she'd taken it. What was that? Target of opportunity? No, Janet Lace could have any woman she wanted. It was just that she wanted Wendy. Nothing else to it. After all, it wasn't like this was Jane Austen and she was trying to marry into a well-to-do family… Well, Wendy was from a well-to-do family, but it still wasn't Jane Austen!

And then, just like that, Janet snapped shut. Wendy saw a flicker of doubt in her eyes, some inner decision-making tilting to one side, and then the mask was back up. Janet regarded Wendy like something on the side of the road. She rose to her full height, her fingers tapering off the desk.

"I believe I asked you to leave," Janet said. "Please return to your office and resume your work."

Wendy bit the inside of her cheek, weighting her options, whether to press Janet, whether it was unthinkably insane to try to press Janet, then realizing that her best bet was to sweat Janet a little and she'd already done that enough, insouciantly lingering in her presence. "All right," she said. "And I won't even make you promise not to watch my ass as I go."

And as she went—feeling like she had more sway than her iPod—Wendy wondered if she'd actually been cool for a moment there.

ÅⱯÅ

Janet thought of starting up the *Kee Bird* like playing a symphony, note by note, every key struck lingering in the air as pregnant as a thunderhead. There'd be the quadruplets of the control panel, one for each of the Wright R-3350 Duplex-Cyclone engines: Polly, Ida, Norma, and Pat.

She'd start with Norma; her first cat had been named Norman. The battery switch would set voltage meters flickering, the needles moving like the twitching finger in a zombie movie. Then the rest would follow in satisfying sequence, each a little crescendo: the auxiliary power unit and the mixture levels and the throttle and the booster pumps; the circuit breakers and booster coil; the start and prime switches.

That would do it: there'd be a metal scream from the starter, the propeller jerking like a body hit by a bullet, the slow spin that followed, and then the magneto, like a flick of a horse's reins sending it into motion once it'd been saddled. The deeply held breath of the exhaust would finally exhale, hacking up flame wrapped in smoke, and the prop would twirl faster, faster, oil pressure rising, oil temperature rising, reaching for the green…

Janet imagined that the smoke didn't stop with the engine clearing its throat, but continued: a never-ending purge of oily black that surrounded the cockpit in a sheath of night. The rattle of the engines growing jarring, hard, unfriendly; shaking the ship that held them like a hound with its prey. The smoke seeping into the cabin, the gauges malfunctioning. The fire now: heat pushing into the cockpit, flame following, pushed by the smoke or pulling it along, some terrible symbiosis devouring the plane between the two of them. The metal groaning as it was rent. As it blistered, bubbling, the entire plane the surface of a skillet, the air filled with the hazy distortion of the heat, stinging the eyes even before the smoke hit, the fire struck. If you were lucky, maybe there was enough fuel left to explode and rip you out of the plane the only way that you could get loose…

"Mrs. Lace?" Mary Borchardt called.

Janet snapped to attention to see that the room's gaze had turned to her. She was in the middle of a meeting—a meeting scheduled for two hours, which meant it was now at three and a half hours. And she had spaced out. She never spaced out.

She stood, adjusting her jacket for a beat as she reoriented herself, noticing a sheen of schadenfreude as those present enjoyed her being caught in an unprofessionalism. Very well. Let them have their fun. They wouldn't get another laugh at her expense.

She moved to the head of the table to begin her presentation.

ᛆᚥᛆ

The sun set, the lights switched off, and Janet's workday ended about an hour after Elizabeth had left. She decided she needed a better time management system. There was no reason she should be working these late hours. In the morning, she would ask Elizabeth to find her some decent applicants. With any luck, a few of them would work out, and she'd be able to delegate better.

Maybe Roberta was right. She couldn't do everything herself. She had to let others do some of it before she became a holy terror of micro-managing. Napoleon on Elba.

As she left her office, pulling on her gloves, Janet looked across the floor to the front partition of Wendy's office and was relieved to find no light pushing through the opaquely pebbled windows or under the door. Then she was amused, if darkly, at her own relief. What did she have to fear from Wendy Cedar?

Why did she still have a flutter in her stomach *after* she'd decided it was inadvisable?

She walked through the darkened offices, exchanging greetings with the cleaning crew as they filtered in, and then she entered the elevator.

Wendy Cedar was inside.

She wore the same respectable suit she'd had on when she'd entered Janet's office—a dark knee-length skirt, a white blouse with subtle polka dots, the sleeves rolled nearly to her shoulders. Her jacket was in her hands, folded over her purse, and Janet could see the power of her musculature, trickling down her arms in tension and tautness.

Janet faced her evenly as she stepped beside her, then looked straight ahead. "What floor?"

"Whatever's good."

"Were you waiting for me?"

"I thought you might have something to say to me."

Janet pressed the button for the lobby. She pulled her hand back, seeing her and Wendy's reflections in the glossy metal that surrounded the white buttons. Even blurred and stretched by the impromptu mirror, Wendy drew her gaze.

Wendy's finger went back. It pressed the Stop button. With a shrill jangle of an alarm, the elevator stopped. Without the hum of its movement, the silence begged for something to be said.

Janet turned her head slightly toward Wendy, barely enough to see her out of the corner of her eye. "If I had fucked you, you'd know it."

"That's what I said," Wendy insisted. "The way you talked to me, the way you looked at me—"

Janet turned her attention fully to Wendy. Looked her in the eye. Nothing more than a vexing issue. An itch. A tingle that had to be addressed.

She could deal with that. "You'd know it," she reiterated. "And right now, you don't."

"Okay," Wendy said. "I don't. But you got to at least third base with me."

"This is a lesbian relationship, Ms. Cedar. Third base is as many bases as there are, to my knowledge."

"Okay, second base. There are a lot of things that count as second base, and that was one of them."

Now Janet turned slightly. Canting her hip as she placed one heel closer to Wendy. "Is that what you've waited all this time to tell me?"

"I wasn't waiting to tell you anything," Wendy said. She dropped her purse and jacket between them. And, her cheeks flushing, her eyes demurely glancing away, she reached to the hem of her skirt and pulled it up her thighs.

Janet watched. She watched idly wondering if she should, could, look away, even when she could think of no reason to. It *itched* that she couldn't look away—that she didn't want to.

Wendy's thighs were firm and flat, not rippling with muscle, but potently taut with it. They gleamed with a little gold sheen, and if Janet could've thought, she would've registered envy. But Wendy's side was facing her, and she was turning slightly as she raised her skirt, so that her ass was facing Janet. Her panties. There was no crass logo on the back, no forced slogan, just the simple fact of white fabric stretched to translucence by her pert buttocks, the simple heft and lift of them revelatory, taking everything of Janet's away but lust.

It didn't make her lust for Wendy. It just stripped away everything in Janet until she was aware of the sheer *want* that was in her.

Then, with her skirt raised high above her ass, Wendy let go of it with one hand and brought that hand down on her cheek with a sudden, resonant *smack*. Air shot into Wendy's mouth as she inhaled sharply, sounding discordantly loud; the flesh jumped with a jiggle beneath Wendy's panties as red flooded in under the gauzy fabric. She'd struck with real force, even mewled a little with pain, and long after the bounce had settled, Janet found herself staring at the skin. The little bit of suffering it was imbued with, that fading, replaced with the creamy hue of Wendy's girlish health.

Her eyes flicked up to Wendy's expression and her heart skipped a beat. Something about Wendy's look was even better than her little display. There was something of pain—that grisly pride some took in being injured that always struck Janet as tomboyish. But there was also an eagerness to please, a keen curiosity as to whether she *had* pleased, even an affection, all of which Janet found utterly irresistible.

Wendy exhaled, a breath that was dragged out of her, flowing softly out from between parted lips.

Janet inclined her head to Wendy, putting her hand around the fingers of Wendy's left hand and pulling it back from her skirt to let the thing fall back down. With her other hand, she smoothed it out, plying it back down Wendy's legs to fix her appearance.

"Does it hurt?" she asked, feeling unnecessarily solicitous, but wanting to know.

"Not anymore. It was just one slap." Wendy smiled at her, looking pleased with herself.

As pleased as Janet was.

"You think I've never had my ass slapped before?" Wendy asked.

Janet saw her and raised her. "If it doesn't still hurt? Not really."

Wendy bit her lip, giving Janet a look that was mostly curious, and all Janet could think was that most of the time when you were trying to fix a plane, even if it broke down again, you could always fix it up some more.

The elevator's phone rang. Wendy jumped nearly out of her skin while Janet instinctively reached for it, tightening a vise-grip around everything she'd just felt.

It was building security. They wanted to know if everything was all right.

Wendy didn't push after that. She seemed satisfied, even if Janet wasn't. And if *she* wasn't, then she at least understood there was only so fast Janet could go. A pace she set that she wouldn't be rushed through.

Still, Janet lingered in the elevator after Wendy had gone. On her phone, looking up where Wendy lived.

CHAPTER 7

"Jesus Christ, what are you doing here?" Wendy demanded the moment she came through her door.

She had a small apartment and with the way Regan was bustling around, finding new spots in Wendy's cupboards to stow non-perishables from grocery bags, then finding stuff to be thrown out to go into garbage bags (also from the grocery bags), she seemed to take up all of it. "Keith bought groceries at the same time I did. I'm letting you have them. Do you know how few fresh vegetables you had in your refrigerator? And where's your bottle opener?" She set a bottle of Pinot on the counter. Not that Wendy had much of a counter left with Regan's bags on it.

"I actually use a corn cob holder. And don't drink wine."

"Where's your corn cob holder then?" Regan asked in exasperation.

"Silverware drawer."

"You mean the one with all the plastic utensils?"

"Hey, you date a girl who works at KFC, there are certain perks."

Regan yanked open the drawer with a clatter of plastic, found a corn cob holder, and started in on the wine bottle. It wasn't easy for her, but then, she was straight.

Wendy took the bottle from her and started working the tines into the cork. "Keith?"

"Keith," Regan seethed. "He deleted a bunch of shows off the DVR—which I was *going to watch*, I was waiting to binge them—just so he could record some James Bond marathon. And I got him a DVD boxset of those a few years ago. For his birthday! He forgot! What other gifts from me has he forgotten? His son? My virginity?"

With the makeshift bottle opener inserted, Wendy clutched the wine bottle under her arm and started wiggling the cork out. "What about Bobby DiMino?"

"Bobby DiMino doesn't count, we just went halfway."

"Still, half a donut isn't really a donut."

Regan glared at her. "All right, it was forty percent, Keith was sixty, we round up."

"I'll let Bobby DiMino know." With a grunt, Wendy popped the cork out. "He'll be crushed." She pointed at the cork. "Eh?"

"Yes, every time you do that, you save more of the one dollar that a corkscrew would cost." Regan sighed to herself. "You do have glasses, right?"

"Sure!" Wendy popped the bottle into Regan's hands, tossing the cork aside, and went to a cupboard. "Do you want Winnie the Pooh or Piglet?"

"Sis…"

"They were at a garage sale!" Wendy stressed, holding them up in her hands. "It's called being thrifty. How do you think grandpa got so rich?"

"Whatever you say, Wendy. But just so you know, this bohemian act is not going to look good in your thirties."

"How would you know? Are you still in your thirties? I can't really tell with all the…" Wendy gestured about her face.

"Fuck you. Drink some wine with me."

Wendy's phone buzzed. She dropped the glasses on the counter and dug it out of her pocket, quickly checking her messages while Regan poured for them.

"At least you don't have a flip-phone," Regan commented.

She had a text from Janet.

I would very much like to see your pussy. Please show it to me.

Wendy went dead still. God, she had it bad—she could just *hear* Janet telling her that, her chilled voice feigning disinterest, but roiling with attraction underneath, pushing Wendy in turn to try to force her hand. Make Janet show just how badly she needed.

"Everything all right?" Regan asked. She'd filled her glass all the way full, and with the brim teetering with liquid, she bent down to suck a little through her lips.

Wendy almost would've felt proud of her, except—*Janet*. "Yeah, it's all fine. Just let me go freshen up."

"Uh-huh," Regan said, taking their glasses to the bed. She crouched down to lean against it, setting the glasses down on the hardwood floor.

Wendy hurried into the bathroom, locking the door securely. She considered turning on the shower for good measure, but no, too secret agent-y. She looked at herself in the mirror. "Okay. We're sexting. We're sexting now." She fixed her hair, as if that was what Janet was interested in. "No problem. I'm sexy. I'm sexy as hell. Janet's sexy and she likes me. Sexy likes sexy. Brangelina. Bennifer. The other Bennifer. I'm good. Face. Boobs. Stomach area. Why should my vajayjay be any different? I've got a good-looking pussy, a beautiful pussy. Who wouldn't want to see my pussy? Whoever they are, they're not named Janet Lace, that's for sure."

She set her phone down on the sink, carefully—this was no time to crack her screen—then reached under her skirt and scooted down her panties. One last second of spiritual meditation—she did not achieve enlightenment—and Wendy lifted her skirt.

She looked at it. She wasn't sure what spot adjustments one could make to a pussy…she wasn't Hugh Hefner or anything…but lesbians went for the natural thing, right? There wasn't some lesbian contingent who wanted women to wax, was there? You never knew, what with all the people coming out these days. Maybe Aubrey Plaza would start a trend and ruin it for everyone. She was bisexual now.

"Screw Aubrey Plaza," Wendy told her area. "You look fine. You're great. It's a great pussy…okay, it's a little weird. It has eccentric good looks. It has character. What does she want, an Amazon.com pussy? I'm an Etsy pussy. My pussy is homemade, it's hand-crafted, it's assembled with love!"

She picked up the phone, stood on her tiptoes to get her area above the sink, and aimed the camera at her reflection.

Maybe she could google Emily Ratajkowski's twat, send that instead?

No, no, she'd taken the picture; she would send it. Her relationship with Janet would be based on honesty and communication.

As quickly as possible, Wendy pulled up her panties, pulled down her skirt, and left the bathroom. Regan was where she'd left her. Half of her wine was not.

"I'm fine with Keith being the breadwinner," Regan was saying, as if there had been a conversation to resume. "But breadwinning is just one job! I cook. I clean. I babysit. Laundry! He does one job, I do five. And I delivered the baby! You think there are UPS drivers who have to build their own trucks before they go to work?"

"No," Wendy said, sensing an opportunity to agree.

"Hell no!" Regan agreed with her own agreement.

Wendy sat down beside her and tried her wine. Like most wine, it wasn't to her taste, but at least it wasn't beer. "I totally get you. People call me lazy, but not only do I work, I clean up this place. I shop, I cook, I take care of Godzilla—he's an outdoor cat, but he's very needy."

Regan stopped her, snorting on her wine. "Are you comparing us?"

"Yeah, we've got the same—"

"We really don't."

"We have loved ones who depend on us."

"You have a cat!"

Wendy's phone buzzed. She quickly swallowed her wine—mindful of the possibility of spit-takes—and checked it off to the side.

That was nice. Now can I see what it'll look like when you hold it open for me to eat?

Okay, that was disturbingly hot, since Wendy couldn't *exactly* imagine Janet saying that, so her imagination ran wild. Would she say it in the same cool tone as everything else? Would she make eye contact as she planted the thought in Wendy's head? Would she lick her lips? She had to lick her lips at some point, right? Everyone's lips got dry.

Then again, without so much as dinner, Wendy had given her full frontal. Maybe that was how they did in high school these days, but this wasn't high school, not even college! She shouldn't just allow Janet to run roughshod on her, even if the thought prompted a mental moan of 'Mmmm…run roughshod.'

Wendy texted back hurriedly:

Maybe you should show me something first.

Regan scrunched up over her shoulder. "What are you doing?"

Wendy hid the phone behind her back. "Pokémon."

"What?"

"It's a new Pokémon app."

"Can I see it?"

"No. It's private."

"It's not some hentai thing, is it?"

"No! How do you even know what hentai is? You're a mom!"

"Moms can use the internet," Regan reasoned.

Wendy furrowed her brow. "Okay, now you're making me picture *Mom* using the internet."

"Just as well she can't work an internet browser to save her life. She'd go Wyatt Earp on the place. Make everyone look at pictures of her knitting instead of naked people."

"Maybe they could compromise and she'd knit naked people."

Wendy's phone buzzed and Wendy felt the most curiously dualistic sensation. She was both going 'oh shit' at the top of her mental lungs, and was also breathlessly excited to see what Janet had sent at the same time.

Grabbing hold of her bed's post, she worked her way to her feet.

"Oh no, I have not finished venting about my husband yet!" Regan cried. "You were my maid of honor, you have to hear this."

"I'll be right back," Wendy promised. "I just have to—" *Possibly masturbate.*

She walked for the bathroom instead of saying that.

"While you're up, get me some more wine!" Regan called after her.

Wendy closed the bathroom door behind her. Locked it. Braced her body against the door just in case Regan tried to break it down.

Shit. Holy *shit*. It was Janet. Smiling.

Not just smiling, of course, Wendy wasn't that easy a lay…even if Janet had *dimples*, holy shit, who knew?

The smile was at the top of the picture. The picture went down. Down Janet's chin. Down her throat. Down to a vertical bar pendant, finely wrought silver worn tight to her neck, giving unneeded accessory to the expanse of flawless flesh below the graceful hollow of her throat.

And then there were her boobs. They took up most of the screen of Wendy's phone, bursting out from an unbuttoned blouse and a demi-cup bra, the cleavage that James Bond's latest conquest would show right before they lost the PG-13 rating. Holy *shit*, Wendy could see the division between the orbs, the entire curvature, and a mole. It was a feat of engineering for a bra to be able to cover all of that and still be revealing all of THAT. It was a cute bra, too. Surprisingly lacy and frilly and wait, no, no way Janet wore that at the office. That was a fun-time bra. What did it mean when someone sent you fun-time bra over the phone? Better or worse than just showing nipples?

Her phone buzzed and Wendy nearly dropped it. Shit, Janet wasn't even giving her time to process! Just two minutes was not enough time to take her boobs in, there were two of them!

Janet's text read, remorselessly:

I've shown you mine. Now why don't you show me something else that's mine?

Holy fucking shit, she was dating Catwoman all of a sudden. This was exactly what Batman went through every time Catwoman showed up. But he had dead parents to think of to kill his boner. Wendy was too damn small and too damn gay for this. Fuck, what if Janet called Wendy hers in person? No one was gay enough to handle that!

"Hey, Wendy, can I use the bathroom?" Regan pounded on the door behind her. "You're not smoking a doobie, are you? We're not thirteen anymore!"

"Just a second!" Wendy replied, automatically, since she was still kind of thirteen still. She pulled down skirt, panties, and sat on the toilet. Tried to spread her legs. Skirt and panties in the way. *I knew I should've worn shorts to the office.*

"Wendy, c'mon, I drank more wine, I need the toilet more!"

"Go in the sink then!" Wendy kicked off her panties, kicked off her skirt—skirt didn't want to go, clung to her ankle like a shed skin that wouldn't take the hint. Wendy flapped it wildly in the air before she realized, barring yoga, a beaver shot wouldn't include her feet.

"You know, you're just like Keith. You don't appreciate me. I bring you groceries, I bring you wine—"

At this rate, anything I take a picture of is going to be sealed up like an airlock. "Regan, come on, let me wipe in peace!"

Regan grumbled, but Wendy heard her moving off. Very quickly, Wendy spread herself, tried not to think about it, positioned the camera, tried to think of something sexy, tried to center herself to give her crotch at least the appearance of belonging to a poised and dignified lady, and made a duckface just because. The camera flashed, Wendy sent it, and was struggling into her lower garments as the little letter icon shot off into the ether.

This is why dick pics are a thing and not vag pics, she thought to herself. Men had it easy. They could just unzip, whip it out, and there you were. Wasn't like the things could look any weirder. Her, she had to think about lighting. She hadn't even put a filter on it. She should've used a filter! Everyone used filters! Cat pictures had filters!

Despondent about being a filterless vagina in a filter world, Wendy stepped out of the bathroom and saw Regan turning away from the front door, opening a box in her hands.

The last box Wendy had gotten hadn't been a bad sex toy, for a GoBot, but it was still a GoBot sex toy thing too far for her to want her sister to find. "Regan, Regan, I think that's mine—"

"It should be, it was on your doorstep." Regan reached into her package.

Wendy prepared herself to have to explain what Ben Wa balls were.

"One glove? Who'd send you one glove? Are you getting Michael Jackson's mail by mistake?"

Wendy snatched it from her. It was one glove. One black, leather glove. Janet's. "Hey, Regan, you think we could do this some other time? Work's been buzzing me all night, I need to get on my computer, yeah, let's do this tomorrow."

"What about Keith?" Regan protested as Wendy worked her toward the door.

"Yeah, sure, he's an awful husband, you should divorce him."

"I'm not going to divorce him, I love him!"

Wendy got the door for her. "Then you should forgive him."

Regan crossed her arms. "Don't take his side!"

Wendy pushed her out the door.

Her phone was buzzing. Even that was pleasant. Only Janet wasn't texting her. Janet was calling her. Wendy walked back to her bed, picked up her wine off the floor, and swigged before she answered.

"You did as you were told," Janet's voice said at a steady clip, every word measured, considered, precisely cut. And dripping with sin. "That's good. I find it very pleasing when you do that."

"You should see me put together an IKEA desk," Wendy said, then regretted saying. "You know, you kinda picked a bad time for this."

"It was good for me," Janet replied. Her voice licked through the phone, nibbled at Wendy's ear. "That's the important thing. Now, is it still a 'bad time', or would you like to play another game?"

Wendy's lips clung together wetly as she opened her mouth to answer. "I'd like to play another game, Ms. Lace."

Wendy could hear Janet's smile like a switchblade flicking out. "I'm so happy to hear that, Ms. Cedar. This game is very simple. I know you liked the picture you got of me—I could see it in how eager you were to show yourself *spread*—so that will be your reward. Every picture I send, I'll remove one item of clothing. And I'll send one picture for every finger you take. You'll be wearing the glove, of course."

Wendy locked her door, then threw the chain up. She started struggling out of her skirt and panties again, flopping down onto her bed, the phone nestled against her ear. Shorts. She definitely had to wear shorts to work. "And how many items of clothing are you wearing?"

"In the pictures? Well, that depends, Ms. Cedar. You saw me at the office today. How much did you think I was wearing?"

Wendy set the phone to speaker mode and dropped it beside her pillow. "I know you're wearing a bra."

"For now," Janet retorted. "Are you touching yourself?"

"Not yet," Wendy said, trying to keep her voice from trembling. She didn't want to admit that the sudden volume of air on her lower extremities, between her thighs and on her ass and pressing in on her sex, was already more intense than she thought she could bear. It just wasn't like this when she touched herself without Janet. And she thought she needed a vibrator…

"That's all right. I'll wait. I'm a very patient woman. I can spend… hours…making sure something is done right."

Wendy groaned. She knew that Janet knew what that had made her think. Didn't matter if she had a filthy mind or not. Carol fucking Brady would think dirty with the way Janet had said it.

Hours, Christ, she didn't know if she could survive one minute!

Wendy slid her right hand into the glove. It fit like, well… She reached downward, stopped herself, heard Janet's breath over the phone—was it a little strained or was that her imagination?—used her left hand to cup her breast through her clothes. It didn't matter that she still had a blouse on, didn't matter that she still had a bra on. Right through both of them, her nipple responded to the touch. It was almost painfully hard, her nipple pebbling right under her fingers, grinding with just the slightest bit of pain and so much more pleasure against its confines.

"I'm…touching now," she said, barely breathing as her hand rolled between her thighs, over her sex. She had to hold herself back from penetrating herself—it felt like her pussy was burning and her fingers were ice water making it just cool enough to bear—but she didn't want to hurt herself, she knew Janet wouldn't want that. The cool leather felt magnificent on her body, like she'd never touched herself before.

"Good girl," Janet replied. "Take your time. Do it *right*."

Hold back, she had to hold back, *don't,* she told herself firmly as her middle finger stroked between her labia lips, the opening just starting to open. *Don't.* She was so wet, when was the last time she'd been so wet? *You know you're not ready yet, can't be ready.* It felt so good, the pad of her fingertip on her inner flesh, the supple leather, the little flecks of stitching, just this close to giving her inner muscles something to clench on, something they desperately needed. *Please,* she begged someone, herself, the universe, Janet Lace wherever the hell she was.

She pictured Janet, and the craziest fucking thing was that she didn't imagine her in her underwear, or in the shower, or getting a thorough massage from Angie Harmon. She pictured her like she was at the office, her hair neatly styled, her glasses on, her maroon blouse fully buttoned, her gray skirt running down to her knees, like who the fuck got off on that, the Victorian Era? But that was how she thought of Janet, all centered and powerful and imperial and precise, and a sigh drew out of her as luxuriously as she'd savor a Godiva chocolate.

"It's…" Wendy bit her lip. Shit, her nipples hurt, they were too damn hard to be wearing a bra, but she couldn't care about them when she was feverishly rubbing between her legs, her middle digit twitching like a gunslinger's trigger finger. And she didn't know if she decided to, on some level, or if it just *happened* from wanting it so much, but her middle finger slipped inside, slick and slender, went inside to the knuckle, and it didn't hurt at all. "It's in," Wendy gasped, hearing an answering intake of breath from Janet. Was she?

"Show me." If she was, her voice showed no sign of it. Didn't tremble, didn't crack.

Wendy took her left hand, picked up her phone, aimed it down her body. *You have me,* she thought as she took the picture. *Here I am.*

"Goooood girl," Janet drawled, and the phone lit up with her answer.

Wendy *clenched* on her finger, the gloved impalement she couldn't quite think of as herself, couldn't feel as anything but Janet.

It was Janet, dressed exactly as she'd been at the office, her dark blouse and her woolen skirt, but she'd unbuttoned her blouse. It hung open down her torso, revealing marble skin, the inner roundness of her cleavage. She'd taken off her bra, and though maybe Wendy had seen more of her breasts in the last picture she had sent, it was just something about seeing Janet that way. No bra between her and Wendy. Just the blouse to separate their touch. And if she slipped her hand under it…

Wendy stirred her middle finger inside herself, to sensations so sharp it seemed she could cut herself on them, and with her other hand she wrenched her own blouse open, she found the clasp between her breasts, she exposed herself shamelessly and flushed as if Janet could see her. The leather of her glove wasn't cold anymore, it was warm; it was bottomless, it was a pool for the liquid heat filling her body. She was burning all over, but her finger was where it was centered. That was where she would explode.

"Would you like to see more?" Janet asked, her voice every bit as poised as it would be if she were at the head of the table in a conference room, as if her breasts weren't rising and falling beneath an unbuttoned blouse, as if her bra wasn't on the fucking floor.

"I would," Wendy replied meekly.

"Because you could get off with one finger. Don't you think I could get you off with one finger?"

"I want more." Now Wendy's voice was just a breath.

It was hard for her not to whimper as she acutely *felt* her ring finger on her pussy—not pressing any harder than before, but she knew it was going in next, she could feel her body's hunger for it, a tightness inside her that was too much for just her middle finger. Her body arched unconsciously, the plush, expensive material of the mattress beneath her cradling her, and she was so attuned that she could hear the bedsprings as they tensed under her. Her ring finger dragged over her sex, already spread wide by her middle finger, the glove leather making it feel like it was someone else, like her hand was someone else's, like the pleasure at the end of her fingers had to be connected to the voice on the phone that she was listening for so intently.

Both fingers centered inside her and she clenched on them so tightly that their presence felt huge, impossible, like she was spread wide open and filled full and laden with almost too much sensation to bear. Her other hand clawed at the phone, fumbling about the bedspread, finally picking it up and she could barely hold it with how her body trembled, tremors going through her body, the San Andreas Fault of her body finally opening after so long.

She took the picture and heard a distinct moan from Janet. She couldn't even think that Janet was touching herself, just that she'd pleased her. That she'd given Janet something she wanted, because Janet wanted *her*.

Janet's next message had her turned partly away from the camera, her skirt crimped up the backs of her thighs as she removed her panties, the side of one breast hanging below her bent torso. Jesus, had Janet hired a professional photographer to take her goddamn nudes?

Wendy brought her other hand down to her clit and rubbed it hard and slow, trying to force some calm into her body as she answered its need. Tension coiled in her belly, pulling tighter with each wet stroke, until the need forced her hips to cant, jerking against her own hand hungrily, third finger inside her and she felt so full, so *complete*, she didn't know how she could take anymore. She was too damn sensitive; it was almost too intense for her. Every touch on her engorged clit sent jagged bolts through her.

"I can hear your fingers," Janet said, "pumping in and out."

"Jesus!" Wendy replied cleverly.

"You can't take anymore, can you?"

"Uh-uh, uh-uh…"

"You're going to come?"

Wendy whimpered as she nodded, tears brimming in her eyes, looking over at that fucking pin-up pose like it was talking to her. This just wasn't *supposed* to feel so good! It was supposed to be a distant second to sex—it shouldn't feel like the real thing!

Janet must've just known that was her answer, because she proceeded as if she'd actually been able to see Wendy. "Come for me. Right now. *Do as I tell you.*"

115

Wendy parted her lips to say yes, but a moan escaped instead, howling out of her body to tell Janet what was happening to her, all because of Ms. Lace.

Her fingers moved with a speed she hadn't known they possessed, the glove giving them a mind of their own, and Wendy stopped trying to fight it, let it do whatever it wanted to her. Her eyes closed, the sight of Janet's beautiful face sharpening in her head. It was right after they'd kissed, leaving those full lips slightly swollen, almost bruised, and a hunger and a fury and a challenge in Janet's eyes that Wendy hadn't been able to see at the time, but now all she could think of was how it felt to be burning under that look.

She remembered the press of Janet's lips to hers, the softness of them; the feel of Janet's tongue darting between her lips and into hers, as she responded, as she'd just *begun* to respond.

Wendy's hand was a blur between her legs, her hips throwing her up against them, holding her in the air with burning thighs as her arm pumped and she strummed her clit and everything inside her went to her core, tight and hot and exploding slowly.

I'm going to come for you, she thought, her muscles straining, sweat pockmarking her body. *You told me to come and I'm going to do it.* Her lips parted, forming words even she couldn't decipher. *Ms. Lace.* Her head thrashed to the side, pressing her cheek to the cool of her pillow. *Ms. Lace.* Her back arched, muscles tensed, all of her centered on her sex as she lifted it up to the sky, her hand. *Janet.* She came, a ragged version of the name escaping her as pleasure flooded her, filled her, then leaked out of her in slow degrees, her fingers continuing to play between her legs.

She collapsed to the mattress, it letting out a groan that mirrored hers. All the strength drained from her body, and she just barely managed to maneuver a clumsy hand to the phone and take a picture of three fingers inside herself before the feeling became too overwhelming. When the glove slipped out to rest against her thigh, the relief was both blissful and frustrating. *More.* She could've taken more. Janet would've made her take more, if only she were there, if only she could see how much Wendy needed it, her, them.

A rich laugh from Janet poured over her like honey. "Well, now we know how many fingers you can take. I'll adjust my expectations accordingly."

"Yes, Ms. Lace." Wendy sent the photo she'd taken.

"Another picture. You follow orders well. Would you like your reward now or are you done playing for the night?"

"One more," Wendy said, surprised she could speak when it felt like the air was flying out of her body the moment she breathed it in. "But I don't want to see your body. I want to see *you*."

The sound of Janet's breathing stilled, quieted, and Wendy wondered for a dire moment if she had hung up. But no, the little timer on the phone call continued to flicker along. A moment later, it lit up with a new photo.

Janet's glasses were off, her hair was down. And her face was different. It took Wendy a moment to realize what. She wasn't smiling, not exactly—there was a tightly buttoned grin at the ends of her lips, but it was more of satisfaction than anything else.

But there was an openness there too. Not a vulnerability, but the cultivated blankness that Janet armored herself with was gone. And if there wasn't a maelstrom of emotion on her face, there wasn't a void of it either. Wendy had the uplifting feeling that if she told Janet a joke, she would laugh; that if she told her a tragedy, she would frown. No minute adjustments of a carefully composed visage, but what she was feeling, written boldly on her face.

She didn't think it was 'the real Janet' or some sophomoric nonsense like that. The Janet who chose to be a businesswoman was just as real as the Janet who smelled roses or whatever. But this most definitely seemed like *her* Janet. Something no one else was privy too.

"Thanks," Wendy said.

"Get some sleep," Janet told her fondly.

Fondly. Wendy could absolutely put that tone with that face.

"I expect you to do your usual excellent work tomorrow." She hung up without anything more.

Wendy struggled out of her top, pulled the covers over herself, and went to sleep staring at her phone and the new glimpse she'd been given of Janet Lace.

ΑΨΑ

The gay bar was not Janet's bag, even after what she'd done, but she was too keyed up to sleep and there was a certain ambience she wished to absorb. Wendy had said she'd fucked her in her office, reading that e-mail, and now Janet understood what she'd meant. However far apart they were, she felt *fucked*. Perhaps it was just knowing Wendy felt the same way.

In a strange way, her own muted reaction to the 'lesbian scene' was comforting. There'd always been that trepidation over her attraction to females—such a relief to meet Roberta, to fall in love with her, to not have to be *gay* so much as dating another woman. On her own, there was this worry, incomprehensible to her younger peers, that she'd go from *her* to one of *them*, a dyke, a lesbian—someone who now had to meet criteria and follow a code of conduct. But she was still her, no different. She felt more herself in a way, but she thought that was just Wendy. Someone else wouldn't have done, male or female. There was something especially pleasing about her that Janet couldn't define, but that she was very much looking forward to finding.

She was a woman who fucked other women, in the presence of women who fucked women. If it didn't feel quite right, it also didn't feel odd, strange. It was relaxing, in its own way. To sit and sip her whiskey and be in the room where other women were kissing, dancing—falling in love.

"How about we put that on my tab, darlin'?" a woman said, and Janet looked up to see her—tall and well-built, with an intriguingly symmetrical face—standing over her. *So that's the level I'm operating at. Not bad.*

"No thanks," Janet replied, and the words tasted sweet. "I'm seeing someone."

CHAPTER 8

WENDY WAS AT WORK AND not working. Not at the moment, at any rate. Her phone was on her desk and she kept looking at it like it was the prop in a magic trick. She had pictures of Janet naked on it. It was crazy. It was *insane*. Playboy didn't even do nudity anymore. She had more nudity than Playboy, on her phone, and it was of her boss. She could look at it anytime. Right this second. Or this second. Or *this* second.

"Got a second, Ms. Cedar?" Janet asked her, head in the door.

Wendy resisted the urge to snap up her phone and hide it. It wasn't even powered on. "Sure. Come on in."

Janet closed the door to the partition behind her and Wendy felt her pulse race. Just being in the room with Janet—and with Janet's nipple, which she'd *seen*—was suddenly something intoxicating.

"There's a war games event coming up at the proving grounds in Yuma. DARPA will be showing off all their latest toys, basically a sales demo where they'll decide what to order and how much." She came around Wendy's desk and laid out a brochure over her keyboard. Several, in fact. There was one for a modest hotel, another for the event itself. "Frederickson's going, he's asked me to put my best people on a sales pitch he can deliver. I'd like you to familiarize yourself with the exhibition and prepare the necessary stats. How our bird compares to this and that. It's not a very glamorous piece of work, but it could help our contract."

Janet was leaning on Wendy's desk, over her, and her blouse was not as tight as it usually was. Wendy could see not just her cleavage, but how it curved inward. God, how had she ever not stared at that? Well, she had, but surreptitiously. The way she was trying to now. "I'll get right on it," Wendy promised.

"Just so you know, Ms. Cedar, this assignment has nothing to do with last night. Your performance has been exemplary, regardless of any interpersonal interactions."

"And I do love performing for you," Wendy replied, while her brain inwardly went WHAT?

Janet smiled fitfully. "Not to discuss events outside the office which hold no bearing on our work—"

"Perish the thought."

"—but do you have any…notes?"

"Notes?"

Janet flicked her fingers against one of the brochures. "Whoever designed this pamphlet received notes," she reasoned.

"Last night wasn't a pamphlet."

"Then no…issues? Not even ones you in particular might have, but more what a reasonable adult might have?"

"No issues," Wendy said, smiling reassuringly. "Very much no issues."

"Good." Janet made a face that expressed an attempt to laugh it off without coming anywhere near laughing. "I'm sure sometimes the brochure designer gets it right on the first try too."

"One thing?"

"Yes?" Janet asked, a flicker of doubt crossing her face.

"Being called Ms. Cedar is nice and all, but my name is Wendy. And yours is Janet, if you don't mind my saying so."

"You're quite right. It is Janet. Janet Pauline."

Wendy grunted a little. "Huh. Really."

"Please don't take a page from Ms. Smile's book and start calling me Jan."

A heavy footfall outside the door jerked Janet's face up, and they both watched as a blurry business suit passed alongside the pebbled Lexan.

Janet straightened, her voice chilling from the husky register it'd fallen into. "On another note, please delete the files I sent you last night, for security reasons. Any further reference to them that you need, I can provide personally."

"I will do that," said Wendy, who would not do that. "Anything else?"

"One small question." Janet straightened, ready to head for the door. "Did you wash your hands after you fingered yourself? Because I didn't."

Wendy blinked. As a self-defense mechanism, her brain struggled for something other than the mental picture she had just gotten. "So you masturbated this morning, right? It's not like you haven't bathed or washed your hands since last night? Because...because you had to have eaten breakfast..."

Janet put a finger to her lips. "Sh."

"What's the best moment in your life?"

Wendy puffed air into her cheeks and blew it out slowly. She was at Wednesday dinner with her sister, and with her brother-in-law and nephew at the table, she was in no mood to complicate the digestion of a perfectly good pork roast with figuring out the answer to that.

"What're yours?" she replied.

"Birth of my child," Regan ventured.

"Marrying the love of my life," Keith said.

"Can you have the same one?" Wendy asked, handing Mac what was left of her roast. He proved to have a great future career as a human garbage disposal.

"Well, if we can't have the same one," Regan said, "I should get the marriage, because I wore a pretty dress, and Keith, you should get childbirth, because," she lowered her voice drastically past the range of Mac's hearing, "your vagina wasn't in two pieces."

"Oof," Keith said.

"What's your problem?" Wendy asked. "You don't even have a vagina. You're never going to be in that position."

"You're a lesbian," he pointed out.

"I can still adopt...oh. Right. I see what you're getting at." Wendy leaned back in her chair. "There is such a thing as in vitro fertilization. I find George Clooney, borrow some spooge—"

"You're giving it back?" Regan asked.

"Point is, I could do it."

"But are you?" Keith insisted.

Wendy looked over at Mac. His face was covered with food. "Point taken." Then, because that didn't count as the last word, "But if my son was going to be John Connor, leader of the human resistance, I *could.*

And you're missing my point, which is that I don't think it's fair to count marriages and small human beings. Because then whatever I say, I look like an…" She glanced at Mac. "Like an anus."

"What's an anus?" Mac asked, inevitably.

"Go do your homework," Keith said. "I'll be up in a bit to help you."

"Okay," Mac said dutifully, taking his glass of water with him.

Wendy frowned seeing it. She'd drunk wine out of that same commemorative glass.

Keith cracked his neck. "So, best moment of my life, besides getting married or becoming a father? You remember my cousin Bob and that party at the beachfront?"

Regan nodded. "You weren't here for this," she told Wendy.

"Well, he did this sorta eloping thing where he and his fiancé invited all their friends and family, and instead of spending a ton booking a chapel and everything, they just got married in the middle of the party. I was best man, Lauren Kelly was the maid of honor, they had a priest there. I don't know what everyone thought, having this priest there at the party before they announced it—"

"Wait," Wendy interrupted. "The best moment of your life was your cousin's wedding?"

"Oh, no, I was wearing a tuxedo, but since the wedding was a surprise, I couldn't be at this party in a tux. So when he said they were getting married, I just ripped out of my clothes to show that I had my tuxedo and bowtie and everything under it. Just like James Bond in Goldfinger. It was pretty dope. So what's yours?"

Wendy blew air through her lips again. "Still thinking."

"Okay. You done with your plate? My turn to do dishes."

"Oh, yeah." Wendy handed it to him. "Have at it."

He piled it atop his, and then Regan's. "One day Mac's gonna be old enough to do this, and then all the diaper changes will be worth it. Thanks for the meal, hon." He gave Regan a quick kiss and Wendy went 'aww' as he left the dining room.

Regan stared at her. "You thought that was cute? You never think that's cute. The last time you saw us kiss you said I had cooties now."

"I might've been wrong about that one." Wendy cracked up a little. "But admit it, Keith did go to Jupiter to get more stupider," she giggled.

"What's up with you? You're acting all weird and happy and optimistic, like you just got back from Narnia or something."

"Like I time-traveled to a dystopian future where you're dead and Mac is an evil cyborg, and then I came back and prevented it and everything's better and I've learned to appreciate my situation?"

"Yes, that's the most specific explanation of your present vibe that I could imagine."

Wendy shrugged, picking up her water and downing it. "I just had a really good flick."

"You watched a movie?"

"No, I, ah…flicked. Down… I flicked down. Okay, you're married, you're not dead, you know what I'm talking about."

"Oh! Were you flicking someone else or…"

"No, just me."

"Who'd Wendy flick off?" Keith asked, as he came back drying his hands on his jeans.

"No one. That's the problem," Regan said as he sat back down. "We're trying to figure out why she's so happy all of a sudden."

Keith snapped his fingers. "Easy. One of her TV show people turned out to be a lesbian."

"You really think I'm so shallow that a character from a TV show being gay could have a measurable impact on my personal happiness?"

"She's right," Regan said. "Movie character."

"We're gonna see the next Marvel movie and Black Widow's going to be living with some woman and Wendy's just gonna be beaming."

Regan groaned in dismay. "She's not gonna end up with Bruce?"

Wendy gaped at her. "Okay, not that Black Widow is gay, unfortunately, but I thought I could count on your support." She jerked a thumb at Keith. "I knew I had him in my corner."

Keith shifted in his seat. "I just like when ScarJo does stuff."

"Natasha and Bruce are cute," Regan said. "What, it's okay for Wendy to want her to be with a woman because she thinks women are sexy, but I can't want her to be with an older man because I *know* older men are sexy?"

"Honey? I'm younger than you."

Regan reached across the table to take Keith's hand. "You'll get older."

"So you're just waiting for me to get gray hair?"

"And a beard."

"And good at sex," Wendy chimed in.

"Well, that's never gonna happen," Keith said. "But I'll keep an eye out on TV for any lesbian activity, see what Wendy's Prozac is."

"You're a straight man, you do that anyway," Wendy retorted. "And I hope you realize how immaturely you're characterizing me."

Regan was looking up the stairs. "Mac should be done with his homework by now." She called. "All right, who wants dessert?"

"Me!" Wendy said. "I do! I do!"

"Keith, if you'll do the honors?"

Keith stood up again. "Four bowls of cookies and cream, coming up."

"Don't give me a bowl without any cookie bits," Wendy called after him. "I was in this family before you, I have seniority."

Regan laughed at her. "Okay, I don't know what has you in such a good mood—or throwing your sister out on her ass and keeping her wine all for yourself—but I'm liking it. I really am."

Wendy snorted. "Feed 'em a little ice cream and they get all emotional."

She moved to stand, but Regan took hold of her wrist. "I know you won't believe me, but if I have to pick a best moment that isn't Keith or the munchkin: it's you. Smiling that way. So, try to make it last? For me?"

"It'll last," Wendy told her. "I don't think I have a best moment, but I'm pretty sure it's coming up."

ΑΨΑ

Score one for career women. Janet was known to take her lunch in her office, and commonly invited co-workers to quickly touch base on business. So it didn't raise any suspicion for her and Wendy to dine together, given they were both working on a project.

"Grilled teriyaki chicken with romaine salad," Janet announced, opening up the Tupperware. Wendy hadn't noticed earlier, but Janet had a chessboard set-up along one side of her office, with a little table and two chairs and a view out the window. It was *made* to seduce impressionable young employees. Wendy couldn't believe Janet hadn't seduced one before. Was there a dearth of impressionable young employees at the company?

She held up her plate and Janet served her, before serving herself and sitting down at her end of the table, where the report Wendy had filed was cued up on a tablet. Wendy opened her mouth to say something, but Janet was already focused on the tablet, idly chewing—very politely—as she flitted through it. Wendy took a bite of her own meal. It tasted very… nutritious. In a good way, mind you, but that's how it always started.

"You know, I could bring lunch sometime."

Janet didn't look up. "Would you make something or would you get burgers from Five Guys?"

"Burgers. But I would carefully sleuth out what you would like on yours, it wouldn't have onions or anything."

"I don't like onions," Janet confirmed.

"See? I know my stuff."

Janet carefully cultivated a forkful of chicken and salad as she glanced up. "Are these specs accurate?"

"Absolutely."

"We're slower than the Helios."

"We're slower than the Helios's *specs*," Wendy countered. She spun the tablet sideways and leaned in to point out a column. "Manufacturers, they all like to tell fairy tales. No way that a bird with that load and that carriage makes that speed. Any engineer can tell you that."

"So our bird is faster?"

"Absolutely. It's the lightest, fastest thing out there. And if they ask you why it can't level a building, just remind them that's not its job."

Janet's lips teased a smile. "Very good. I don't suppose you have the Helios's actual specs?"

"I made some educated guesses in the attachment. It's got a fat ass. The Army will order it, but not to do what our Hawkowl will do."

"Fantastic," Janet said, and bit into her meal with a moan like it just grew five times tastier.

Usually Wendy wore trainers with her slacks, but she wasn't so butch that she couldn't pull off pumps, stockings, even garters. And she hadn't worn pumps with her pantsuit because Janet was a tall woman.

She slipped her stockinged foot out of her shoe. "You know, this is our lunch break."

"Yes? So?"

"We're not being paid to work. It wouldn't be out of sorts for us to talk about something non-work-related."

Janet had the poker face of Doc Holliday. "Such as?"

Wendy stretched her foot out and ran it along Janet's calf, their stockings sliding together like Wendy imagined a livewire would sound. Instantly, Janet sat bolt-upright—as if her posture hadn't been great before—with her eyes growing nearly as wide as the frames of her glasses. Her mouth flew open, though she didn't actually squeak. It was a very squeaky kind of expression, though.

"You're adorable!" Wendy laughed.

Janet picked up a napkin to dab at her lips. "I have not been referred to as such often."

"You're beautiful," Wendy corrected herself. "You're sensual. You're effervescent."

"Good word choice."

"My sister's married. Less drinking games, more Scrabble." Wendy stirred her salad. "Look, I'm not saying we have to necessarily…"

Janet leaned forward, resting her elbows on the table and steepling her hands below her chin. "Yes?"

Wendy flushed. She licked her lips. She recovered. "Well, there being a lady present, I won't say. But it involves a moderately smaller version of that bathysphere you got me."

"All right, bathysphere? Now you're going too far."

"Withdrawn. My point is, we can just talk about stuff. Our—insert scare-quotes if you want—relationship."

"Mm." Janet put her thumb at the corner of her lip. "I have been wanting to talk some things over with you."

"All right." Wendy clapped her hands. "Hit me."

"You're very good at inviting emotional intimacy," Janet said dryly.

"It's what I do."

"Well, it's not some gothic family secret or anything." Janet tapped the tines of her fork delicately against her plate. "It does have to do with intimacy, sexual intimacy, but I'm sure we can be open and honest and mature about that."

"Absolutely," Wendy agreed, crossing her fingers.

"It's just that, I noticed in your fantasizing about me, and in the phone call that you responded to so dramatically—"

"Are we having a conversation or are you issuing a press release?"

Janet canted her head. "Ms. Cedar, I'm sure you're aware that if I went into indelicate detail, I'd have to worry about you lunging across this table."

Wendy gulped, feeling suddenly too gay for this conversation. She needed a translator or something. Someone who'd gotten laid recently, and not with a glove. "Point taken."

"Now then," Janet continued, sounding much more centered. "I've noticed that what you respond to tends to be…kinky."

Wendy laughed. "Is that a problem? I mean, c'mon—" She waved her hand around. "Office. Fucked me. We've been over this."

"Yes. Indelibly. But…with Roberta…many of these sorts of things have the participants talking about what they fantasize about, planning scenarios…"

"Yeah, I get that, I read *Fifty Shades of Grey* too, well, I read people making fun of *Fifty Shades of Grey*, but it's not like we're pouring candle wax on each other or anything. We're just having fun."

"I'd still like to know what your preferences entail."

Wendy grinned at her. "This is you trying to get me to send you another smutty e-mail, isn't it?"

"The last e-mail was really more of a movie recommendation."

"True, but *Ella Enchanted* was pretty good, right?"

"It seemed to try a little hard for my tastes."

"Wow," Wendy enunciated. "I know, not the time or place, but you'd better like *The Princess Bride*."

"No, you caught me, I'm a robot." Janet adjusted her glasses. "All right. You're uncomfortable with planning out activities."

"Well, don't handcuff me out of nowhere or anything, but if you're just gonna tell me your fingers are all—jilly, I don't need a trigger warning."

"All right. A list, then, of what you'd be comfortable with."

Wendy hiccupped a laugh. "Would you like our kinky sex to have a mission statement too?"

"Wendy, this is serious. I don't want to do something that's going to make you uncomfortable."

"And I trust you not to. Look, I'm not saying I'm down for anything, I can come up with a few things that I'd prefer to die not having on my hard disk. And if you're worried something crosses a line, *of course* ask me if it's cool. I'm not gonna think you're weird if you want to pee on me." Wendy added quickly, "I mean, I'm not gonna let you do it either!"

"Wendy, please, I worry about hygiene enough without adding that to the mix." Janet speared another chunk of chicken, and Wendy noticed she let out another unconscious little moan when she bit into it. Wendy smiled. *Happy Ms. Lace.*

"I'd just like it if you were a little spontaneous, in the moment. Give me a one-minute warning. But even if we make a list, I'm not going to freak out if you order off the menu."

"Very well. That does leave the matter of a safe word," Janet continued, holding the tines of her fork aloft, rotating them idly.

"Yeah, we should probably have one of those. I didn't ask for one before because, y'know, I could've hung up."

"Obviously, it shouldn't be something we might say in casual conversation, so I was thinking it could be 'trichotomy'."

"Okay," Wendy said, "I can't remember that *now*, much less when you'll have me bent over your knee."

Janet gestured flippantly. "I'll defer to your expertise."

"Well, it's supposed to be the watchword for 'not all good', so how about 'watchword'?"

Janet nodded. "Acceptable." Then she stopped nodding. "You know, this doesn't have to be that sort of relationship."

"The sex kind? Because the phone calls are great, don't get me wrong, but I like to get more out of a relationship than a free phone sex hotline."

"The kink," Janet said. "Sometimes I'm not sure I understand why you're interested in that. Being degraded. Punished. Hurt. If you think that's a requirement to be in a relationship with me, it certainly is not."

Wendy grew serious. "And I'm not the sort of girl who goes along with some shit she's not comfortable with just because you're really hot and generally amazing."

"Why then?"

Wendy kneaded her fingers together. "I don't know…just something about it all, I guess. Feeling something, feeling it so *intensely* that you almost can't stand it, that you have to *endure it*. It just seems like that's what you want out of a relationship, right? Not just 'pleasant,' not just 'okay,' but…" She circled her hands in the air. "Greatness. Even just feeling something that's sublime."

"You put great expectations on me, Ms. Cedar."

Wendy mirrored her aristocratic manner. "You invite them, Ms. Lace." She checked her watch. "Now if you'll excuse me, I need to go look at some funny cat videos. Work! I meant work."

Janet glared at her, but in a fond way. And Wendy had a feeling that whatever expectations she might have of Janet, Janet was plainly determined to meet them.

ÅⱯÅ

Janet held her hands under running water in the executive washroom, thinking of Lady Macbeth, out damned spot; thinking of how you could have the exact opposite problem for the exact opposite reason. She didn't want to wash away Wendy's touch, her feel, her kiss. But she was a little too particular not to.

What a wonderful thing to be able to go and get Wendy back on her skin, whenever she chose.

"Nothing like a long lunch break when you don't eat, is there?" Mary Borchard asked, coming up to the sink beside Janet's and washing her hands.

Janet removed her glasses from where they hung at her neckline, putting them back on. "Depends on the company, I suppose."

"Too true. Hear about Frederickson?"

"Yes. Leukemia, right?"

"Right."

"Shame."

"Shame," Mary agreed. She dried her hands. "Won't even be able to make it to Yuma."

"I suppose they'll just have to send someone else."

"Wonder who?"

They walked out of the washroom together. About to go their separate ways when Mary called "Lauren, there you are, how've you been?"

Janet turned, watching a bit bemusedly as Mary cornered one of her employees.

"It's Leslie, actually," she said, sounding apologetic at the correction.

Mary pointed at her wedding ring. "Well, you're married, I remembered that much right. How is your husband?"

"He's great."

"And the children?"

"Good," Leslie said, brightening, before wincing. "Well, Timmy's a bit of a struggle, but they always are at that age."

"Good, good," Mary said, nodding. "Give them my best, won't you?"

"I will, Ms. Borchard."

As she bustled off, Janet joined Mary at the elevator bank. They both reached for the call button, but Mary pressed it first, stabbing the light into it.

"She's being let go at the end of the week," Mary said, apropos of nothing, and watched Janet's reaction. "You flinched. That's why they won't send you. You let your emotions be a part of the equation. But don't worry. The world needs plenty of middle managers."

The elevator arrived. Janet let Mary take it. She was in no mood to share a ride with her.

"Besides," Mary said, "not much point in climbing the ladder. Once Old Man Savin dies, either his shithead kids or shithead grandkids or shithead nephews will take over. They'll strip this place and sell it for parts. You're never going to get the brass ring."

"And you?" Janet asked.

"When the hammer comes down, someone's gonna have to help swing it. Too bad you don't have the balls."

The elevator doors closed between him. Another set of doors dinged, and Janet stepped over to them as they opened up.

Grinning.

"Too bad you're not going to Yuma."

CHAPTER 9

WENDY HAD BEEN DRINKING. Tina had been managing her. She'd come home too buzzed to sleep, worked on cleaning her Bonneville's wheels and hubs. Then, covered with grease too stubborn for Ajax to get off, she wrapped herself in a shower towel and passed out on top of her bed, too gross for the sheets.

The purple bunnies were just about to swarm when the world abruptly had a ringtone. Wendy opened her eyes and saw something far scarier: she'd left her phone on the other side of the nightstand and to get it, she'd have to leave her bed, which was suddenly the most comfortable place in the world.

She was this close to letting it ring—it couldn't be that long until it went to voice-mail—but then she remembered that she was in a relationship now and really couldn't tell her phone to fuck off just because *someone* wasn't courteous enough to text.

Besides, someone could've died or something. And now she was worried someone had died. How could she enjoy her bed when someone might be dying?

Cracking inactivity out of her bones and groaning, Wendy shuffled herself out of her bed and picked up the phone. She sagged back down on the bed as she answered. "Yeah?"

"Ms. Cedar, good, you're up." Janet's voice was a strong jolt of espresso, even if Wendy could only manage a weak smile. Four hours later, this call would've made her day. But it wasn't four hours later. It was four in the goddamn morning.

"We have very different definitions of 'up'. You know, if you feel the need to wake me up, you could at least do it by crawling into bed with me, wearing mink…"

"This isn't a social call—"

"And it's Saturday, right? Because I don't know who told you I spend my Saturdays masturbating, but they're sorely half-mistaken."

"Yes, I'm afraid there's no time for pleasantries." Janet kept the faux-professionalism in her voice, to the point where it didn't sound so faux. "Our current marketing director was diagnosed with leukemia yesterday. He's starting treatment immediately, so I've been chosen to go to the conference in his stead. Very last minute, they just settled on me being the one to make the trip. I'll need someone to assist me, so since you already worked on the pamphlets, I take it you're familiar enough to be of assistance?"

"Yeah. Go to Arizona, I'm cool with that. Do we get hazard pay?"

"If you could pack a bag and come down here, I'll drive us to the airport. It'll just be for the weekend, and I'd really appreciate it. I'm afraid we would have to share a hotel suite, but I trust that won't be a problem?"

Wendy rubbed some errant sleep from her eyes. "Okay then, we spend three hours doing a sales pitch, the rest of the weekend finger-banging and watching cable porn. I like it, I like it. Should I bother packing underwear?"

Janet faked a laugh. "I'd love to hammer out those details, but I'm with the board of directors finalizing the arrangement, so use your own best judgment and we'll attend to the little concerns later on. Please come right away, you don't have time to shower."

"Yeah, no doubt, no doubt. What's your favorite color? Because whatever it is, I can probably bring a dildo that color. There was a sale and I thought, 'Wendy, why not treat yourself?'"

"All right, glad to hear I have my best man on the job," Janet said with false cheer. "Please get in touch with my secretary if you have any further inquiries, she probably knows more than I do at this point."

"Are we taking a plane? Because, Mile High Club? Very easy with two women. Unless you're really into scissoring, and I've always found that pretty overrated."

"Thank you again and I will see you here." Janet hung up.

Wendy cracked some more stiffness out of her joints, going around her apartment and unplugging her appliances. While she tried to remember every gizmo that needed to stop leeching electricity, she rang Regan. She got her answering machine. "Hey, sis, can't babysit this weekend. Work thing. Janet needs me to go with her to Yuma."

The phone abruptly picked up. "'Janet'? You're going to Yuma with a 'Janet' now?"

"Yeah, she's my boss."

"I bet she is."

Wendy held the phone away from her ear while she worked on a straight face. Regan could detect a snicker at five hundred yards. "I need to go. And we're not having sex." Technically true.

"I'm looking her up on Facebook."

"Do not send her a friend request!" Wendy hung up. She didn't have any clean clothes. She'd have to take her laundry and do it at the hotel.

It was true what they said. Nothing good happened after 2 a.m.

ΑΨΑ

"Need any help with your bags?"

Still stretching after the long car ride, Wendy jerked in surprise. That didn't sound like her Uber driver, and she should know after listening to him talk about dolphins for thirty minutes, like geez, dude, host a nature documentary already. Although it was kind of cool that killer whales were just really big dolphins.

She looked over to the speaker, un-spacing out. It was a small woman, thin and seemingly frail except for a steely, spindly aura of strength she possessed. Her hair was dryly styled, her face neatly made up to hide the fine bones of her features in suggestions of volume. Wendy couldn't place her exact age, but had the idea that calling her an old soul would be taken as an insult. Still, she was beaming a pleasant smile and Wendy returned it.

"Sure. Hate to make two trips."

Wendy wished the driver a good day and agreed to give him five stars, or whatever system Uber had nowadays. Then she handed the woman her carry-on bag while she lugged the suitcase, acutely aware of her arm muscles against her shirt sleeves. She thought that perhaps her commitment to bohemianism should stop at using secondhand luggage, and include buying something with rollers.

She'd packed only the essentials. She really thought they'd be lighter than this. "Wendy Cedar," she greeted, nodding thankfully.

"Mary Borchardt," the steely-eyed woman returned. Her gaze was disconcertingly intent, like it had weathered at twice the rate of her body. "I know who you are. You're going with Janet to make the sales presentation."

"You know Janet?"

"We collaborated on the Hawkowl. She's a firecracker, isn't she?"

"That's one word for it." *A word like hootenanny or skedaddle.*

They'd made it to the lobby, and the place was like Count Dracula's office space with almost, but not quite, everything closed for the night. The few hints of movement she could see on higher floors and infrequently lit offices seemed vaguely frenetic. Maybe it was just her imagination; the excitement at the prospect of barely having to share Janet with any of her responsibilities. Wendy just had to kick the presentation's ass and cue one grateful Janet Lace…

She had to remind herself not to think about that one in public. She was liable to start shooting gay out of her eyes like laser beams, mooning over Janet.

"Could you tell Janet Lace that Wendy Cedar is here?" she asked the receptionist, dropping her suitcase by the front desk. The receptionist obligingly relayed it up the first of however many rungs were below Elizabeth Smile. If Elizabeth was even still at work. Wendy yawned.

"Crazy, isn't it?" Mary asked, all rhetorical as she set the carry-on down by Wendy's suitcase. "All this hard work and aggravation, and it all comes down to getting people to want to buy the damn things."

"Yeah," Wendy agreed. "Funny."

"Would you mind giving me a little sneak peek of the pitch? It's hard for me not to worry."

"No time," Wendy said, seeing that the elevator was on the way down. "This is kind of last minute, have to make my flight."

"Yes, of course, of course. Just tell me if you'll be mentioning the RadarVoid system?"

"RadarVoid?" It sounded familiar, but woken up from a deep sleep and then tranquilized again by the car ride over, Wendy felt too frazzled to fully place it.

"One of the new features of the Hawkowl. My team implemented it and we're all very concerned it won't get its due. We're mostly women, you see, sort of the girls' dormitory you might say, and, well, you know how it is." Mary reached into her jacket pocket and brought out a file folder. "Here. Take it. The project overview. I'd hate to see it buried just because *someone* up there doesn't see it as important."

The elevator emerged into view, Janet visible through the glass wall, arms crossed in consternation, gloved fingers rattling against her biceps.

Wendy fought against a smile, remembering that she was supposed to be helping a fellow employee out. She took the folder. "I'll see to it that Janet gets it."

Mary grinned and seized Wendy's hand in a firm shake. "Thank you! Thank you very much. It's so wonderful to be appreciated for, well, not for *once*, but sometimes it does feel like it!"

"Think nothing of it. Us girls have to stick together."

"Exactly." Mary nodded. "Exactly, exactly, exactly! Well, have a nice flight and, yes, try not to work too hard? It may be business, but it's still a trip!"

Wendy laughed. "You too!" she said, as if Mary were going on a business trip, *stupid, stupid*. She shook it out of her head and picked up her suitcase and carry-on just in time for a beefy intern to take them from her. Another one was pushing Janet's rolling suitcase ahead of him—it looked so easy—leaving Janet only grasping her usual briefcase.

Wendy held still as a statue as Janet passed by her.

"Come," Janet said, giving her a raised eyebrow.

Wendy followed her back to the curb, where a limousine had pulled up.

Honestly, who knew Janet Lace could be so fucking extra?

ΑΫΑ

The limo ride was long and smooth. Wendy had done it before, of course, and even if she did want to shove her head out the sunroof, she would hate to embarrass herself that way in front of Janet. Her boss, meanwhile, sat dead center in back of the bench seating, casually checking off engagements she was deferring on her phone—sending texts to all the poor bastards who wouldn't get to see her because she was in Yuma. And not seeming to notice at all how the limo was flying from the hundred bucks she'd slipped the driver to get them to the airport 'toot sweet'.

Funny as hell—all that just so they would be there two hours before their flight took off. Not that Wendy cared. She was just looking at Janet. All the way in the back of the stretch, lioness in a rolling den, going over her phone like it was the bone of a picked-clean carcass. The Yuma trip was a big opportunity for her, and her smile was smeared with red. A fresh kill. A delicious kill.

And every so often, her eyes flicked up from white-painted glasses to take in Wendy. And each time, Wendy felt, in a very real way, honored to be noticed by her. To get her attention when there were so many other things it could be on.

The ride settled: they got on the highway, and the stop-and-go traffic just *went*. With balance restored and the speed smooth, Janet finished with her phone.

"You're aware, I trust, that you're accompanying me because of your diligent work ethic and excellent performance, not because of any… superfluous factors?" Janet asked, a near-match for the Voice of God.

"Yeah, I know, I'm awesome," Wendy replied. She got up. She sat down beside Janet. Beside those long legs, skirt leaving them bare, crossed thighs leaving them hoisted up close enough to touch…"What are you thinking?" Wendy asked, to avoid thinking what *she* was thinking. The partition may have been rolled up, but it wasn't soundproof. And Wendy may not have been a screamer, but she also wasn't sure if that'd be the case with Janet.

Janet looked her over, with a smirk that showed she knew exactly how much Wendy liked being looked over. "I'm wondering what you'll let me get away with."

"I'm pretty flexible," Wendy replied. "Both in terms of my body and with gay stuff."

"Not in bed, I know you'll let me do anything I want to do to you there. I'm referring to intensity. I'm referring to something for you to *endure*."

Wendy gulped. She'd never actually gulped just because someone implied she was about to get a break-off-a-switch whooping. Then again, no one had ever implied she'd get a break-off-a-switch whooping. And it wasn't like anyone fantasized about being sent to time-out.

"Have I been a bad girl?" Wendy asked, trying to sound sultry and fearing she mostly sounded like she needed a cough drop.

Janet nodded slowly. "The phone call. You're a smart girl, Ms. Cedar. You clearly realized that was a work call, to be taken seriously, and not an appropriate venue for your antics." She leaned toward Wendy. "Do you enjoy the thought of me trying to attend to important business, with respected colleagues, while imagining *you*? What I'm going to do to you? How I'm going to do it?"

Wendy bit her lip. "I do like that thought," she said. "I like knowing that you think of doing things to me as much as I think about it."

Janet shook her head. "Naughty. So naughty. And willfully disobedient."

"I need to be taught a lesson," Wendy agreed. "Tamed with a firm hand…"

She could almost see Janet shiver. "Pull up your skirt."

Wendy did. But slowly. Not to be dramatic, but so that her hands didn't shake. "I liked how it felt, that day in the elevator. I couldn't stop thinking of how it would feel if you did it. I still can't."

"Do you think I'm going to reward you or punish you?" Janet asked. Her eyes burned into Wendy, nearly making her whimper before they dropped down to bare thighs. "Pink panties, Ms. Cedar. That's very cute. Did you used to wear cute panties like that for your college girlfriend?"

"No. Just for you."

"I like them," Janet said. "But your behavior has to come first. I'm taking away the privilege of wearing panties. From now on, whenever you're at work, you'll have to put up with knowing that you're exposed. That anyone can see you, or feel you, at any time, and there's nothing to protect you from it. That I'm the only person who will know. And I will check to make sure you're being obedient, Ms. Cedar. If you're not…" She trailed off.

Wendy shuddered. It wasn't in fear.

"Well? Take them off. You're not allowed to be covered."

Wendy couldn't stop herself from shaking as she planted her shoulders against her seat, arched her hips, worked her panties down. She felt Janet's eyes on her sex, saw the look in Janet's eyes as the woman saw her exposed, and she was suddenly aware of just how much need there was in her body. If Janet had asked, she would've done anything for her.

She set herself back down in her seat, and her skirt hadn't fallen back down. Her bare ass touched the cool leather of the seat cushion and she remembered the glove and she remembered how good it had been just for Janet to hear her and she clenched and tightened until it was almost painful, until she wanted to beg Janet to finger her just so she wouldn't implode. But she had to be good. She'd disobeyed enough for one day.

She bent over—Christ, everything was such a fucking porno with Janet watching her—and scanted the panties down her legs. Over either one of her feet. As she lifted them, one by one, the pressure on her womanhood crested. She thought she could get off just by squeezing her thighs together. Instead, she picked her panties up off the floor and held them out to Janet.

Janet took them and put them in her pocket. "I hope you brought a pink dildo," she said. "It's my favorite color."

When they arrived at the departure gate, Wendy patted her skirt down about half a billion times in ten seconds before the chauffeur got the door and she got out, following a Janet who appeared cool as a cucumber. As if she didn't have another woman's panties in her fucking breast pocket.

Janet stood beside the door as Wendy got out, being more careful of her skirt than she'd ever been. "Remember, Ms. Cedar," Janet said, continuing their conversation as if it had been about the market value of legumes. "Next time I expect you to follow my instructions implicitly."

"Yes, Ms. Lace," Wendy replied. She meant every word.

ÅѶÅ

Wendy would've expected nothing less: Janet had airports gamed down to a science. Before they were even out of the limousine, she had given Wendy slip-on shoes and clear toiletry bags for her personal items. She double-checked Wendy's documents for her, then fitted them to her own, and put them in her jacket pocket. Not the same one she had Wendy's panties in.

Wendy couldn't stop thinking about how bare she was. If she bent over too far, took a long stride, walked down a flight of stairs, anyone could see her. It was probably one of her better reasons for not taking the stairs, all told.

She handed over her laptop case at security, took off her shoes, and could feel the inside of her skirt on her thighs, her hips. Of course, she could always feel it there, but it felt so much more intimate with nothing to stop it from going through her. If Janet touched her, right through her skirt, it'd be like she was wearing nothing at all.

She looked over at Janet. Janet was watching her. Smirking. She put her shoes back on. Very carefully. She imagined Janet declaring her panties at the customs desk. Wait, they didn't go through customs to go to Arizona, it was part of the US, technically.

Janet did it again with the flight. The plane was medium-sized, cramped but not claustrophobic, with a wide aisle and two gangly seats on either side. There were few passengers on the red-eye, and they were able to space themselves out into bubbles of privacy: a skeleton crew occupying a vast, insurgent territory.

Janet and Wendy sat in the middle, by the wing. From the aisle seat, Janet gave the wing a quick check and an approving nod through the window, as if it were a horse she were about to take for a ride.

Wendy stowed her carry-on—Janet hadn't even taken that much, just her purse—and sat by the window. She wondered just how comfortable she should get; it was a long flight. "So, when do you want to...go to the bathroom?" she asked, glancing about at the other passengers. None of them were within earshot and she hoped it stayed that way as more boarded.

"This is an Embraer E-Jets 190," Janet said. "You'll be lucky if you manage to pee in the bathroom, let alone masturbate, let alone mutual..." Janet silenced herself as a flight attendant started down the aisle. "Maybe on the flight back."

"Then maybe you should've taken my panties off on the flight back," Wendy suggested. She got up, struggling past Janet's aisle seat. "Trust me, it'll be fine, I did gymnastics in high school."

"High school is always farther back than you think," Janet needled, starting her book.

Wendy paused in front of Janet, making one long step to the aisle, stretching her skirt up her thighs. "Maybe I got held back a grade."

Janet looked up over the rim of her glasses. "It's not me. It's physics."

"Uh-huh. Well, I'm gonna go have a word with physics."

With that, Wendy went to check out the restroom. She came back in thirty seconds. "That thing is a chamber pot. Not a room with a chamber pot—an actual chamber pot."

Janet patted her hand. "I'll try to find us a nice 747 for the return flight."

Wendy caught Janet's hand in her fingers and gave it a squeeze before she let Janet pull away. She wondered if Janet had known this was an E-Jet 190 when she booked the tickets. And whether or not it was worse if Janet *had* known, but not thought of how much Wendy would want to touch her, kiss her. Be in love with her.

ÅⱯÅ

Their stopover was in Chicago and it felt like they had to wait as long as they'd been in the air for the connecting flight. All that haste, just to hurry up and wait. They had the gate all to themselves. Wendy considered coffee, considered trying to get some sleep on the chairs—curling up horizontally was an impossibility for obvious reasons—and finally settled on washing some of the grime off in the bathroom so she could at least feel clean on the flight.

Janet went with her to the restroom.

"All you're doing is giving material to the stand-up comedians of the world," Wendy told her.

Janet was quick but thorough, checking under the stalls, then double-checking them by nudging the doors open. Finished with that, she exited the restroom and jiggled the handle on a small door adjourning it.

"Janitors never lock these," Janet said, and pulled out an Out Of Order sign, which she neatly slotted over the women symbol on the restroom door before pulling Wendy back through it.

And Wendy would've thought that if anyone in this relationship had a system for bathroom quickies, it'd be her.

"Come on. Let's not press our luck," Janet said, going to the line of sinks and pulling hotel-sized soap and shampoo from her purse.

Wendy took off her sweatshirt, suitably embarrassed by the fresh tank top she had on underneath that had supported her through sobering up and coming awake and had been repaid with toxic levels of sweat. But Janet didn't appear to notice, dragging Wendy by the hand and giving her arms a quick once-over. Wendy helped out, struck by the absurdity of trying to wash one arm while Janet washed the other; by having Janet lift her tank over her shoulder blades and scrub her back, or hold it up to her breasts and wash her stomach. By the end, her tank was soaked through anyway. She'd have to put her sweatshirt back on just to avoid looking like she'd been on the set of *Coyote Ugly*.

"Lean your head down," Janet told her. "Turn your head to the side. Eyes closed."

140

Wendy did, forgetting she was mooning the handicapped stall until the air conditioning picked up and flicked her skirt at least once. She moaned unhappily; Janet ignored her, giving her hair a good rinse, then massaging shampoo into her scalp while Wendy hung on to the sink and concentrated on not taking a header into the linoleum.

"When I was your age, I did this every week," Janet said. "Much easier with a second pair of hands."

"'When I was your age'? People actually say that?"

"When I was in my twenties," Janet corrected. "The company had a plant in Germany, and many of the NATO countries were interested in our products, so I did demos. Troubleshooting. Taught the mechanics a thing or two about maintenance. It was all terribly exciting. And Roberta *loved* having me gone for weeks at a time."

"It was your job, though," Wendy reasoned, eyes still shut against the shampoo. She thought that was why Janet had picked now to bring it up.

"I didn't say that so you could defend me. I said it because you were thinking it, just too polite to say so. There we are."

She held Wendy's head under the faucet a moment, long enough to comb through her hair one last time, then she pulled her up. Wendy straightened her skirt. That was going to become a nervous tic, she knew it.

"How do you feel?"

Wendy wrung out her hair into the sink. "Halfway human. That was certainly the most hygienic thing that's ever happened to me while I was bent over a sink not wearing panties."

Janet kept a stiff lip. "Sorry I didn't bring conditioner. Short notice."

ÅⱯÅ

Once they boarded, the plane couldn't take off. They were grounded.

An hour into the wait and Wendy was too awake to sleep, too tired to do anything else. She made a good-faith effort, asking for a blanket from the flight attendant and snuggling under it when it arrived. Maybe it was suddenly having senior prom modesty over her legs, but she felt more at ease. She tilted her seat back, eased down with it, and turned on her side to look at Janet.

In profile, the woman was stunning. Her keen intelligence focused on a paperback, a manicured thumb turning the pages like some Roman emperor might accept a grape popped between his lips. In the darkened cabin, her glasses shone with the light reflected in them.

"Good book?" Wendy asked.

"Good book. Great subject matter," Janet replied.

Wendy adjusted her position, staring at Janet meaningfully.

Janet turned another page. "It's about a B-29 Superfortress that crashed in Greenland after WW2. It was abandoned for decades, but perfectly preserved. Some men went to repair it and fly it back. Nova did an episode about it."

"You think I watch Nova?" Wendy asked. "That's the sweetest thing anyone's ever said to me."

"No, it isn't."

"You callin' me a liar, city slicker?" Wendy said, putting on a Yosemite Sam voice.

"I think people must say sweet things to you very often," Janet said. "Because I'm not a very affectionate person and it's all I can do not to say sweet things to you all the time."

"And I think you are a very affectionate person." Wendy grinned. "You're just not having a particularly affectionate week." Her hand wandered between the seats, dropped down, tickling the stream of warm air that ran under the seats, keeping the plane from being as cold as the condensation that formed outside the windows. "Read to me?"

Janet blinked. "Why? I could just let you have it when I'm done?"

"Because I like hearing your voice," Wendy said. "And I like watching your lips. But I would love for you to let me have it."

Janet glanced sidelong at her. Then returned her attention to her book. She cleared her throat.

> "Bob cooked and helped wherever needed, as did the Nova crew, as the normal distinction between journalists and their subjects dissolved in the all-consuming fight to stay alive and get the job done. The task was so overwhelming, the life so hard, there was no place for anyone who failed to contribute."

As she read, Janet shifted the book to one hand and dropped her right arm between the seats, behind the armrest. Wendy felt her open palm and stroked it. Traced her fingertips over Janet's palm and the back of her hand and the sides of her fingers and the hardness of her knuckles and the chill of her fingernails. Thinking of the tiny hairs she felt, the capillaries carrying blood, the sinew that tightened and loosened for each and every motion. All the things that went into Janet Lace's hand. All the things that made it fit around hers.

"And, in addition to survival, they had a shared interest. Without an airplane to fly, there wouldn't be much of a film or a story, and without six more useful bodies turning wrenches or cleaning or lifting, the airplane would never fly."

ΑΨΑ

By the time they took off, Wendy had long since fallen asleep, her grip limp on Janet's hand. Janet didn't know why she kept reading aloud, her voice low, barely a whisper. And she didn't know why she liked the thought of Wendy falling asleep a little closer, resting her head on Janet's shoulder. It wasn't as if Wendy would care where her head was while she slept.

Janet tucked her finished book into the pocket of the seat in front of her, then called the flight attendant for her own blanket. She slept the six hours left in the flight, waking up with the gentle, golf-commentator tones the captain used to announce their approach. Somehow, it was always more of an alarm clock to her than announcements about the in-flight meal or turbulence; some trigger word about descent always jogged the air traveler in her awake. She took a moment to watch Wendy sleep, the girl looking as peaceful as ever, then gave a light tug on one lock of her hair.

Wendy squeezed her eyes shut tighter, groaned, then yawned and woke. "I cannot believe I slept with you on the first date."

"It's amazing the jokes you can come up with on a full night's rest."

"That's nothing. I'm still tired as…I'm still very tired." Wendy yawned again, pointing a finger at her mouth in demonstration. She checked her phone. "And cold! The low is *thirty degrees*? We're in Arizona! I thought this was a desert."

"Cold front. El Nino. Climate change. Take your pick."

"I didn't even bring a coat."

"You can have one of mine. Yes, I brought a spare."

"You bring spare coats on business trips?"

"Needed it, didn't I?"

As they disembarked and went to claim their luggage, sluggish and sedated with jet lag and the hours of confinement, Janet nevertheless felt a palpable excitement. It was the crush of the responsibility placed on her, the trust she'd been given, the opportunity that she'd doggedly pursued until this moment, when it was hers. And it didn't hurt to have Wendy sharing that.

She didn't know what it meant, but she knew it meant something. And she was growing more comfortable with not knowing.

She had traveled light, only two bags on the carousal for her, and only one for Wendy, although Janet suspected that had more to do with Wendy planning to buy what she needed here rather than having thought through everything she needed. No one knew how to save money in their twenties.

She unzipped one of her bags, found a gray wool and cashmere coat. It was heavier than the long camel one she would be putting on herself, but she felt indebted to Wendy for agreeing to this on such short notice and not being able to dress appropriately for the weather. She was wearing a skirt, for Christ's sake. Not even a modest skirt—it disappeared under the hem of her coat.

"Wait here," Janet told her, pulling the coat tight around Wendy before shrugging her own on. "I'll hail a cab."

"And I will try to sort out if this is the most uncomfortable I've been for fashion. Probably not. I'm wearing flats."

Janet hurried out, wishing she'd had more time. She'd been able to arrange for the limo *to* the airport, but getting one to take her *away* from the Yuma main terminal was outside her timeframe. It embarrassed her, having to smuggle Wendy about in a cab. That certainly hadn't been her experience on her honeymoon. That had been first-class, all the way.

Only you're not on honeymoon, you're barely even on a date, you're on a business trip with, what, your work-wife? Your office fling? Your slightly-more-classy-than-banging-the-secretary? Just because she's the same age you were when you got married doesn't mean she wants damaged goods and—

Whatever existential episode she was having was interrupted by a taxi cab pulling up. She signaled for the driver to wait, hurried back inside to fetch the luggage Wendy was guarding, and together they got everything into the trunk of the cab. The cabbie didn't offer to help, seeing they could manage three bags on their own, and probably not getting out from under the cab's heater for love or money. Even if it wasn't actively snowing, there were hailstones on the glossy-wet ground that Janet assumed had come with recent sleet. The airport had been chilly, the outside was *cold*, and when they finally piled into the back of the cab, it was all Janet could do not to help out as Wendy rubbed herself warm. She did offer a sympathetic smile and promised herself she'd get some hot coffee into Wendy at the earliest opportunity—her treat.

The ride was through light traffic, the driver careful with slick streets. There was a peculiar melancholy to being driven in that haze between morning and night and overcast skies. The natural tendency was towards sleep, lulled by the motion of the vehicle, buffeted by the darkness sweeping by on all sides. It soothed frazzled nerves, not that Janet had let her nerves get frazzled. She'd been remarkably calm in her dealings with Wendy, despite the eagerness of the move. The stupid, silly conspiring between libido and circumstance to rush her into this. She felt breathlessly afraid that a wrong move would spoil everything beyond repair; a misstep that she would be entombed in for the remaining days of the conference, the error festering with the close proximity she and Wendy would be in, if she moved too fast, if she moved too slow, she could ruin it all.

Janet stared out the window and tried not to let any of the anxiety reach her. It wasn't like with Roberta. She wouldn't let it be. When was the last time, with Roberta, that Janet had wanted so keenly to feel her hand again? She laid her hand down on the bench seat between herself and Wendy, palm down, gripping the coarse leather of the water-damaged seat. Wendy could lay her hand down alongside Janet's, and if she left it there long enough, it would be perfectly natural for their fingers to brush together, for her to feel the warmth of Wendy's pinky along hers.

She was smiling, thinking of something so small—gripping the leather in hopes it would happen. She hadn't had that with Roberta for a long time, if ever. She wouldn't let it go now. She'd find a way to make it stay.

Wendy set down her carry-on bag, light as it was, atop Janet's hand, and Janet shot her a look before Wendy slid her hand underneath the bag and gripped Janet's.

Maybe she wouldn't have to make it stay. Maybe it would last.

"Oh, Janet, before I forget," Wendy said, as if she weren't holding Janet's hand, but with a secret little smile because she *was*. "I read on the plane about one of the Hawkowl's new systems, a RadarVoid project?"

"I've heard of it," Janet said. "It's one of the upgrades we're planning to implement after the Hawkowl's gone into production."

"It sounds revolutionary. You might want to lead with it."

"The thing about revolutions is sometimes they fail," Janet reminded her gently. "I'd rather promise what I can deliver."

"I've seen the project reports. They sound very promising."

"I'll consider it. But when we get there, leave the talking to me. You're there to learn and observe, not participate."

"Sounds like my high school love life."

A light drizzle started halfway to the hotel, clattering at the roof of the cab with enough volume to be rhythmic, and Janet knew if she leaned her head against the window, the cool glass would rock her to sleep. She kept awake. Dragging her thumbnail along the skin of Wendy's hand, seeing the muscles in her arm clench right through the sleeve of her coat. Two days… an eternity!

The drizzle cut off, too abruptly to be natural, and Janet realized that they'd passed under the awning of the hotel. Wendy slipped her hand away in a smooth motion, seeming to pick up her carry-on bag more than anything else. "I really need to use the bathroom."

"Would you like a hall pass?" Janet asked, trying not to tease too hard with her smile with the cabbie so close at hand.

"Just wanted to know if you could handle the luggage."

"The porter will handle the luggage. This isn't a Holiday Inn."

"Oh. Right." Wendy glanced out the window. "You know it doesn't have automatic doors?"

"The bathroom's probably inside," Janet pointed out.

"I'm just saying, is it not a Holiday Inn because a Holiday Inn wasn't available?"

"It's the best I could do on short notice. My predecessor was going to stay with friends in the area, and everywhere else was booked. We're lucky to get a five-star hotel at all."

"Five stars!" Wendy guffawed. She got out her end of the cab and came around the car, stopping once more at Janet's window. "This is a three-star hotel, four if they got the reviewer on a good day, but *five*? As what, an Airbnb?"

"Would you prefer to go around town, seeing if any of the Shriners have canceled their reservations?"

"There's a Shriner convention in town?"

"Yes. I triple-checked."

"I can't believe Shriners are still a thing. I thought they went extinct or something. Where've they been all this time?"

"Apparently, here."

Janet got them checked in, the porter handling the bags with ease. He had them to the elevator long before Wendy had returned from the bathroom, and Janet found herself wondering why Wendy was taking so long. And why she had taken her luggage with her?

Maybe she packed a book. No, she would've read it on the flight. *Makeup?* For what, she looked perfect? What else would someone bring on a trip? Change of clothes? But why would she need to change her clothes?

Then Wendy came back and Janet realized her coat covered her entire body. There was no way of knowing what she had on underneath. No way of knowing what she might have changed into.

As they rode the elevator up, the porter and the luggage cart and the elevator's cramped interior conspired to push her toward Wendy. She felt like she had to pull back to stop from pressing into her. And she couldn't stop thinking about what Wendy had on. Was her bag bulging? Just how much had Wendy taken off to put in there?

Janet imagined some black mini-dress that would show off Wendy's body while barely covering it, like her shadow had reversed itself to cling to her. Or some glossy leather corset that would hold her from chest to groin, so black that light would bounce off its curves, desperate to touch her too. Maybe a cheerleading uniform—God, she was getting too into this. She had to stop looking at Wendy. Nonchalantly, Janet looked up at the floor indicator. Six, seven, eight... She glanced back down, unthinkingly, and saw Wendy looking over her shoulder at her.

Wendy smiled.

She was wearing a strap-on, Janet just knew it. And a concert T-shirt, something ratty and worn, the Beastie Boys maybe, just something she'd thrown on, she'd have slept in it too, *why was any of this turning her on?*

147

The elevator dinged and the rumble of the cart was impossibly loud as it left the elevator and she could've sworn she felt the weight shift as Wendy stepped off and Janet followed her, feeling a dizzying half-second of weightlessness as she stepped out from atop a ten-story drop and on to relatively solid ground. It didn't feel that way, though.

The carpeting was, frankly, tacky, in the way things were when they had no thought put into them, but it was full enough to absorb her footfalls, the clicks of her high heels sheathed like a cat's claws. That didn't make her feel any less weightless. Ahead of her, she saw Wendy's bare legs. The muscles along the back of them, from mid-thigh to the calves stretching her socks, as they bunched and contracted in seamless harmony. The hem of Janet's own traitorous coat cordoned off the actual divide, the scissor stroke that terminated each step. The thing drooped, it sagged—there could be something so much more interesting underneath, swooping and swishing. A schoolgirl's tartan skirt, maybe. Okay, it would be a little insulting on Wendy's part to presume that would appeal to her—that and a tied-off white blouse, while she was at it—well, it *would* appeal, but no more than any short skirt and belly-baring top. So Janet would forgive her.

Was Wendy even Catholic? If not, was it problematic for her to dress as a Catholic schoolgirl? *I'm losing my mind.*

"Here you are," the porter said, unlocking the door for them. Janet looked at it, forcing herself sane by memorizing the number and its placement in the hallway. "Sorry we had to double you up like this. But hey, at least there are two beds."

"And one shower." Wendy pouted at her. "Good-bye warm water."

The door swung open. The porter pointed around inside. "The minibar, channel listings for the TV are on that nightstand, there's a list of take-out places in the drawer—"

"Thank you," Janet interrupted, sweeping past him. "I'm sure it's all fine. We'll get our bearings ourselves."

Wendy slipped him a twenty. "Thanks for everything."

He set their luggage down and wished them well and was gone, the door soundly shut behind him. Trapping Janet with Wendy and herself and whatever Wendy was wearing.

She looked at the evacuation plan on the wall, committing it to memory over and over again. All her life, she'd tried to give herself time to think—now she was trying not to.

Wendy picked up the do-not-disturb hanger from their side of the door, looked it over curiously, then opened the door just enough to put it on the doorknob outside. She closed the door. She locked it.

"Are you still interested in knowing how many fingers I can take?"

Janet's brain couldn't respond to that, so her mouth let out a flat "What?"

Wendy played with the belt on her trench. "It just occurs to me, as an engineer and a woman of science, that using just one set of fingers doesn't objectively prove anything. We'd need a larger sample size of fingers before we conclude how many can fit in my cunt."

Janet looked at Wendy, then with a weird tic, glanced back at the evacuation plan, then back to Wendy. "You mean my fingers?"

Wendy smiled at her. "I mean, unless you have Elizabeth in one of those bags."

"Wendy, I haven't even unpacked," Janet said helplessly.

Wendy gave the belt one last tug. The two halves of it fell down her lower body. They dangled. Her coat opened. Wendy put one hand on the left side of the coat and drew it open, then her right hand on the right side and pulled that away from her body as well. She stood there, displayed, as Janet had never seen her before.

She hadn't put anything on. She'd taken it all off.

Janet's eyes trailed down Wendy's body like water running over her. She could barely even get to Wendy's nudity, not when Wendy's face was so… open, her eyes full of lust, her mouth set in a cocky smirk, knowing how good she looked, knowing Janet couldn't resist, knowing as Janet didn't just how good this would feel. Then the swan curve of her neck, the delicate set of her shoulders, belying the subtle, understated muscle in her arms, in her flat stomach, in her firm thighs. Her cleavage crested her torso in perfect teardrops, just enough for her long, lean frame, for the miles of midriff that led to neatly swelled hips, the peacefully eddying current that flowed from belly to pubis to thighs to groin. Then the long, slender legs, the graceful part of her thighs, even the cute little rustle of motion as she realized she still had her slippers on and kicked them off to stand in white socks on the floor.

She was magnificent. She was willing. She was naked.

"What if you'd fallen down the stairs and broken your neck?" Janet asked, aghast.

"Then I'd be more worried about my broken neck than someone seeing my nips," Wendy replied, crestfallen.

"I mean, don't get me wrong, you're—"

"I know."

"You're just so…"

Wendy grinned. "I know!"

Janet forced herself to calm down. She really wasn't taking this nudity in as much stride as befitted someone with an internet connection. And she had to be in control, had to be the one with the power. For Wendy as well as for herself. It was what the girl wanted from her, after all.

"I want you to hold the coat open," Janet stated, her words coming out of her like they were delivered by conveyer belt.

"I am."

"No. Not like that." Janet went to her. She took Wendy's hands, moving them to the lapels of her coat, and had her hold it apart just so, the lines of it falling like a cape over the outer curves of her breasts. Her breasts full, but not oversized, overstated, just perfectly *becoming* to her body, to her sexuality, to her—*get a grip, Lace.*

"Like this," Janet finished, squeezing her hands to tighten Wendy's own grip on the lapels. "Don't let go. And don't move."

Wendy helplessly cracked a grin before affecting a look of solemn submission. Her eyes couldn't help but sparkle with excitement though. "Certainly, Ms. Lace."

"I'm going to see how you like to be touched, Ms. Cedar. I'm very curious to find out. But I can only do that if you follow the rules."

"Don't let go. Don't move."

Wendy nodded, and Janet could see her having to stop herself from doing it more than once. "Got it."

"One other thing." Janet cupped Wendy's chin between her thumb and forefinger. "You're not allowed to be silent. Whatever you feel, you have to let out. In fact…" She insistently tugged downward, pulling Wendy's mouth open. "You're not allowed to close that pretty little mouth. Should be a familiar sensation for you."

"Yes, Ms. Cedar," Wendy said, sneaking another grin before parting her lips again.

God, Janet wanted to touch her breasts. They were right there, Wendy was literally offering them to her, and she knew they would be warm and smooth and soft in her hands, but she didn't know just how warm, how smooth, how soft, and to find out...and Wendy wanted her to find out, too. Wendy had barely been able to wait for the door to be shut for Janet to find out.

But Janet wasn't sure if that was what Wendy needed. Because Wendy wasn't a sex toy, wasn't a bitch in heat, wasn't any of those things she might play at being. She was a young woman on her wedding night, even if that wasn't the right word anymore, wasn't even a *thing* anymore. She needed to know she was beautiful. No, she already knew. She needed to feel it.

Janet raised her hand and stroked Wendy's face, feeling the sleek curve that led irresistibly from a high cheekbone and down the apple of her cheek, down to the strong curve of her jaw. There was warmth, a slight glimmer of sweat, a thrum of blood that she could just barely feel. It reminded Janet of a beach at night. Everything soft and smooth and secret.

"Oh," Wendy said, looking chagrinned with herself for responding already, to something so innocuous, but Janet nodded. She cupped her face in her hands, and leaned in and was kissing Wendy before she even realized it. It was as easy as slipping into warm water.

She could've sworn she felt the flush in Wendy's cheeks warming her palms, the blood of her throbbing hard enough to rattle down Janet's arms, and Janet kissed her again, again, Wendy's lips clinging to hers as if they didn't want to let go, Wendy continuously returning to Janet's lips almost before she could kiss her again, a soft panting behind every parted lip. The only thing that stopped Janet from devouring Wendy was a sweetly whispered word breaking against her lips.

"Janet." Wendy was almost whimpering. "If you keep doing that I'll let go of the coat."

Janet stayed there, inches from her, frozen with her, and saw Wendy shake as her words drifted against wet lips. "You're not allowed to let go of the coat."

Wendy gulped. "Then don't make me so horny I want to hump your goddamn leg…Ms. Lace."

The last words were not an afterthought.

Janet smirked. "I think you're going to want to hump my leg a lot, Ms. Cedar. It'd be best if you got used to it."

Janet reached for the hollow of Wendy's throat—it looked so vulnerable, so tender, and *God* how she wanted to feel it inside her hand—but stopped. Curled her thumb and her ring finger and her pinky. Reached out with pointer and index finger to touch Wendy's throat. Felt her swallow. Heard her sigh. She drew her fingers down Wendy's body, between the swell of her breasts and the slight ridges of her rib cage, down the center of her belly and her navel and the fine, rich hair that waited to net her fingertips. Wendy breathed like the waves coming in at high tide, sweeping out as far as they could, then sucked back in just as far. Janet took her fingers away before the hair darkened into black. Wendy bit her lip before she forced herself to open her mouth again. Her lips curled into a coo next.

"You like being touched with two fingers," Janet said smugly.

"Yes, Ms. Lace."

Janet reached around Wendy—the action pulling her close to Wendy's body, so close that her coat touched to Wendy's—and she drew her fingers down Wendy's back. There was muscle just below the skin, muscle packed hard with tension, and Janet petted it firmly, pushing into the corded tightness. She thought it would be very good to massage Wendy, some day. To take her from this rigidity into absolute softness. But right now, she lived for how pitched Wendy's breathing was.

She dropped her hand to Wendy's ass, groped it suddenly, remorselessly, and Wendy's mouth fell open and there was a keening exhale, unexpected and all the stronger for it. Wendy rubbed her thighs together. Janet wondered if that was how fruit felt before it was harvested.

"I didn't say you could move."

"I'm not moving, I'm just…getting comfortable."

Neatly, nicely, Janet wiped her hand on Wendy's coat. It'd gotten a little damp with Wendy's sweat. Then she reached down and fitted her forefinger to Wendy's sex, like she was placing a key at a lock, and it felt like she was touching an ocean.

"Jesus," Wendy moaned, her breathing peaking and twisting and turning, as Janet fingered the lips of her sex to one side, to the other, seeing how it opened for her, how it welcomed her in, how it wanted her with such intensity that even Wendy couldn't quite show it all. Except by this. Except by touch.

"We're not so different... I like to be touched this way, too."

Janet took her hand away. Wendy whimpered and Janet put her finger to Wendy's lips, felt them quiver, felt them part, felt Wendy suck as Janet fed her finger to her. When she took her hand away again, Wendy was moaning. She didn't even need to be touched.

"Did that taste good?" Janet asked.

"Yes, Ms. Lace," Wendy answered, just between pants.

"Do you think I'll like it?"

"Yes, Ms. Lace."

"Do you think it's good enough for me?"

"Yes, Ms. Lace, please, Ms. Lace..."

"Do you want my hand?"

"Yes, Ms—"

"Will you come if I give you my hand?"

"Yes—"

"Will you scream when you come?"

Wendy could barely speak, she was breathing so hard. "I'm screaming right now, Ms. Lace."

Janet smiled. She didn't know how it was she could think this woman was adorable when her finger was still wet from Wendy sucking herself from it, and yet... "Do you know how wonderful it is just to touch you?"

"No, Ms. Lace." Wendy met her eyes. "Show me?"

Janet touched her where it would feel as good for Wendy as it would feel for her, thumb on her clit, palm on her cunt, four fingers between her legs and under her and almost lifting her up. Giving her heat and pressure and touch, almost everything she needed to come, but Wendy would have to put up the friction herself.

"Fuck my hand," Janet told her.

Wendy did. Rushed against Janet almost hard enough to knock her over if she hadn't been so firmly planted, trapping her hand between their two bodies, rutting against it, pleasuring herself on it, plunging herself down to

Janet's rubbing thumb and her clenching hand and the moisture she herself was spilling on Janet's palm, everything warm and wet and beautiful for her, and Janet felt it in the palm of her fucking hand when Wendy came, felt her throb, felt her clutch, felt a little liquid rush skip between her fingers, one-Mississippi, two-Mississippi, three, four, five, six, seven, eight, *goddamn, either I'm that fucking good or she has been waiting too fucking long,* then it stopped and Wendy went boneless, held up only by Janet's arms around her and body against her and then a whispered command in her ear: "Stand the fuck up."

Wendy whimpered—practically sobbed—and got her feet under her. Janet put a hand at the small of her back and walked her, on tender feet, to the bed. Wendy collapsed there as if she'd run from New York instead of flown.

"Did I scream?" Wendy asked.

"You moaned," Janet replied. "That's enough for now."

Somehow, Wendy managed to raise her head. "Ms. Lace?"

"Janet," she corrected, getting a bottled water from the minibar. Wendy had earned it.

"Janet," Wendy said, her voice cracking as she relaxed with the game's end. "Can you put your arms around me again?"

"Uh-huh." Janet took her glasses off and lay down beside Wendy and held the bottle as she took a long drink. As soon as she'd finished, Janet screwed the cap back on, dropped the bottle off the side of the bed, and fit herself to Wendy like she was another layer of clothing against the cold.

Wendy moaned sweetly. She put her hand over Janet's on her body. "I've always believed that it's better to say this early than too late—I love you."

Janet kissed her. From the way Wendy returned it, it seemed like enough. It seemed like more than enough.

It felt bracing, having Wendy sleep against her, so comfortable, so at ease with her. Like a puppy falling asleep on Janet's lap. Yes, it seemed odd to think of her as 'adorable' after what they'd just done—or, looking at the clock, what they'd done an hour ago. But she couldn't think of any other way to describe it.

Janet enjoyed it implicitly, but she couldn't quite trust it. It felt wrong. She knew it was just nerves, the flight, the presentation, but it was impossible to feel drowsy with Wendy curled up next to her, sexual and innocent all at once. Janet tried shifting away from her—Roberta had never minded sleeping apart—but as if the thought of her ex-wife turned Janet's body coarse, Wendy stirred.

"Wha-? What time is it?"

"Not yet noon. Go back to sleep."

"Sleeping till noon? I'm corrupting you already."

"We're on presentation time. Sleep while we can, up and at 'em four hours before the presentation. We can have a sleep cycle at home."

"Then I guess it's all you corrupting me," Wendy tittered, and drew close to Janet, putting her hand to the rise and fall of Janet's breasts, her body tucked under Janet's arm.

Again, Janet tried to force herself to sleep, but again, it was impossible. Too warm, too naked, unfamiliar sheets and unfamiliar skin. "Wendy," she said. "The sex acts…they were all right, correct?"

"The sex acts?" Janet felt Wendy's lips curl against her skin. "Oh yeah. Very tolerable. Practically adequate."

"Because I actually don't…Roberta and I didn't…" Janet squeezed her eyes shut and wouldn't have opened them again, only now Wendy was looking at her. "I do like…being in control," she said at length. "I mean, *obviously*. Especially after Roberta left. But we never really tried that. It was just this thing that interested me. And when I saw that e-mail of yours, I thought that's what you wanted, too."

"It is. I mean, kinda." Wendy shrugged. "It was a weird dream, what can I tell you?"

"I'm not some sex goddess, Wendy," Janet said bluntly. "I've done research, I've watched—" She saw Wendy's eyes light up and almost could've been amused. "*Documentaries*, but I haven't actually done anything like that before. It's just things I would like to do. Sometimes things I'd like to have done to me. I never know if you'll like them or not. I can't promise it'll always be that way…I got lucky."

Janet could see Wendy struggle to pass up the pun. "One, you *are* a sex goddess. And two—" Wendy snatched Janet's hand up while she was distracted like it was made of a precious mineral "—you being a sex goddess is not why I'm interested in you."

"It's not?"

"I'm interested in you because you gave me a job when anyone else would've buried me on the off-chance it would make them look good. And because you're smart and a really good boss—absolutely the kind of person I want to be in twenty years, divorced and childless or not…and you're beautiful, that helps, you are just…Roberta's an idiot."

"Well, she managed to snag a woman who's younger than you are and teaches yoga, so…"

Wendy gave Janet's hand a squeeze. "She's an idiot."

Janet nodded. Wendy was holding on to her hand—she didn't have to. She couldn't think of anything to do with it but pull it to her chest and not let go, but she hoped that would be enough for Wendy. "I really thought… with the vibrator, that that's what you would like. I mean, women these days, you have so much more experience, you go to rainbow parties…"

"Me? Experience? What's a rainbow party?"

"You know, you…people in high school, they put on different color lipsticks and they take turns…well, you know what every single Van Halen song was about?"

"Yeah, they taught us all about it in preschool."

"Well, that happens, and so at the end, there's a rainbow—"

"That's disgusting. And no, no way anyone has ever done that. If anyone ever tells you that young people are having kinkier sex than you had when you were their age, it's someone trying to sell papers. Or blogs, whatever it is these days."

"Really?"

Wendy pulled herself up onto Janet by way of her grip on Janet's hand, straddling her waist and hugging her torso. "Trust me, Janet, I've been in, like, two actual relationships and one of them was being catfished. I go to gay clubs and I stare at girls and I wait for someone to make the first move and I spend way too much on overpriced drinks. I give a subsidiary to the alcohol industry every time I try to get laid. So you don't know about this stuff because you've been married for the last fifteen years or whatever? *I* don't know about this stuff because I'm a weirdo loner with a massive crush on her boss. But if you want to figure it out, we're two reasonably smart people. I think we can figure it out."

Janet smiled. "And you really wouldn't mind maybe a little of the e-mail stuff? If it wasn't all the spirits talking?"

Wendy petted Janet's hand. "I went as Ella Enchanted for Halloween last year. But maybe we could also just cuddle on a couch and watch Game of Thrones? Because honestly, I fantasize about that a little more than collars."

"Game of Thrones?" Janet looked down at her hand and liked the look of it in Wendy's. "I can work with that. *Wendy*."

"Good, because I'm eighty percent sure that Yara and Daenerys are gonna bang. In fact…" Wendy undulated her body just enough for it to rub against Janet's. "I kinda have some thoughts how that would go."

"Wendy," Janet took her shoulders and rolled her on to the other side of the bed. "I'm rather used to sleeping alone, at this point. Do you think you could stay on your side of the bed? I promise I'll try to get used to sleeping as a matched pair again, but for now, with the presentation, my rest?"

"Yeah," Wendy said, sounding so certain that she couldn't possibly be. "No problem. We're in the same bed, at least. That's way better than I thought I'd do."

"Thank you for understanding," Janet said, and with only the cool blanket for company, she was asleep as soon as her eyes closed.

CHAPTER 10

ALL THAT WAS MISSING WAS a haze of cigar smoke.

The bunker at the Yuma Proving Grounds was lushly furnished, for a room built to withstand the hit of a stray shelling or crashing plane. Rich carpet covered the floor, flags and framed pictures tried to obscure the bulkheads that made up the walls. Wendy examined a few: military porn. A Lockheed Martin F-16V IN Super Viper in flight, a squad of F-22As dropping JDAMs, a few of West Point graduates posing or USMC Scout Snipers in full gear, walking the desert. It made her wonder just how many stories had ended up, after all the blood and sweat and tears, as set decoration.

The crowd was a robust mix. Mostly colonels, if Wendy was getting her stripes right, and from all branches. Lots of full birds, lots of lieutenant colonels, lots of medals as well. Purple Hearts, Silver Stars—if Wendy had to guess, she'd say this was grunt work, but still *important* grunt work. These guys might not have been primetime, but they were the rising stars, and what they said today would influence the top brass decisions in five, ten, fifteen years' time.

Then there were the defense contractors like her and Janet. Business suits so dark they were practically a uniform in and of themselves; their only medal was that they'd gotten an invite over here. Wendy straightened the lapels of her jacket. Dress code, informal as it was, meant no skirt and panty fun, but it also meant Janet in a pantsuit. Small blessings.

Janet returned from schmoozing a DARPA chief, with two cups of coffee. Styrofoam.

"You'd think sixteen percent of the national budget would get them some mugs," Wendy said, taking hers.

"You'd think twenty-four percent of it would get my nana better social security benefits, but there you go."

"Oh my God, you call her your nana?"

Janet drank her coffee. So did Wendy, suddenly feeling a wave of guilt. Speaking of grandparents, she hadn't exactly been honest...

"If everyone is ready? We're about to begin," said the major in charge of the exercise. He was easy to distinguish, wearing fatigues to emphasize that he was on active duty. The room was one long hall, the entrance at one end, at the other an open viewing port that ran the length of the wall. Covered by bulletproof glass, it looked out over the gunnery range, HDTVs mounted over and below to show off footage being recorded by chase planes and drones. *Now all we need is a jumbotron and a hot dog vendor, we're in business*, Wendy thought to herself.

She drew close to the glass, looking out at the range. It reminded her a bit of period pieces about Hollywood: films where Marilyn Monroe or James Stewart were characters. Someone always visited the backlot, an Old West town with facades of buildings that were just plywood when seen from behind. These buildings had four walls, but not much else. Junker cars and retired tanks were laid out on the unpaved streets, as well as dummies dressed in black bad-guy uniforms. The few acres formed a reasonable approximation of some blocks in an enemy city, if bisected and transported on to government land. "We'll begin with our new AEW&C, the Boeing 898 Sentinel, which will fly overhead to perform area search, and command and control duties..."

The monitors showed various views of the aircraft, a big pelican of a thing, feeds showing its crew, the view from some of its many cameras, and the view from within the 'city.' Wendy craned her neck to see it in the sky. There was barely a dot.

It went like that for the better part of an hour, though rarely that peaceful. Many of the planes being demoed were refinements—theoretically, at least—on old classics—again, theoretically. So Wendy saw a lot of old news. F-22s with upgraded weapon systems flew trailing colored smoke to show off their moves, lobbing off flares as if they were being shot at and dropping new PGMs on a few targets. They saved some for the H4 Self-Propelled Howitzer, the Multiple Launch Rocket, airstrike after airstrike after airstrike, the targets being reduced to rubble and smaller rubble and then into dust.

The major kept up his narration, gesturing with a laser pointer to a model of the alleged city, pointing out how an attack would target this building in particular, or this floor in particular, or this wall in particular. It was all a bit moot when saturation bombing left the whole thing a parking lot. A parking lot with a lot of potholes.

"Kinda scary, isn't it?" Wendy whispered to Janet, watching another explosion punch at the air.

"It's a scary world," Janet replied. Then, as the fireworks went off, their noise demanding attention, she reached casually into Wendy's pants and felt her bareness. Just a taste of Janet's hand before she took it away. "No panties. Good. I love a woman in bare skin."

"You have a cavewoman fetish? I'm not that butch!"

There was a hill on the far end of the range that took the really big hits, the ones that just showed off how big a bang they could make. Wendy wondered how long it would be there. If one day it would just be worn down, like a boulder in a river.

The final bomb fell, a bunker-buster taking out a fortification that could've been theirs, as the major almost gleefully noted. And then the meat market was open. Her, Janet, the Boeing boys and the Lockheed Martin guys and Raytheon and Northrop Grumman, all trying to cast aspirations here, suggest improvements there, find a way to get their hat in the ring and someone else's out of it.

"As you can see," the major concluded, "we're quite confident in the current range of warfighters in suiting any power projection need, from destroying a single room with a Predator drone to complete area denial. Any questions?"

"I have one," Janet said. She finished her coffee before continuing, having nursed it all through the demonstration. She handed the empty cup to Wendy. "I assume, in the field, this will all be integrated with forces on the ground. Tanks, Humvees, troops…"

The major nodded, not feeling the need to verbally confirm such an obvious question.

"So then…" Janet gestured out the viewing port, where the smoke of the bombardment lingered like morning mist. "What happens to them in this onslaught? Say you have a squadron of Marines cut off by enemy fire here." She tapped a rooftop on the model city. That it was still standing while its scale approximation was rubble struck Wendy as slightly surreal; cut-rate David Lynch. "Or here, where you have hostages you want to extract. There, let's say a high-value target who's been taken captive, but needs to be transported away for interrogation. I know the major has aptly demonstrated that you can fire *around* them, but that doesn't get them medical assistance."

Pausing to see if anyone would take issue with her—and they didn't—Janet reached into her pocket and brought out a scale model about the size of a Hot Wheels car.

"The NA-44 Hawkowl, our new helicopter, already in testing. It's light, nimble, but with enough armor to withstand virtually any small-arms fire. You give it ten seconds, it can get in, defend itself with electronic and physical deterrence, and then evacuate with any asset you want. Because the enemy isn't going to be a bunch of empty buildings. It's going to be people. And to fight people, you need boots on the ground, and when you put boots on the ground, you need a way to get them back. Without getting brought down by a rickety Soviet RPG that any teenager can get off the Dark Web for two hundred bucks."

Someone cleared his throat and Janet set herself, staring across the model at the Sikorsky representative. Janet had fired a shot across his bow, reminding everyone of his Blackhawks going down in Somalia. Even if she wasn't looking to take his slice of the pie, he'd have to respond. "I've heard of your Hawkowl—a weapons platform with peashooters."

"Less ordinance means more room for passengers, increased maneuverability. And we all know the future of directed munitions isn't a man in a cockpit pushing a button on his joystick, it's someone an ocean away on a computer telling a Predator drone to launch a Hellfire. But you can't provide battlefield support with a laptop. The Hawkowl will let the aerial drones do what they do best, while increasing support for troops in the field. Better a master of one trade than a jack of all."

The rep smiled tidily. That was the only way Wendy could think of it: tidy. "You paint your girl here as invincible against small-arms fire. Well, these ships won't be going up against street gangs. What will your Hawkowl do when it's targeted by enemy armor?"

"Explode, I expect. The same as your Blackhawks do. The Hawkowl isn't a miracle, no weapons system is, but it can evade enemy fire, work in conjunction with escorts to—"

"The Blackhawk can engage enemy armor directly."

"With all respect to a distinguished colleague, not very well. You don't use a Swiss army knife to cut your steak and you don't use a steak knife to open a bottle of wine. The Armed Forces can't afford to pretend that one size fits all on the battlefield of the future. We need specialization."

"Overspecialization," the rep corrected.

"What war has ever been fought without a man holding a weapon? That man needs support, and the Hawkowl will give *him* support, not treat him as cargo. We've designed it with modular support for ambulatory duty, mass evacuation, even a skyhook system for supply delivery—"

"There's also the RadarVoid system," Wendy said.

Janet snapped to her, as shocked by Wendy's voice as she would've been by her blood gushing over the floor. "Yes, the RadarVoid is one of many proprietary technologies being developed for future incarnations of the Hawkowl," she said, trying to recover.

"And what's it do, exactly?" the rep demanded.

"Large-caliber fire," Wendy answered for Janet. "Which these days is all directed by electronics. The Hawkowl's electronic signature is specifically designed to be easily spoofed, so with the RadarVoid system engaged, it's impossible for the real one to be locked on to among a…a plethora of duplicates."

"I'd like to see the data on that."

"I have it right here," Wendy said, taking Mary's folder from her jacket. She dropped it on the model. "The Blackhawk simply can't disguise its signature the way the Hawkowl was designed from the ground up to do. You're looking at a helicopter that can't be hit."

The representative said nothing. Especially as the major stepped in and picked up the folder to read.

It was a long drive back to the hotel, even with an MP chauffeuring them.

"You're upset," Wendy said, much as she hated stating the obvious.

Janet was going through the RadarVoid report backwards and forwards, so fast and so intently it was like she was trying to commit suicide via papercut. "I'm not upset. I'm concerned. You'd know if I was upset."

"Look, I'm sorry, I know I wasn't supposed to tag myself in, but it shut him up, right? That was exactly the opening we needed to drop the bomb; I bet they're saving their pennies for the Hawkowl as we speak."

"You do understand that makes it worse, right?"

"Huh?" Wendy asked eloquently.

Janet rapped the sheaf of papers against Wendy's knee. She lowered her voice. "I can't speak to the efficacy of the RadarVoid system. If I knew it worked, fine, you spoke out of turn, it's not a big deal. If it doesn't work—"

"You think it doesn't work?"

Janet lowered her voice even farther, shushing Wendy with the sheer intensity of her words. "I don't know if it does or doesn't. That's what concerns me."

Wendy flicked her finger against the papers. "Look at the tests. They all show it works fine."

Janet let out a long-suffering sigh and paged through the reams of test results. "They all *look* aboveboard, but really read them. You know at Savin, our R&D department assigns every test a unique code. Month, day, year, hour, minute, second, location. Look here. D/C/16/I/AA/B/JJJ. So that's April the third, 2016, 9:27:02 AM, and I believe the Kirkwood lab. That's test one. Test two should take place maybe an hour later. A few hours at the most, because they go to lunch, someone pulls a fire alarm, what have you. It doesn't, the code's completely different. *All of them are like that.*"

"So? Kirkwood ran one test for the RadarVoid program, then some different tests, then they came back to it."

"For all of them? Or are we just looking at the most successful ten tests out of fifty? Out of a hundred? Out of two hundred?"

"C'mon, we don't do that."

"We don't?"

"No. Savin Aerospace has a reputation to uphold, we don't cook the books like that."

"You said it yourself. Everyone cooks the books."

"You're being paranoid."

"I didn't get this far by being something else."

Janet's phone rattled. She took in a sharp hiss of breath before she answered it. "Roberta, hello…"

They were still going at it hammer and tongs when the MP dropped them off at the hotel. Wendy made it through the lobby before watching Janet's reverse-massage wrack her body up into knots became too much for her. "I'll take the stairs," she said, and left Janet in the elevator not even noticing her.

Ten flights of stairs later, she was keenly aware of the difference between her fatigue last night, when Janet had wrung her out just enough to be comfortably exhausted, and just hating her legs. Sore, and really regretting going with kitten heels that morning, she went down the hallway and heard Janet shouting right through the walls.

"It was a trial separation, Roberta, a trial separation! Not a hall pass to go fuck your way through the nearest sorority!"

Wendy let herself into the room. Might as well have been invisible. She went to get herself a glass of water.

"You thought I'd be okay with it, *fuck you*, you thought I'd be okay with it, if I was okay with it, I would've told you to take a weekend in Ibiza and be done with it!"

No ice. Wendy picked up the bucket, went around to the ice machine—conveniently right next to their Shriner-free room—filled it, came back, added ice water, took a drink, sat down.

Better. Much better.

"If you want to run off and play trial lawyer, fine, but you can do it on your own dime! You are not getting one red cent for abandoning me, it is *my* money, *I* earned it, and I would rather *burn it* than let you use it as your goddamn safety net. Have some fucking balls and live in a studio apartment like the twenty-year-old you so *desperately, obviously want to be*!"

Wendy had not known a cell phone could be slammed. But she guessed if you pressed the disconnect button hard enough… She slipped off her shoes and stood up, groaning, wondering if she could talk Janet into taking a bath together. Flying for half a day, hours in taxis and Humvees, sleeping on an unfamiliar bed…they deserved a hot tub, something.

"Janet?" Wendy called, stepping out onto the balcony with her. Stupid of her—she should've thought to pack massage oil, have something on hand to rub Janet down with when the tension got to her. Good move for a girlfriend to have. "Is everything all right?"

Janet wheeled on her and was kissing her so abruptly it was like Wendy had just breathed her in. Wendy stumbled back into the hotel room, practically carried by Janet, and suddenly felt Janet's hand sliding down her pants, stroking at the neatly trimmed hair between her legs, and Wendy didn't know how girls could stand to be bare down there when it was so much better to have something for your lover to run their fingers through, something to tug on.

But Janet wasn't just touching her, Janet was *scraping* at her, making Wendy tense, making her close her thighs instinctively, trap Janet's hands, because while there was a hint of moisture inside her, there was not much, not enough, and if Janet tried to enter her it would hurt.

Wendy expected Janet to realize this, having Wendy's thighs squeezing her hand still, but Janet forced her hand farther, kissed Wendy even harder. It wasn't overwhelming, it was noxious—the warmth of Janet was too hot, the scent of her stung Wendy's nostrils, everything was too fast and too much and not enough *Janet*.

"Open your legs," Janet hissed. Her voice rose with frustration. "Open your fucking legs, I'm not going to tell you again, this is what you wanted, this is what you like!"

"Watchword," Wendy said, shocked at how weak her voice sounded, how her eyes stung, and she felt itchy and sweaty all over, not how it'd been before but like she was being touched by someone else, a stranger. "Watchword, *Janet*, watchword—"

Janet took her hand away. She stopped kissing Wendy. And after a moment, she took a step back, letting the air rush back into Wendy's personal space, and Wendy realized just how hard it'd been to breathe. It'd only been half a minute, but she still gasped in air.

"What's wrong?" Janet asked. She was forcing calm, regulating herself, and it gratified Wendy to read not a trace of her aggravation, not anymore. It was replaced by concern, and if that still chafed at Janet's fraught temperament, it was at least not directed at Wendy.

"I don't mind a little kink," Wendy said, "but at least one of us should enjoy it."

"I thought you would like that," Janet insisted. "That you liked it like that."

"Well, I don't." Wendy sighed and went to the bed, slumping onto the mattress before her feet could get in on the act as well. "It's not your fault. Last night—last night was great. That was just too much, you know? And it felt like you weren't even thinking of me. You were just…"

"Roberta," Janet said. She sounded gratifyingly guilty. "I'm in control and I'm *me* and then she calls me and…seems like the first time either of us has cared in years."

"Do you want to talk about it?"

"No, I think I've troubled you enough for one day." Janet went to her toiletry bag on the nightstand and dug into it, coming up with some sleeping pills. She kept her back turned to Wendy, like a child believing that what you couldn't see couldn't hurt you. "I'm going to try to get some rest before our plane leaves." She stopped with the bottle in her hand. "I'm very sorry, Wendy. I didn't mean to upset you."

"It's all right. No harm done." Wendy smiled reassuringly at her and did a little shimmy. "Want to spank me? Maybe something else? That leather belt of yours looks fun."

"I should sleep." Janet poured out a few pills and dry-swallowed them. "Maybe in the morning, if there's time before our flight."

"Yeah. Sure. It's okay if you need to blow off some steam, Janet—Ms. Lace. It just has to be that you're venting, not exploding."

"I'm not sure either one is okay." Janet waved her hand in the air. "Help yourself to the minibar. My treat."

As she undressed, Wendy knew she would be expected to sleep in the other bed. That bothered her more than anything else.

ᛉᛉᛉ

They flew back home on a 747, but Wendy didn't suggest doing anything in the bathroom. She'd seen Janet calm, serious, solemn, but never thought that might be some sort of depression. Now she'd gotten so good at reading Janet that she could see when there was no sparkle in her eye, no glimmer of rich amusement to bely all her self-seriousness.

Janet barely got her carry-on put away before she was looking over the RadarVoid research again.

"You've been going over that since last night," Wendy told her. "Why don't you give it a rest? Read your book?"

"I finished it," Janet said, not looking up from the papers. "The Kee Bird never makes it off the ground. The fuel tank on the APU failed. They hung the tank so it would gravity-feed and forgot to disconnect it. The take-off was bumpy. Fuel spilled out of the tank, hit the APU, it was hot, started a fire... The whole plane went up. It broke in half. It exploded."

"Well, that's a wonderful story to tell before a cross-country flight."

Janet flipped from one page to the next so fast it was almost a slap. "What would you prefer?"

"I don't know—tell me about your childhood."

"Father drank."

"Well, at least your mom—"

"She might've. I wouldn't know. Not around."

"Ah. You want me to leave you alone?"

"Just for a few...states."

Wendy nodded. "All right." She fetched her earbuds from her pocket. "I'm right here if you want to talk or anything. I answer to Wendy, Cedar, Ms. Cedar, Dub-dub, hey you..."

Janet made a 'mmm' sound and minutely adjusted her glasses, turning the page back.

Wendy put her earbuds in and set out to find how many podcasts she could listen to before New York.

ÂⱯÂ

A limo picked them up at the airport—weird to be looking for someone else's name on one of those chauffeur signs, but there it was. They went to drop Wendy off at her apartment first, and Janet helped her take her bags up. Inside, the first thing Janet noticed was the wall art. Wendy smirked a little; she'd expected no less.

"Aluminum two-blade prop from Hamilton Standard," Janet reeled off, eying it, coming closer to run a hand over the blade. "Controllable pitch... damage to one of the pitch stops just below the guide ring...someone flew with this."

"Uh-huh." Wendy wrapped her arms around Janet from behind, felt Janet stiffen in her embrace, but also breathe a little easier. "I know your chauffeur is keeping the meter running, but have I ever introduced you to the fine American custom of the quickie?"

"Wendy…" Janet started to brush her arms away, and Wendy held on a moment longer before letting her. "It's been a long flight. We can talk about this tomorrow."

"Talk?" Wendy shoved her hands in her backpockets, felt like scuffing her shoes. "Hey, I don't want to rush you into saying any three particular words, but…you still want me to kiss you, right?"

"Yes."

Wendy hovered closer, brushing her upper arm against Janet's. "And you still like me touching you?"

"Yes."

Gently, Wendy leaned in and butted her forehead against Janet's shoulder. "And you like it when I say that I love you…"

Janet took off her glasses to knead her sinuses. "Wendy, how I feel isn't the issue. The issue is whether what I feel is a good idea or not."

"You don't feel something because it's a good idea. You feel it because it's what's inside you."

Janet sighed. "I'm sure it must seem that way at your age."

Wendy felt ice water going all through her. "Look, I know I fucked up—whatever, don't take me on the next business trip, or leave me in the hotel room. If all you want to do is date, that's fine, we don't need to be business partners."

"I'm not sure it was a good idea for us to get together." Janet pressed on while Wendy was still stunned. She fiddled with the earpieces of her glasses in uncharacteristic reticence. "We have to work together and all this does is confuse you about our boundaries and that's my fault, not yours, but it has to stop. We need to be co-workers again."

She set her glasses down on a drawer, forcing herself to stop playing with them.

"So that's how you're going to play it then?" Wendy crossed her arms. "You just find someone you like around the office and you seduce them and you fuck them and you make them think…and then you just drop me off at the curb?"

"It's not like that…"

"Maybe you don't remember how that feels since you're two hundred years old, *but it's pretty shitty at this end.*"

Janet nodded. "All right. All right, I deserve that. I never would've started this if I'd known—"

"Known what? That it would be hard?"

Janet put her fingers to her brow. "I don't want you to be mad. I just want you to understand that this isn't you, it's the situation. It's just an untenable—"

"All right then, I quit."

Janet let out a short, shrill laugh. "You can't quit."

Wendy tightened her crossed arms. "What, you want my two weeks' notice?"

"It's just a relationship, Wendy, it's not some kind of—"

"It is to me. And don't tell me it isn't to you, because I've seen the way you look at me and I know, *I know*, how scared you are. *That's* why you're doing this, not because you suddenly have a bug up your ass about workplace romance."

"Wendy, you have a bright future at Savin, a promising career, you cannot give it up for anyone."

"You are not just anyone."

Janet took a deep breath. "I don't accept your resignation. And I don't want to continue this relationship. When you've had some time to process this…I'm leaving now." Her lips trembled a moment; the urge to say something more. "If you have any…questions, you can still send me an e-mail."

"Oh, for fuck's sake, you'd think a divorcee would know *something* about how people get dumped!"

Janet stiffened again, took the hit, and moved for the door.

Wendy took a moment to just grind the heel of her hand into her forehead, then she turned around to follow her. "Janet, I didn't mean—"

Janet shut the door behind her. She was still in control enough not to slam it.

CHAPTER 11

A QUICK WASH OF HER hair with Aveda to start the day, then saltwater hairspray and some oil to keep it from drying overmuch. Janet massaged her hair, fingers along her scalp, hair between her digits; the lushness of her hair making it seem longer and fuller than it really was. She imagined doing this as a young woman: her hands trailing down her back, finding curling, luscious softness belying that firm flesh underneath.

Then she picked up her hairbrush and began to pull it through her hair. She wasn't a young woman.

Janet made dried pear arugula salad. Simple, but good practice for something more complex. Mostly it was just hunting down the ingredients, feeding them all to the food processor or the salad bowl, whisking it around, then watering it with apple cider vinaigrette.

The taste was decent, the meal filling.

Janet kept few plants. A cacti or other succulent in each room. She enjoyed their self-sufficiency—that without her, they could get along quite well. Not forever, of course. They would die without her. But there was no need to coddle them.

She'd already watered them: the sand collar cactus, the bishop's cap, the saguaro, all the rest. But she knew that in the active period, they were watered more frequently, they were given fertilizer. She checked again when the active period was.

It was later in the year. Much later.

She treated herself to a Greek yogurt. She had a whole carton of them in her refrigerator. It tasted of almosts: almost ice cream, almost fruit, almost milk. When she finished, there was still yogurt skimming the sides of the cup.

She called Elizabeth as she opened the bottle of wine they hadn't finished. The thing was, if she drank it straight from the bottle, that was one less glass she'd have to wash. Smart. She was so fucking smart.

The speaker phone picked up. "Jan? Hey. Didn't expect you to be back from your trip so soon?"

"Why not? We sold the damn things, didn't we?"

"Yeah. Good job. You and Wendy celebrating?"

"I'm celebrating."

"Don't tell me you haven't sealed the deal yet. Look, if fucking her is that big a deal, I can always sit in, give you a little constructive criticism…"

"No, no, I fucked her. Just like you said. It was nice. And now we're moving on. Onward and upward."

"Okay then." Elizabeth sounded less than enthused, but Janet couldn't judge her. She herself didn't sound especially…anything.

"Elizabeth?"

"Yeah, Jan?"

"I don't think I was happy with Roberta. I wasn't sad, but… I wasn't happy, either."

"I know, Jan."

"I know what happy is like. It just isn't for me."

"You want me to come over?"

"No. I should be alone now. I've had enough practice at it."

ÅⱯÅ

Wendy hated herself and wanted to die.

Naturally, Regan was having a great week.

"Look at how much my husband loves me in floral form!" she cried, hoisting a bouquet like she was Miss America.

"It's like porn for bees," Wendy agreed, very happy when it was out of her face.

Regan lugged it over to the dinner table, where she had a glass of water waiting, and she took some posies out of the bouquet and put them there.

171

"I mean, I'm sure he had a coupon or something, this is a lot of flowers to buy when I'd just settle for a dozen roses—"

"You would?" Wendy asked sarcastically. "Geez, get some standards—"

Regan ignored her, smiling over the posies now sitting in a vase on her table. "Go get me some more glasses."

"Half-full or half-empty?" Wendy quipped, headed to the kitchen.

Regan gathered up a fistful of begonias. "These would look great on the windowsill… Wendy, c'mon!"

Wendy came out of the kitchen with three glasses in either hand, another two caught between her arms and body. "Just for the record, what do you intend to drink out of?"

"I'll pick up some Dixie cups," Regan said, taking one glass, filling it with flowers, and setting it picturesquely on the sill. "I could get addicted to this. I think I'm a little high. Let's put one on the stairs!"

"Let's!" Wendy agreed with false cheer.

"Okay, fine, you're in a snit," Regan conceded as they moved to the staircase. "Do you want to get it off your chest or do you want to be a little shit all day because I'm getting laid tonight? Well, Keith's getting laid, but I'm doing the honors."

"Trust me, I'm a professional, I can be a little shit regardless of your sex life. The bluebells would look good there."

"They *would*!" Regan agreed, setting a glass between the banisters on the landing of the staircase. "C'mon, I'm really not going to be able to enjoy railing Keith with my favorite sister in mourning."

"And I'm not going to be able to enjoy food ever again with that mental image."

Regan stopped to smell the roses—Wendy suddenly got that expression. "No more banter. Come on now."

Wendy set all the glasses on the landing and sat, drinking from one of them. "What would you do if Keith left you?"

Regan laid the bouquet between them and sat down next to her. "Oh God, what is this?"

"Just tell me."

"I wouldn't let him."

"You wouldn't let him? How would you stop him?"

Regan guffawed. "Jesus, Well, he wouldn't *want* to leave me in the first place, but if he did, I could only assume there'd be something wrong, something he was struggling with—I'd find it and kick its ass and get my husband back."

"What if it's not something that you can ass-kick? What if he really wants to go?"

Regan leaned back against the railing, sighing. "You need to schedule this introspective stuff before I get flowers. You're really harshing my buzz."

"Hey, you asked."

"Yeah. The burden of a big sister is a heavy one. Okay, you remember when I was pregnant? You were off at UCLA or wherever, building model airplanes?"

Wendy resisted the urge to correct her. "Yeah, I ordered you pickles and ice cream online. That's what pregnant women like, right? I'm gay, it's really not my scene."

"We'll discuss that if Mac ever gets a little brother."

"Little sister," Wendy corrected.

"Anyway. You weren't here, but when I first got pregnant, Keith really got cold feet."

"What? I'll kill him," Wendy said jokingly.

"No, he had, like, stripper-level daddy issues. He didn't know if he could be a good father, he thought maybe he wasn't even a good husband because suddenly we were in this situation where the shit was hitting the fan. He thought maybe it might be best to have a procedure done and then if the relationship didn't work out, at least we wouldn't…well, you can imagine we argued a bit."

"Yeah, you'd think!" Wendy cried. "Where is this coming from? Does he also kill people for a living?"

"It was a long time ago," Regan assured her. "The point is, I fought for him. I told him that of all the men in the world—and also Angelina Jolie, if she were interested—I was with him, I only wanted him, and the baby would feel the same way. Mac wouldn't want someone else. I wouldn't want someone else. We wanted every part of our family." Regan reached over and nudged Wendy. "Including Vodka Aunt here."

"I actually prefer tequila." Wendy grinned.

"So he came around and he studied how to be a good father and I studied how to be a good mother and we did the Lamaze classes and ate a lot of pickles and ice cream—"

"Ha! Told you!"

"Actually, he liked the pickles a lot more than I did. And Mac was born, you were there for that, the rough patch was over, we moved on. It wasn't the first time we fought, it's not gonna be the last, but we got through it. And now my arms are full of flowers and I'm waiting for my son to get home. And making fun of my sister a little bit, so I'm feeling that was a good call."

"Yeah, okay, so you're a success story. But you seriously never thought to just let him go?"

Regan looked back at her. "Is that what you're thinking?"

Fucking sister psychic spider-sense bullshit. "No," Wendy replied, leaning her head back. "Maybe I should be. Maybe she's right, it'd be best if I found someone better for me and she found someone better for her."

"And flying cars would make road trips easier," Regan interjected. "If you love her, you love her. You can't just swap her out for someone you think is better suited for you. She's it. I mean, God knows Keith isn't perfect, but I wouldn't trade him for…Mr. Darcy or whatever. He's my guy."

"Ugh…" Wendy flopped down onto the steps behind her. "You are not making this 'getting over her' stuff any easier."

"Wendy Cedar, you turned your back on your inheritance, raked up a frankly unholy amount of college debt, worked as an intern, and you live in an apartment building that I am honestly not a hundred percent on letting my son visit. Because it's what you wanted, you fought for it. Now you have this woman—and she's definitely not good enough for you, you're my sister—but she means enough to you that you are going—" Regan laughed "—full Enya on the emotional spectrum. And you're not going to fight for her? Bullshit. You want my permission, you've got it. Go kick some ass. I'll bail you out if you get arrested."

And suddenly, Wendy was smiling. "You know what I need to do?"

"What?"

Wendy snatched a white rose from the bouquet. "Get her flowers."

Wendy played with Janet's glasses on the elevator. Janet had left a pair at her apartment—she definitely had spares, given how she hadn't broached their inelegant silence to ask for them back—and since then they'd lived in Wendy's jacket pocket. The longing Wendy had felt for her had been growing unendurable, but now that she'd decided to win her back, there was a sweetness to it. It felt like an itch being scratched.

The elevator dinged. She slipped the glasses back into her pocket.

The key to infiltrating someplace you weren't supposed to be, as Wendy had learned from sneaking into horror movies from age twelve, was to look as if you knew exactly what you were doing and were absolutely where you belonged. This was hard for any twenty-something to do, but Wendy thought she had the hang of it. She went through Mary Borchard's division like she was slightly bored of it, an everyday fixture dressed in the same slacks and Oxford shirt and sweater as everyone else. When she got to Marlon, it took him a moment to recognize her.

Marlon was a tall, springy guy with a toothbrush haircut that he either thought was cool or was waiting to loop around back to cool. He'd come up through the intern program with her and they were still friends on Facebook, right alongside everyone Wendy had been in elementary school with.

"Marlon, hey—" she said, dipping into his cubicle. It was about big enough for the both of them, which told Wendy she wasn't overeating.

"Wendy? What are you doing here?"

"It's a long story," Wendy said, crouching down beside his desk. If she stood up, she was tall enough to be seen over the cubicle partitions, because apparently Mary had gotten the things secondhand from the Lollipop Guild. "But you know how I got hired by Janet Lace?"

"Yeah—what's it like having a job? They pay you? You have insurance?"

"Yes," Wendy agreed, trying to remember if she'd been quite so underpaid.

"You have dental? You can just go to dentists?"

"Marlon, honestly, if you help me out here, I will get you a job over in my division. Promise."

Marlon lowered his voice. "Deal! What's the 411?"

"The 41—never mind. My boss thinks your boss is misrepresenting the RadarVoid system, so I need a copy of all the test results on it, unedited."

Marlon's brow furrowed. "God…they might be on the cloud servers. No one ever deletes the old files from the draft folder—and you think Borchard is lying about this stuff?"

"Suspect."

"Yeah, wouldn't surprise me. The woman's a witch, works us like dogs, doesn't even learn our names, barely recognizes any of us. She has these nicknames and I don't think bread rises around her."

"What?"

Marlon was typing frantically. "You know, witchcraft? Horses sweating, cream going sour, bread not rising? I brought some creamer from home and it went sour in the office refrigerator! After one day!"

"That is definitely a *Warlock* or *Warlock II: The Armageddon* type situation," Wendy agreed. "Found it yet?"

"Yeah, she ordered something like fifty tests done. You want all of them?"

"Each and every."

"All right." Marlon picked up a USB drive from his desk and plugged it in. "If there are any other files on this, don't open them?"

"Not even a little bit," Wendy promised.

She heard the hard drive in Marlon's tower buzz as it started spinning, grinding the data down into the thumb drive. And then she heard heels on the hardwood floor.

Wendy threw herself under the desk as Mary Borchard leaned over the cubicle partition, staring down at Marlon.

"Bradley, where's the JW report? I assigned it to you two hours ago. You didn't go to lunch, did you?"

Marlon nonchalantly rolled his chair in front of his desk's footspace. Wendy could've kissed him. Just not when she was under his desk.

"No ma'am—it's Marlon, actually—and I sent the JW report to your e-mail."

"Not finished, you didn't include the PCS file."

Wendy looked over at the computer tower next to her, in a special slot of the desk opposite the drawers on Marlon's right. She could see the green light on the thumb drive blinking as it loaded. She knew the model—once the light went out, the file transfer was complete.

"I didn't know I was supposed to include the PCS file—you didn't ask for it, and that's Bill's job—"

"Should I have to tell you *every* aspect of your job? If I want the JW report, of course I want the PCS file too! Either have it in my inbox by the time I walk back to my office or security will be showing you the way out! They're very good at removing undesirables from the premises."

"Yes, ma'am, right away—"

"What's the matter with you, anyway? You seem sweatier than usual. I'd like to think that's all me, but somehow I doubt it."

Wendy heard typing above her. The green light of the thumb drive was out. If she grabbed it, checkmate. Even if Mary caught her, she could smuggle it out. But if Mary caught her, noticed the thumb drive—hell, if she was smart enough to have security search her—she'd assume Janet was behind it.

Not exactly the peace offering Wendy wanted to send.

"It's just I heard there was an opening in Upper Atmosphere," Marlon was saying, "and I was thinking that maybe you could write me a letter of recommendation if I decided to, er, go for it."

"I think the only thing you could get me to recommend you for is a vasectomy, but it does seem a little pointless. Are you ready to send the PCS file, or should I insult you a little more to give you time to do your job?"

"It's sent! It's sent!"

"Good," Mary said, and Wendy swiped for the thumb drive, yanking it from its USB port and jamming it under the tongue of her shoe.

"What was that?" Mary demanded.

"What was what?"

Wendy heard a few footsteps as Mary came around for a better look. "What's under your desk?"

She pulled her hair into a ponytail, ripping an elastic from her wrist to tie it off. Slammed on Janet's glasses. Affected a broad Jersey accent as she crawled out on her hands and knees. "Oh hi, boss lady, you must be Marlon's boss, he talks about ya all the time—"

Mary stared in a way that made Wendy feel as if she were on a slide. "Who the hell are you? You don't have clearance to be in here."

"Oh, no, I'm Marlon's girlfriend. Jocelyn? He's mentioned me? Listen, this is *super* embarrassing, know I'm not supposed to be here, but it's his birthday and I thought who'd it hurt to come over and wish him a happy birthday? Y'know? A really happy birthday?"

"Uh-huh. Get out."

Wendy got to her feet. "I'm really sorry, Mrs. B, Marlon said you'd understand." She put an arm around him. "I just love my little guy so much!"

Mary crossed her arms. "Well then—*Marlon*—since you see fit to attend to personal business on my time, I'm sure you won't mind attending to my business on your time. Saturday and Sunday. Be here. And your *friend* had better be gone by the time I've called security. Which I'm doing right now."

Wendy smiled ruefully at Marlon as soon as she was gone. "Sorry," she said under her breath.

"Don't be, I was working this weekend anyway. Plus, if anyone overheard that, I could be very popular around here."

Wendy did think someone gave her a thumbs up as she left.

ÅⱵÅ

One plus to having a girlfriend, even a presently head-up-her-ass girlfriend—no more gay bars. Wendy got to meet with Tina at a café. It was nice. Quiet music, drinks with names that weren't euphemisms for anything, actual chairs to sit in. It was like going to grandmother's house, with bottle service.

Wendy liked it. She was getting too old to pretend to be good at dancing.

"So here's the thing," Wendy said, "if a guy hits on you, first you turn him down, right? See if he's okay with rejection. Better to know that now than when he's hitting you up for anal."

"That's not a real thing people do," Tina said.

"Yes, it is, it totally works! It's like getting a mammogram. Wouldn't you rather know than wonder?"

"Okay, how many dates have you been on that you're suddenly the master of relationships? That is why we're in a place that plays actual music, right? Or did you just woman up and make peace with dying alone?"

"Does it have to be one or the other?" Wendy reached into her purse and brought out her tablet. "But let's set aside my expertise at having sex and being in love, and go to your expertise in radar shit."

"Whoa, whoa—" Tina held up her hands. "You know I don't have security clearance for any of this?"

"You don't need it. It's proprietary technology, hasn't been sold to the military yet. As far as they're concerned, it might as well be Microsoft Flight Simulator."

"That's some flimsy shit right there."

"Tina, c'mon, no one knows this stuff better than you. Just look it over and tell me if I'm on the right track. After you tell me which track I should be on."

Tina groaned and took Wendy's tablet. "You're picking up the tab."

"Yes. Oh hey—" Wendy slightly inclined her eyes to Tina's left. "Hottie on your six, coming your way."

"How would you know?"

"Just because I'm not ordering doesn't mean I can't read the menu. Remember, turn him down first."

"This is stupid—"

"Trust me!"

The man put his hand on the table. "Hi there. Tom Willis. Mind if I buy you a drink, miss? You look like you're running on empty."

"That's all right," Tina said. "I'm just not in the mood right now."

The man shrugged. "All right. Enjoy your evening."

"Hey there," someone said, and Wendy turned around to see a woman gesturing from the neighboring table. "If that money's burning a hole in your pocket, I could use a refill."

"Sure thing," the man said, moving over. "What'll it be?"

Wendy turned back around to find Tina glaring at her.

"Barkeep," she called, "could I get a bottle of your finest brandy? Thanks."

$$\text{A}\,\forall\,\text{A}$$

First thing the next morning, Wendy rued how fucking bright it was. But second thing, she rode to the office. "Janet, you are not going to believe—"

Her seat was taken. By Mary Borchard. "Mary. Hi there. I knew I recognized you from somewhere. "

Wendy only let herself be abashed for a half-second. Then she slapped the tablet down on Janet's desk. "I know what you're up to."

"Do you now?" Mary asked.

Wendy faced Janet. "RadarVoid works *too* well. It doesn't just screw up the instrumentation of computers targeting it, it messes with everything. Other helicopters can't engage their targets. Planes can't accurately drop ordinance. As soon as the Hawkowl's in the area, the entire C2 breaks down."

Mary wasn't fazed in the slightest. "That was a problem in initial tests, but we corrected it."

Janet spoke for the first time. "You mean you changed the tests not to check for that. Then you mixed them all together so no one would ask why you ordered multiple series of tests."

Mary shrugged. "So this is it, then? You found a few bugs in my program—is that really why your little helper monkey's been sniffing around my people? Well, I'll raise you."

She picked up a file folder from Janet's desk, dropped it on top of Wendy's tablet.

"What's that?" Wendy asked. No one answered. She reached for it—

"Don't," Janet said, but Wendy ignored her.

They were pictures.

Blown-up, glossy, perfect reproductions of the pictures Janet had sent to Wendy. In exchange for her fingers.

"I'm sure it would interest the higher-ups very much to know that Janet here is sleeping with someone in a different security classification. One whom she's let run amok with proprietary technology. It really doesn't take long to look like corporate espionage, if not counterintelligence."

Wendy tightened her fists into neutron stars. "You wanna see counterintelligence, lady?"

Janet held up a hand and Wendy froze. "You must know this'll come out, Mary. As soon as the military finds out the tech doesn't work, the contract won't be worth the paper it's printed on."

"But it'll still be printed," Mary said. "And thanks to you, *Wendy*, everyone will know the sale was made on the strength of the RadarVoid system. I've already gotten offers from Boeing and Lockheed. So years from now, when the Hawkowl is in production and I'm making eight figures at a new company, I don't think it'll really matter what happens to Savin Aerospace. For any of us."

"Fuck you," Wendy said.

Mary stared into Janet. "Is that your answer, too? Savin's a sinking ship, but you can get in the lifeboat with me. That tablet won't change anything, but it's still aggravation I don't need. Make sure no one sees it and I can get you through the door right behind me."

Janet sat still as a statue behind her desk. It seemed to take a great deal of effort for her to rotate her chair, for her to be turning from side to side, lost in thought. And it took her a long time to raise her downcast eyes.

"You heard her," she told Mary. "This company's been good to me. I've devoted my life to it. I'm not going to help slit its throat so you can get a corner office."

"Fine. Don't help. Watch its throat get slit anyway." Mary rose from her seat. "Tests that you obtained, how? And that you checked, where? I have my sources, I would've known if you'd gone through any of the right channels. All that tablet has on it is supposition from God knows where based on God knows what, fucking up a sale that's already being made, and no one's going to hit the brakes on a billion-dollar contract just on your say-so. Especially once they find out you've been fucking the intern here."

"Hey! I'm a structural dynamics engineer, bitch."

Janet silenced her with a gesture. "People will listen. We'll take this all the way to the CEO if we have to."

"'We'"? Mary mimicked. "I'm sure your *intern* is good for a lot of things, but getting a come-to-Jesus with the Old Man isn't one of them."

Wendy walked up to her.

"What?" Mary asked. "Are you going to hit me now? Go ahead, completely destroy your own credibility. I'll sue you for every cent you've got. I can always use change for the laundromat."

"Excuse me," Wendy said, and stepped past her. To Janet's desk. She picked up the phone. "Need to borrow this. Local call." She punched in a number, fast with memorization, then waited while it rung.

Mary watched: amused at first, then impatient to see what her play was.

"It's ringing," Wendy said, then straightened as the other end picked up. "Hi, Grandpa? You told me to call you if I had any trouble? Well, I'm pretty sure this qualifies…"

She took two minutes to lay it out. She was pretty succinct. Mary only had time to look at Janet and ask "What the fuck is she doing?" once.

Then Wendy put her hand over the receiver and spoke to Mary. "He wants to talk to you."

Mary reacted to the phone being held out to her as if it were a loaded gun. Then she shook her head dubiously and took it, sneering at Wendy as she lifted it to her ear. "Yes?"

The Old Man was even more succinct. A moment later, Mary lowered the phone, a dial tone issuing from it.

"I'm fired."

Wendy took the phone from her and dropped it back in its cradle.

Mary shook her head. "That's it? You just—you make a phone call and I'm…no, you can't just…I have connections, I, I'm…"

"You might want to call security," Wendy told Janet. "I hear they're very good at removing undesirables."

Mary darkened, the blow finally cutting through layers of denial and moving into rage. "You know this is bullshit. If I were a man, I'd be CEO by now."

"No," Wendy said, sitting down on Janet's desk. "If you were a man, you'd be an asshole. You're still an asshole. You treat your employees like shit. You only care about yourself. You nearly bankrupted my family's company and sent thousands of people into unemployment just for your own ambitions. Don't flatter yourself by thinking any of this is because you're a woman. It's because you're a piece of shit. Now here. Your severance package."

She reached into her pocket and flipped something small and shiny Mary's way.

Mary caught it.

A quarter.

"For the laundromat," Wendy said.

Mary left between two security guards, about as defeated as she would ever be. That wouldn't be the end of it. She'd sue for wrongful termination and anything else she could think of, try whatever dirty tricks were left in the book, but she'd lost. Everything else was just how bad her losses would be.

Wendy wasn't thinking of any of that just then.

Janet had still not said a word.

"I'm sorry about the pictures on my phone—" Wendy started.

"No, no, that's Mary's fault. She hacked your phone, that's not your fault. Wallace Savin is your grandfather."

"Maternal," Wendy said. "His daughter married my dad, hence Wendy Cedar...and umm...so I'm in high school and I am the smallest avionics nerd you ever did see. Model airplane club, remote control helicopters, everything, everything. I'm already applying to all these engineering schools and I'm getting acceptance letter after acceptance letter and I realize, why bother? It's the family business. All I have to do is turn in a job application with one of my parents for a reference and I'm on the top floor. So I have this idea—more of an experiment. I go to college across the country, I don't tell anyone who my dad is or my mom or my grandfather. And I'm actually really good at this engineering stuff. I mean, I let my parents go half and half on tuition, I'm not crazy, but I get a part-time job to pay for my books, I meet some really cool people who don't have summer homes, and when I graduate, I put in an application for Savin Aerospace's intern program. And they choose me. Not because of my mom or my dad, but because of my work. It's my job, it's mine. And the shitty apartment I live in is mine. And this really amazing woman that I fell in love with along the way... I really hope she's mine."

"Your father's Jacob Cedar," Janet said.

"Yeah."

"He's on the board of directors."

"I know."

"I'm fucking the boss's daughter."

"Do you one better, I fucked the boss, okay, so inappropriate, forget I said that, couldn't resist."

"For me?" Janet asked. She was crying. Not sobbing, just with a kind of leak below her eyes. "All this..."

Wendy took a deep breath. "I would never ask you to choose between me and your career. But you don't have to choose."

"Yes I do. I can't have this. Me, you—*God.*" Her elbow planted itself on the desk, her head falling into her outstretched hand.

Wendy took a half-step forward, going to comfort her, but also kept at bay by the sheer despondency of Janet's grief.

"Trying to seduce a woman half my age, what right do I have…"

"How old are you?" Wendy asked.

"Forty-four."

"I'm twenty-six, you're not twice my age or old enough to be my mother unless you were a Teen Mom and you're the least Teen Mom person I've ever met!"

Janet pried her hand away from her face, eyes suddenly red, and seeing her carefully composed face suddenly all knotted up with emotion was as shocking to Wendy as seeing it covered with war paint. "I'm forty-four, I have no children, I'm divorced, and I'm experimenting with bondage five years after it was cool. It's fucked up. It's all fucked up."

"Listen, Janet—Jan…" Wendy hopped up on the desk on Janet's side, wishing she had the nerve to take Janet's hand. "Tell me about it. Talk to me."

Janet took a deep breath. "Tissue." She held out her hand. "Please, could you just—hand me—"

Wendy realized there was a box of tissues on a file cabinet adjacent to Janet's desk, but Janet's desk was so large that Janet couldn't reach it. She plucked out a swath and handed them to Janet, who first dabbed at her eyes, then blew her nose. The soiled tissues went into a wastebasket that was already half-full.

Wendy plucked another tissue to offer to Janet, but she was already gone. Face closed off, bricked over, the redness in the orbits of her eyes and the nostrils of her nose now seeming like graffiti on her composed expression.

Yet she couldn't quite manage it. That wall she'd put up so many times before had cracks in it. Wendy could see it in her eyes—the thing she'd seen more and more of over the past few days, that Janet had let her see more and more of.

Her sadness.

Janet stood abruptly. Like she was ripping free of something. "I can't have this. I shouldn't even want it. This is just another reason…"

And she was moving, so fast and yet so controlled that Wendy thought of a machine overheating, going faster and faster until it broke down. Wendy trailed after her, knowing that Janet didn't want to be followed, hating that she knew Janet well enough to think that, that she couldn't be ignorant enough to try and comfort her. Maybe she didn't know Janet at all.

She heard Elizabeth say, "Jan, the Carson meeting?" through the open door, but the pace of Janet's footfalls never altered as she left the office.

A moment later, Elizabeth appeared in the door of the office. She closed it behind her. Wendy sat at Janet's desk, not even feeling the warmth of her. Wendy chewed on her thumbnail and thought of all the worries she'd carried that someone would find out who she was. All her self-doubt that she wasn't proving anything to her family except how pig-headed she could be, and then there were the small pleasures in earning something and having it be hers. Her job, her work, and something of Janet Lace. And now…

Maybe it was all a waste of time. Especially the Janet Lace part.

"Did you hear any of that?" she asked Elizabeth, as if just noticing her. Fuck, it was getting awkward, brooding with Elizabeth standing in the corner like a lifeguard or something.

"Mostly the entertaining bits with Mary getting her ass kicked. I tried not to catch any of the stuff where you and Janet…yeah."

"So you got the gist of it?"

"That, and we've been shooting the shit about her sex life pretty consistently over the course of our friendship. It's been pretty dull for the last few years, actually." Then she ventured a question like she'd been called on in school without her hand raised. "Good on you for tapping that?"

"More or less inappropriate," Wendy said.

"Yeah…Janet's used to it. So, uhh…you going to go after her? Seems like your…thing. If you're not, I am."

Wendy stood, stretched. The few moments she'd been sitting felt like a thousand years. "Should I? I want this relationship, but she told me in Yuma that it wasn't right. I don't want to force something on her…I want to be what she wants. Just because I can't see the appeal of not having sex with me doesn't mean…"

Elizabeth held up a finger, went to the drink trolley, and fetched a bottle of cognac. One glass. "This is medicinal," she said, looking around for glass number two. "I mean, what, you thought dating your boss-slash-employee would be easy?"

Wendy pushed her hands together. "Kinda thought the boss and employee things canceled each other out. Not that I am her boss…"

"You own stock in the company?"

"I own a lot of stocks," Wendy said defensively, then winced as that somehow shockingly failed to make it better.

"So you own the company."

"Only some of it."

"You own the company, she works for the company, she works for you."

"Okay, that's not even the problem."

Elizabeth found a clean coffee mug. It did not say 'World's Best Boss'.

"The problem isn't the problem," Elizabeth told her, suddenly fancying herself a philosopher-bartender as she poured. "It's this, it's that, it's that she had an unhappy childhood and her marriage ended badly and her career isn't going as well as she thought it would and she thinks her thighs are chubby…"

"Bullshit! Her thighs are great!"

Elizabeth handed her the mug. "And if she realizes that, suddenly all her issues go away and the clouds clear up and the sun is shining and the Justice League movie doesn't suck? No, because she's got a million things and she doesn't want to share them and she struggles with them every day. And then she has a million other things that are great and smart and funny—maybe not funny—but she'll give me the day off and answer her own phone when I have the flu, she'll take a cut in her own salary before she lets an employee get laid off, and she…" Elizabeth lowered her voice. "She's actually a really big fan of the Babysitters Club."

"Shut up!"

"She has the entire series in this chest she keeps hidden. Have you been to her apartment?" Wendy shook her head. "Keep your eyes open. And make her take you to her apartment, you've been her bitch, you deserve to sleep in her bed. Jesus, what's wrong with you? You're making us all look bad."

Wendy laughed and drank, and made a somewhat gratified, somewhat pained noise when it hit.

"Okay, you can hold your liquor. I'm starting to approve of you." Elizabeth took the mug back and drained it. "Boss isn't here. I haven't goofed off like this in five years…my point is, all this shit she has? It's her shit. It doesn't go away just because she's gone down on you—"

"She hasn't gone down on me—"

"Fuck you, get that shit. Are you a lesbian or aren't you?" Elizabeth slammed the mug down on the desk. "Making us look bad...listen, she is the most amazing woman I've ever met, and she is also one of those Indiana Jones boulders of neuroses and regrets and just, just bullshit. You take the one, you take the other. She can't just toss this away because it's inconvenient for you. Even if she'd love to...be worthy of you." Elizabeth sighed and poured again. "You're young and beautiful and now you're rich. She doesn't want you to waste yourself on her."

Wendy held up her hands. "Okay, I get it; Dr. Phil, no more drinks—"

"This is for me."

Wendy ignored her. "Janet could be getting on a plane to Bora Bora right now, so could you just tell me if she loves me or not? Did she tell you? Did she say those exact words?"

"Wendy, over the past few months, she's said everything about you. All our conversations have had you in them. Either she's crazy about you or she's going to murder you."

Wendy made a weighing motion with her hands. "Fuck it. I'm going after her."

"She'll be at the park."

Wendy didn't take the time to go around Elizabeth, just jumped up on the desk, jumped off the other side, and was out the door.

She thought she heard Elizabeth asking for a raise as she left.

ΛΨΛ

It was a lovely day in the park. Janet could tell from the office—see the blue sky, the white clouds, the green grass. But she didn't really *know*. That only came from sitting on a bench, feeling the wind in her hair and the sun on her skin and hearing the discordant little harmony formed out in nature. Running feet, walking dogs, snatches of conversation, even the cars in the distance, a part of the world along with the birds and the rushing wind.

Roberta Olsen, formerly Roberta Lace-Olsen, was walking with her girlfriend. It had the slowness and comfort of a walk that was entirely unself-conscious. No neurotic notions of exercise or enjoying nature or a feeling of obligation, just a desire to enjoy the day and the company in equal measure. As she walked, her girlfriend told her a story, hands gesturing to and fro, her overly-animated face miming expressions, and

Roberta laughing, laughing, laughing, until she had to pull her girl into an embrace as if to stop her from joking even more.

Janet watched them from the park bench. She wondered if it had ever been so easy. Her discomfort had nothing to do with seeing them together. *That* provoked little reaction in Janet that wasn't scientific. But her office had been her castle—not her home, never her home, her home and Bobbi's—and now it was unsafe. Wendy had invaded it, revealed it to have been compromised so insidiously that Janet had never even noticed, and she couldn't reconcile its sanctity from Wendy's hold on it.

Wendy had come looking for her, found her, she was looking at her even now. Trying to think of something to say to her while her eyes reminded Janet how possessed she was. Her own skin felt half Wendy's. So much of it touched by her, still hungering for her…Janet was losing too much, giving up too much that she had hoped to hold in reserve, safe and sound where it couldn't be lost, but Wendy had been ravenous for it. And Janet hadn't had the will to stop her. She'd signed over so much of herself that she wondered if there was any left. She worried that if there was, it went with Roberta, already too far away for her to feel.

She'd gone to the park to feel safe. It didn't feel that way. Not with Roberta there.

Fuck it, she should probably say something before Wendy got bored and left. "Are you supposed to be a Secret Service agent or something? Sit down. For God's sake, I'm not a deer."

Sheepishly—as much as she seemed capable of sheepishness—Wendy came out from behind the tree she'd been somewhat hiding behind, somewhat leaning on, and collapsed onto the other side of the bench with a kind of relief. Janet guessed she thought the hard part was over.

"I was going to write you another e-mail, but then I remembered you're old, so I thought you'd prefer talking in person."

Janet replied, "Funny."

"Yes, I am. Thanks for noticing." Whatever brave face Wendy was putting up, died in the wake of Janet's apathy. She folded her arms, played with her hair a little, she let Janet stew. Gave her time to tell her to go away.

Janet would've, only she wanted something from her. She didn't know what. Maybe some kind of closure. Something to make it okay that they weren't going to see each other anymore.

"I didn't follow you," Wendy said, her voice slightly bright with false cheer, and it wasn't even very cheerful. Her eyes sought Janet's, but didn't find them. "Elizabeth told me where you were. And it's been an hour, so… I wanted to make sure you hadn't hit your head or anything. Gotten amnesia."

"What's that?" Janet said by rote.

Wendy smiled at her. Janet wished she could look at her. But she felt more fragile than ever—more in touch with her own weakness. She could see the breadth of it, all its dimensions, how far down it went. But then, Wendy already knew.

The least she could do was hold up her end of the conversation. "I assume Elizabeth gave you a pep talk too?"

"Full disclosure: I also got one from my sister, so a double pep talk."

"And I'm guessing Elizabeth told you I just need to open up and let you in and *be happy*, everyone wants to be happy…"

"Actually, it was about how being a little closed off and withdrawn is just who you are. But being alone isn't. You don't have to bury everything."

Wendy left the words hanging, for once not pressing, not poking, not prodding, but letting Janet process. Janet looked out, down maybe a hundred feet to the pond, where Roberta was buying a pretzel from the vendor. One to be shared.

"Are you worried about the meeting with Carson? Think it'd be shallow to bring it up?" Wendy winced, worried she'd put her foot in her mouth, and Janet wanted to reassure her, tell her how cute it was, actually… She didn't. "Doesn't matter, I'll tell you just so I can think I'm considerate. As it turns out, the CEO thinks everyone has been working so hard that they deserve a break, so he ordered pizza for the whole company. It's a one-time thing, though. Don't expect pizza every week."

"All to get me out of a meeting." Janet felt a tear rebel against her control, and wiped her eye. Wendy saw it and didn't react, maybe didn't even think how weak she was, not even being able to have a simple conversation. "Not that it's come up, but this is why I don't recommend employees date shareholders. It conjures thoughts of nepotism."

"I'm not a nepot!" Wendy insisted. She slid along the bench. "I mean—I am Wendy Cedar, but I'm just Wendy Cedar. You know?"

"That's not the point. That's not even the issue. You were right. I am scared. Scared for you. Look at you, Wendy Cedar. You're young and smart and ambitious. You deserve the whole world. You could win it. Why do you want to be saddled with me? I'm not even good enough for her."

Wendy followed her eyes out to the couple, just like any other, and Janet almost laughed at the thought that she probably couldn't even tell which one was Roberta. Someone who could mean so much to her, go through so much with her, and now—a stranger.

"She's moving away soon," Janet continued. "It's a shame, she loved this park. I wish I could let her have it."

"And you?"

Janet shook her head. "I loved the way she loved it."

But Wendy understood. "You know, I did some reading about the *Kee Bird*. It's still in Greenland. You can go there and look at it, it's very well-preserved. It's still standing, Janet. Even if it can't fly. Even if some people aren't interested in it. Isn't that impressive enough? Still being there after over seventy years?"

"That's a very sentimental way to look at an old bucket of bolts," Janet told her.

"And you have a very cynical way of looking at an antique. Makes you wonder why you're looking at it in the first place." Wendy reached out and put her hand on the bench between them, baiting that demon thought. So close, it was so close, it was right there.

She had the audacity not to look affronted when Janet didn't take it.

"I'm not sure," Wendy said. "I might be totally off-base. And if I'm wrong—or even if I'm right—you don't have to say anything. But I think you'd like to talk about her. And whatever it is, I am so fucking okay with hearing it."

"You really can't get enough of me tormenting you, huh?"

Wendy smiled. She kept doing that, making it harder for Janet to convince herself she didn't want her.

Making it impossible.

Janet bowed her head. She could see Roberta without looking at her. "I kept changing. And she kept changing. And finally I wasn't hers anymore. I guess she isn't mine either, now. Wendy, I want you to be happy. And you think we will be, and maybe you're right, but for how long? Ten years? Twenty? No matter how happy we were together—how happy you thought you were—you're better off without me. It's no way to live, being satisfied with whatever dregs of love I can offer."

"You can love a lot more than you think. I've seen it." Wendy held herself there—Janet could see the twitches in her muscles as she wanted, as she needed to be held, the same way Janet did, but she wouldn't move. She just kept her hand laying there on the bench, an offering. "So in ten years I'll fight for you. And in twenty years I'll fight for you. At the end of time, I'll fight for you. Because you don't make me happy. You are my happiness. And I think I'm yours. Even if you aren't, like, physically capable of laughing…"

Janet proved her wrong, in a short burst like a flock of birds taking wing. Her eyes darted to Wendy's hand on the bench. It was still there.

Wendy bit back a smile, but Janet could see her chewing on it. "I didn't fall in love with you because you were a hugger," Wendy said. "I fell in love with you this way. I'm not asking you not to change. I'm saying I would like to see who you're changing into."

Janet couldn't do that. She just couldn't do it. Agree to a life with Wendy, living together, having everything that was *her* shared… She couldn't give Wendy anything she wanted. She tried, she wanted to force the possibility into her brain, but she would think of Roberta and knew, *knew* it would end with her right back here. Watching Wendy with someone else. She couldn't commit to that. But she could reach out and take Wendy's hand. And hope Wendy could wait until tomorrow for more.

"Just this once, I really have to hug you," Wendy said.

Janet shook her head. "Hurry up then, you goose."

Wendy stood up and did. Janet buried her smile in Wendy's throat.

Maybe it was a smile so rare that it demanded attention, because when she stopped looking down Wendy's back, she looked out into the distance and saw Roberta, seeing her. She held her hand up in whatever greeting she could manage. Roberta waved at her. She waved good-bye.

"You know yoga doesn't have any proven health benefits?" Wendy said in her ear. "The science just isn't there."

EPILOGUE

Wendy ignored the fancy fixtures of Janet's building. The dry art pierces on the wall, the potted plants at every turn in trendy eco-friendliness, the wallpaper that was overbearing enough to insert itself into the prints they bothered to frame. It was a little tacky, actually. Thankfully, Janet's own apartment was much more tasteful. She knocked at the door.

"Ready to go?"

"Just one moment," Janet said through the door, then it opened and Wendy realized *oh, yeah, there was a reason people cared about their appearance besides not wanting to be arrested for suspected vagrancy.*

Janet wore a simple, sleek blue mini-dress that left her long legs bare to strappy high heels. There were a few modestly placed transparent panels about her waist, and the short sleeves were mesh as well, adding to the lightness of the dress—as if it were caressing her body, and particularly teasingly in a few places. Her hair was down, in a neat little part that tucked behind her ears and stopped in a bob at the nape of her neck, and she wore her contacts instead of the glasses.

It was kind of a shock. Janet looked beautiful, she always looked beautiful, but this was an entirely different kind of beautiful from Power Dyke Secret Kinky Librarian Janet Lace. It was High-Class Escort Janet Lace. Rich Widow Whose Husband Died Under Mysterious Circumstances Janet Lace. Spy Undercover At A Caviar Tasting Party Janet Lace.

Wendy decided to go with that last one if Janet asked how she looked.

"How do I look?" Janet asked.

"Like a spy undercover at a caviar-tasting party."

Janet smiled, too pleased to admonish except for a little bit. "I don't know where you get this stuff. But it's very flattering."

"You should see the first drafts," Wendy replied. "Just be glad I've never compared you to a sexy Buddy Holly."

Janet's hand automatically went to where her glasses weren't. "Funny. What about you? Are you changing? I don't see a garment bag."

"Not sure I own a garment bag. Sounds like something I'd have if I were a Hobbit. C'mon, or we'll miss the last-week's-episode preshow and Tina will eat all the dip."

Janet tapped two fingers on Wendy's shoulder as she turned to go, stopping her. "I thought we were going to a party. You go to parties dressed like Wolverine, the rugged individualist with a secret code of honor and a heart of gold?"

"Good one."

"Thanks. I've been reading TV Tropes."

Wendy picked at her T-shirt. "It's a viewing party, Lace. Just a bunch of friends sitting around on the couch, or lying on the floor, watching *Game of Thrones*. There'll be chips. There'll be dip. No caviar."

Janet blinked. "There'll be people lying on the floor?"

"Yes."

"The refreshments will be tortilla chips and salsa?"

"Maybe guacamole, I don't know."

Janet looked down at herself. "I'm overdressed."

"Babe, it's fine, it's my sister's place, people wear whatever."

"Yes, and I'm not wearing 'whatever,' I'm wearing Alexis!"

"You name your dresses?"

"I'm changing," Janet announced, swooping around on her heel.

With a sigh, Wendy followed her into the apartment, closing the door behind her. Janet disappeared into her changing room—she had a changing room—and began struggling out of what had no doubt also been a struggle to get into.

"I suppose it would be fun to figure out just how much time Janet takes to throw on a casual look," Wendy mused to herself, glancing at her watch. Then: "Does she *have* a casual look?"

"Wendy?" Janet interrupted her thoughts with a slightly plaintive rendition of her name. Wendy looked over to the cracked-open door.

"Yeah, hon?"

"I may be stuck."

Wendy felt the urge to be noble and also thought, *not now, nobility.* "Well, are you stuck or aren't you stuck? Because if you aren't, I don't see how you need my help."

Janet seethed most pleasingly. Wendy could feel it right through the door. "Just get in here."

Wendy went into the dressing room, and any further dad jokes left her mind as she beheld Janet Lace, the subtle flaxen tan of her skin complemented by cream-colored bra and panties that encircled the most interesting areas of a particularly interesting body in patterns of lace. And there was a dress over her head.

"This is not funny," Janet said.

Wendy glanced at a nearby table, happy to see that Janet's version of dressing down included designer label jeans, a gray wool crewneck, and a *scarf*. Then she resumed glancing at Janet. What was it called when you repeatedly glanced at someone without looking away? Or blinking? And they were sort of naked?

"Wendy—" Janet said seriously, and given everything she said was serious, this was an accomplishment. "If you are taking a *picture*—"

"Oh no," Wendy interrupted, drawing close. "This is all mine." She could see Janet's face through the thin fabric of the dress, inverted around her neck, and just about make out her sourpuss expression. Darting forward, Wendy kissed her.

The time they'd kissed in the office had been overwhelming, intoxicating; a roller-coaster climbing up a hill and coming down it all at once. This was much more…controlled. Not all the sight of Janet, not all the taste of her, just her warmth. Her scent. Wendy felt tremors through her where there had been volcanos, and it was pleasantly teasing.

"*Wendy…*"

She loved that name.

Wendy got down on her knees—easy, when you were wearing jeans— and brushed her fingertips scantly over Janet's ribs, her hips, her thighs. She didn't think she could speak, but she still wanted to ask permission, and when Janet spread her thighs a little, canted her hips forward, it was all the answer she needed. She took hold of Janet's panties and peeled them down her thighs, but not over her knees.

She didn't want Janet naked, not quite, she wanted her to feel her panties down around her thighs and constantly know that they weren't on her hips, that she was exposed, that she was seen. And Janet quivered for her—knowing it.

And there was her pussy. The soft fleece of her hair, the gentle parting of the lips—an invitation Wendy couldn't refuse. She leaned in, already knowing she would love this part. Licking lightly at Janet's folds, kissing along the contours of her groin, the sensitive space between her legs but outside her sex where a woman was so rarely touched. Wendy loved this almost more than the penetration, the taste—before that, the sweat.

Past teasing, going into foreplay, the little space for just the two of them where she could shower Janet with affection. Not fucking her, not quite, not yet, just pleasing her. Showing her how she was loved. And when her tongue slipped farther and farther from her control, when it started to explore the moist part in Janet's labia, felt the beginnings of the pressure inside her… God, she tasted so *good*…

Janet started to shuffle, shifting her weight from foot to foot and trying to take the dress all the way off. She was either not liking how the dress trapped her arms and blinded her eyes, or was ill at ease with how much she did like it. Wendy thought it was the second one. Janet had been wet before she'd even started.

She clamped her hands on Janet's hips, stilling her. "Don't. *Fucking*. Move."

Wendy could've sworn she felt Janet clench from six inches away. She went a little harder, just a little harder—long, slow kisses on her core, crushing her lips to it, letting her tongue push just a little more insistently inside. And Janet welcomed her, hot and tight and wet and *ready*.

Wendy brought one hand away from Janet's hip, keeping the other on her waist as a reminder to hold still, and she took her fingers to Janet's sex and she petted it, gently, softly, letting it learn the feel of her fingertips on every curve, every fold, every glorious inch. She only touched, she didn't press.

She loved the part before, the luxuriating in Janet Lace, but how could she decide between that part and this? Between wanting her and having her? Both ached sumptuously—wanting her meant she didn't have her, but having her meant an end to that delectable tension, the clarity of her lust.

No, she loved all of it, from joking with Janet at the door to this. And she loved just the feel of Janet as she pushed her fingers inside; as her tongue settled in a lazy curl on Janet's clit, so hard, so needy; as her fingers climbed the inside of her, all tense, all taut, and found that secret little place where Janet's pleasure lived.

"There you are," Wendy whispered into her cunt, and felt her, and felt her, and felt her.

Whatever resolve Janet had, and it was considerable, it broke in the face of this final, undeniable summit. What had mounted inside her had grown too large to deny and she let out a cry of sheer, shocked, satisfied surprise. Janet went all liquid around Wendy, and Wendy loved it, and caught her even before her knees started to buckle.

She helped Janet out of the dress. She laid her down on the floor, to pant and open her eyes and realize where she was. And once Janet's eyes were open, once the ecstasy had faded enough for her mind to come back, Wendy kissed her.

She loved it with the dress in the way. But she loved it a little more when it was just Janet—undeniable, indescribable, overpowering Janet.

"That's how sweet you taste," she said as she pulled away—and watched Janet lick her lips.

Janet took a deep breath, pleased, girlishly *bright*, and put her hand on Wendy's cheek and mouthed three words quickly, quietly. Then kissed them into Wendy's lips.

And then, in a fit of motion, Janet was back on her feet, pulling her panties up, throwing on the casual clothes she'd laid out. "Now we are going to be late."

Wendy looked around, not quite wanting to watch *Game of Thrones* with her fingers smelling like—there was hand sanitizer on Janet's vanity. Of course there was. "I don't think so," she replied. "I mean, not only are we both women, but we were only at third base."

Janet tied her scarf into something intricately simple. "You'd better drive. If you make me laugh too hard, I could crash."

Wendy scooped up Janet's keys and handed Janet her purse. "Okay then. Tally ho."

And just as she started for the door, she felt Janet's hand in her hair, jerking her head back just roughly enough, sharp teeth at her ear: "Next time you pull a stunt like that, you'd better have a few hours to spare for you to finish the job. Just so you know."

"Absolutely, Ms. Lace."

"Good," Janet said huskily, and released her, hand dropping down to slap Wendy's ass. "Now, please hurry," she concluded, all business once more. All crazy-hot business. "Punctuality is a sign of respect, you know."

Wendy hurried before her. She didn't know if she loved Power Dyke Secret Kinky Librarian Janet Lace more than Spy Undercover At A Caviar Tasting Party Janet Lace, or taking a little sip of a kiss from Janet versus the overpowering *truth* of really kissing her. But she definitely liked being topped by Janet just a little more than doing the topping.

After all, she'd already done that tonight. Wouldn't want it to get old.

ABOUT GEORGETTE KAPLAN

It was never easy for Georgette Kaplan. She was born a poor child in Mississippi, where she still remembers sitting on the porch with her family, singing and dancing around her. After learning she was adopted, at the age of 21 she hitchhiked to St. Louis, where she worked at a gas station and in a traveling carnival. After a shooting incident at the gas station, she decided to quit and pursue her lifelong dream of a career in writing. She now lives back in Mississippi with her life partner Marie.

CONNECT WITH GEORGETTE:
Tumblr: georgettekaplan.tumblr.com

OTHER BOOKS FROM YLVA PUBLISHING

www.ylva-publishing.com

EX-WIVES OF DRACULA

Georgette Kaplan

ISBN: 978-3-95533-410-9
Length: 338 pages (122,000 words)

Mindy's best friend, Lucia, is a vampire. Every second Mindy spends with her she's in danger of becoming dinner. But Lucia needs help. To keep her alive they need fresh blood, and to cure her they have to kill her sire. So why is it that Nosferatu, the cops, and the chance of becoming an unwilling blood donor don't scare Mindy half as much as the way she feels when Lucia looks at her?

UNDER A FALLING STAR

Jae

ISBN: 978-3-95533-238-9
Length: 369 pages (91,000 words)

Falling stars are supposed to be a lucky sign, but not for Austen. The first assignment in her new job—decorating the Christmas tree in the lobby—results in a trip to the ER after Dee, the company's COO, gets hit by the star-shaped tree topper. There's an instant attraction between them, but Dee is determined not to act on it, especially since Austen has no idea that Dee is her boss.

HEART'S SURRENDER

Emma Weimann

ISBN: 978-3-95533-183-2
Length: 305 pages (63,000 words)

Neither Samantha Freedman nor Gillian Jennings are looking for a relationship when they begin a no-strings-attached affair. But soon simple attraction turns into something more. What happens when the worlds of a handywoman and a pampered housewife collide? Can nights of hot, erotic fun lead to love, or will these two very different women go their separate ways?

THE CLUB

A.L. Brooks

ISBN: 978-3-95533-654-7
Length: 227 pages (72,200 words)

Welcome to The Club—leave your inhibitions and your everyday cares at the door, and indulge yourself in an evening of anonymous, no-strings, woman-on-woman action. For many visitors to The Club, this is exactly what they are looking for, and what they get. For others, however, the emotions run high, and one night of sex changes their lives in ways they couldn't have imagined.

COMING FROM YLVA PUBLISHING

www.ylva-publishing.com

DRAWN TOGETHER

JD Glass

Zoe Glenn Edwards, graphic novelist, is determinedly single and happily married to her work. Dion Richards, author, is trapped in a hostile sham marriage and only happy when she's working. Both creatives are well-known in their respective fields. When they inevitably collaborate on a new project, what happens when two 'unavailables' discover they're unmistakably Drawn Together?

YOU'RE FIRED

Shaya Crabtree

When an inappropriate Secret Santa gift backfires, Rose needs her smarts to save her job, while Vivian, her sexy boss, needs her smarts to save the business. Can they stop bickering long enough to do a deal?

Scissor Link
© 2016 by Georgette Kaplan

ISBN: 978-3-95533-678-3

Also available as e-book.

Published by Ylva Publishing, legal entity of Ylva Verlag, e.Kfr.
Ylva Verlag, e.Kfr.
Owner: Astrid Ohletz
Am Kirschgarten 2
65830 Kriftel
Germany

www.ylva-publishing.com

First edition: 2016

Credits
Edited by Gill McKnight & Zee Ahmad
Proofread by CK King
Cover Design & Print Layout by Streetlight Graphics